# YESTERDAY

the Truth Circle Series

Lisa V. Gallimore

All names, characters and incidents are the products of the author's imagination as this book is a work of fiction.

# Lisa V. Gallimore

This book is dedicated to some exceptionally phenomenal women who are in heaven smiling down. They had a profound impact on my yesterday and taught me how to unapologetically stand in my truth.

Beryl "Betty" Mae Davis, thank you for loving and supporting me unconditionally. Your unending acceptance of me inspired me to go after my dreams with fierce tenacity. You drilled into us that *"Reading maketh a man!"* Mama, I did it…I've added to the reading fraternity! Mama, I miss you with every breath. Your last words to me have brought me tremendous joy and daily motivation: *"Felise mi proud a yuh caan done!"*

Keresa Grooves, I miss you always! I have never been able to recover the part of me that died the day you left this earth. You had my back girl! Thank you for your endless kindness; you will always be "Keresa, the one, the greatest one!"

Joan E. Hill, thank you for always encouraging me to be myself, your words solidified my confidence. You telling me, I was the daughter you never had, made me feel at home in a place where my unique personality was not readily accepted.

-   Love you always!

## Prologue

The officers hastily carted the teens into the dark and hazy station. The stench of stale coffee and gloom ambushed their nostrils upon entry. Each got their very own dimly lit claustrophobia-inducing box to stew in. The officers lowered the temperature in each interrogation room, thus beginning the application of hyperbolic intimidation tactics. They choose to question Beth first, figuring they could break her quickly; she was not a member of the Secret Six. After an hour, the translator had to caution the detectives; shouting was useless as Beth is deaf and her story remained consistent.

Having refused Suva's several requests for a bathroom break, the officers figured she was at the right level of frustrated! Suva stared at the large armed men across the table. *Why did her interview merit an officer and two detectives?* Officer Kade turned on the camera. Suva spoke in a low tone,

"Officer Kade, recording a minor without parental consent is inadmissible in court. Have my parents given consent?" The head detective motioned for him to turn it off. She smiled slyly, "I want to get my protest on record. I'm positive that what Travis got wasn't what he deserved!" Reading that as a ploy to defuse them, the detectives applied pressure. After an hour, the detectives grew warry of Suva's calm demeanor. Officer Kade paused, stared at her for a minute, exhaled and asked calmly,

"How are you the captain of the swim team, having severe asthma, aren't you a liability?"

"Detective Archer has a bum leg, and he is the lead detective. Kade, are you calling him a liability?" Suva responded sharply. Kade blinked profusely. Detective Archer rubbed his arthritic knee, swallowed his shock and roared in anger,

"Suva you will be arrested, we found your hair on Travis' body!" Adrenaline propelled him from his chair, his burly frame towered over Suva. "All we need is a mouth swab to confirm that it's yours, and bingo, you are in jail for the rest of your life." Suva laughed,

"This interrogation is over. How would you know that it's my hair without a DNA sample to match it? Secondly, you don't have probable cause; therefore, you cannot compel a DNA sample. Mr. Bent doesn't have enough pull to get a subpoena with no evidence. Thirdly, I have asthma, so there is no way I could've made it over to the Bents and back as quickly as you said the assailant did." Suva stood and leaned over the table, looked the men square in the eyes, her tone got deep. "As I said, what Travis got wasn't what he deserved." She took up one of the many pictures from the table, ripping it slowly, "It should've been cut off completely!" She flashed her hair and scampered off like a kindergartener going for ice cream. Her statement sent chills down their spines.

They knew she did it but felt some dissonance trying to prove it. She was right, Travis did deserve what he got. Plus, the assailant punched Travis in the face multiple times, neither Suva's or the other members of the Secret Six had bruised knuckles.

The hair they found was red and straight, again no red or straight hair amongst them. They were a close-knit circle; getting the truth would be insurmountable. The case was dead; they didn't have enough to go to trial.

Exiting the station Suva inhaled freedom and smiled at her friends, "Let's get back to her, we will never know what happened yesterday...

# YESTERDAY

## Chapter 1

Suva Atsila Lanaghan enjoyed the comforting sensation of the red-and-white cotton dress gliding over the contours of her body. She was very pleased with the color of the day. Her body was well proportioned, standing at five feet four inches, and when she moved, the loose-fitting dress emphasized her plump 32C breasts, small waist, and voluptuous hips. At the sound of a horn outside, she took one last look in the mirror, grabbed her book bag, and ran out the door. Exiting her room, the delectable scent of her mother's breakfast enveloped her. Descending solid mahogany stairs that overlooked a well antiquely furnished living room with crisp white-tiled floors, she made her way to the kitchen. Entering, she saw her mom over the island, tending a pot that contained something heavenly. Her mom kissed her forehead, Suva straight-lined to the refrigerator for her container of grapes. Her mom pleaded,

"Baby, you have to eat something more, please."

"I'm going to have a great lunch. I promise!" She dashed through the big wooden doors. Suva's face lit up, her body filled with electric joy when she saw him.

"Good morning, Wohali," she blasted, he locked her door and got around to the driver's side. He mimicked her cheerfulness,

"Good morning to you, too, Atsila!" Suva rolled her eyes. He exited the driveway. Tommy and Suva were destined to be in each other's lives. Their parents, now neighbors and lifelong companions were brought together by their rich cultures.

They met at a Cultural Society Club meeting their first semester in college. Their dads were both Irish and were instantly smitten by two very enchantingly vocal young women.

Suva's father, Deaglan Lanaghan, had seen many gorgeous plains in Ireland, but nothing compared to the wonders he saw in her mom, Melissa, a Jamaican beauty. He was breathless the first time he heard her speak; she delivered her speech with such clarity, passion, and eloquence. His roommate, Kyle Boughen, had the same reaction to Melissa's roommate, Atsila. Atsila was her Cherokee tribal name meaning *fire*, and she lit a fire in his heart. Twenty-three years later, their teenagers were carpooling to school in a red Mercedes convertible.

"Buenos!" Sofia greeted, pulling up at the stop sign.

"Hey!" Suva replied, noting a very disgruntled Jason, the passenger in Sofia's blue Mercedes.

"Don't even ask…she took forever to get ready as usual," Jason answered before Suva could voice her concern. With a guilty giggle, Sofia announced,

"Duncan is here." Another Mercedes pulled up, carrying two other teens, completing their carpool group.

"Now that the circle is complete, can we go, please?" Jason asked, amusing the five other teens.  Despite the delays, they arrived at school on time.  Only the intellectually gifted went to Mayberry Academy, its officials took pride in the caliber of their populace. Mayberry Academy had outstanding accolades in academics, and they dominated in individual sports: soccer, chess, football, swimming, basketball, tennis, and cheerleading.  The building looked more like a Citadel pretending to be a high school. The architecture was aesthetically breathtaking; the varying colors of the rocks that constructed the walls that span the parameter of the property captivated onlookers. The Irish/Scottish ancestry influenced the design and culture of the private institution, and every room was decked with modern flourishes.

The student parking lot was located directly in front of the school with staff parking in the rear. Spaces weren't assigned, but social norms specified a section for each clique.  The three cars pulled into their usual areas under the trees.  That spot was coveted because it was strategically located in the center of the lot, allowing easy access to the main offices and the outside gymnasium.

Observing them walk to homeroom seemed to play out in slow motion; they all had on some variation of red and white. That was their thing, to wear matching colors each day.  They have been one of the most popular groups in school since they were in Mayberry Junior Academy.  They were the top six performers in the eleventh grade, and they competed daily for those rankings. They were *Fort Knox*, hence dubbed the Secret Six. Leaving the students to speculate on the juicy happenings within their tight circle.

"I hope Ms. Baker is on time today," Duncan's thick Irish accent denoting annoyance. "I'm excited to try out this new formula. Thursdays are the only time we get extended hours in the chemistry lab."

Duncan was born in Ireland; his parents moved to America when he was seven years old. He was transferred to Mayberry Junior Academy after being the youngest chemist to enter and win a high school science fair.

"Calm down, Mr. Science, you will get to the lab soon enough," Ayesha popped her gum while flashing her bleached-blonde extensions and batting her overly-mascaraed eyelashes. She was the rebel in the group. Ayesha was never shy to use her sparkly blue eyes and full double Ds to get what she wanted. After homeroom, they went to the chemistry lab, Duncan sat with Sofia, Jason with Ayesha.

"Where are the others?" Mr. Depti inquired, "In India, students were never late for classes…discipline." Suva and Tommy walked into the class. "Discipline!"

"So sorry we're late, Thomas and I had to go to our locker to retrieve our lab coats," she pleaded apologetically, the class chuckled.

"Thomas, you are always late." Jason teased in his best Indian accent. Suva whispered to her lab partner,

"Wohali, you need to bring the coats with you to class when it's your week to have them laundered." Tommy affectionately rubbed her right earlobe.

"It's okay, Atsila; I'm sure you'll find it in your heart to forgive me." Their middle names were in honor of Tommy's mother. At birth, Tommy's eyes were so bright and his gaze so penetrating, he was named Wohali, *eagle*. Fourteen months later, when standing beside her best friend, Mrs. Boughen knew at first glance that her goddaughter was strong, but when she stared into those hazel eyes, she recognized some of her fire in the child's eyes. Suva got her godmother's name, Atsila, *fire*. Tommy could gauge Suva's mood by what name she called him. Wohali in public spelled trouble, Thomas equaled business, she was at her most playful when Tommy was uttered.

At lunch, they sat at their table in the cafeteria. Mayberry's cafeteria was huge with different sections that catered to the appetites of all the school's multicultural population. Their cafeteria was similar in design to a shopping mall food court. Ayesha popped her gum,

"What are we in the mood for? Italian pizza, Chinese, Indian, or old-fashioned corner-store deli?" Jason responded first,

"Let me choose, so we don't spend forever deliberating. Large meat-lovers with fries and fruit smoothies."  After lunch, they walked to their next class in their usual pairs; Sofia with Duncan, Ayesha with Jason, and Suva with Tommy. Jason astonished the group by breaking stride and pulling Suva into his arms for a long passionate kiss. There was a long awkward pause.

"Oh, come on, guys, leave it out!" Duncan shouted everyone cheered. Suva smiled to mask her surprise; her boyfriend was not usually into public displays of affection.  She pulled Ayesha's hair,

"You need to stop daring him to do stuff like that!" Ayesha popped her gum and paid Jason twenty dollars. Tommy retorted,

"Look, don't damage my woman." He pretended to soothe Ayesha's hair but not quite because she would have a fit if he touched it. Jason held Suva's hands.

"I missed you last night." They were in their other class by now.

"Sorry, I was exhausted." She responded.  They made their way to the far corner of the class by the window, ensuring privacy. Jason's gray eyes pierced through her.

"Why do you always have to stifle her with a ponytail?" In one swift motion, he pulled the red ribbon loose, freeing her hair from its bondage.

"Jason, I know you are accustomed to getting your way, being a fifth-generation Henri.  My hair is not the real estate industry; its stubborn thickness will not bend to your will." Suva finger-combed the wild tendrils. She and Tommy exchanged a discreet glance. Displeasure was plastered across Tommy's face. Jason's hand was hypnotized by Suva's thick, curly, black hair. He stroked her back-length tresses. She sighed and surrendered.

"What was that about?" Tommy asked quizzically when their class commenced.

"Can we talk about it later? I didn't know he was going to pull the ribbon out," Suva stated quietly, anxious to end the conversation. She never thought that choosing between wearing her hair up or down would have so many ramifications. Thursdays after school were designated for swimming. The championship swim meet was coming up, which meant their lives belonged to the coach. They met in the library after practice to go over the study scheme for the night and finalize their projects.  Later that night, after a soothing bath, Suva readied herself for the study session with Tommy.

"Atsila, we're doing chemistry tonight? Tommy asked, walking through her window, his usual entrance. He used to climb the side of the house to go through her window, so for his safety, their parents built a balcony joining the two houses. Suva responded without even glancing up.

"Yes, Wohali," She gasped at the state of his hair. "You haven't showered? Labs aren't going to write themselves, yuh noe!" He started removing his clothes, he made his way to the bathroom, passing her queen-size, cushioned-filled bed. He closed the door when he was at his boxers. Five minutes later Suva commented,

"That was quick!" Tommy emerged from the bathroom, his lower body wrapped in a towel. "Try hurri ah put on clothes before mommy catch yuh!" He walked over to her large walk-in closet and retrieved his clothes. Before leaving the closet, he saw the beautiful white summer dress that he bought for her a few weeks earlier. He brought it out with him.

"Wear this tomorr—" he stopped midsentence. Suva, sitting in front of her vanity like a Broadway performer glancing at her beauty before a major show. He came up behind her, "Allow me..." He slowly loosened the ribbon, and the curls rejoiced in freedom; each soft tendril seduced his fingers. Their eyes met in the mirror, and time froze, his body reacted in the most primal way. Suva's pulse quickened. The phone on the computer desk rang with persistence until it accomplished the task.

"Alo, Jason. Yes, he's here...we can do the conference now." Putting the receiver down, she pressed the speaker button, and her room filled with the sound of four persons talking at the same time. Suva interjected,

"Can we get to it, please? We have so much work to do." The line went silent.

"First order of business, what's the color for tomorrow?" Sofia was the first to speak up. Suva looked at the dress on the bed,

"White dresses with floral detailing and the guys..." She pictured Tommy's closet. "The guys can wear white pants with blue polo shirts." They wanted to go to the cabin after school, and Jeeps were suited for the terrain. Their three-hour study session was very productive.

Suva couldn't help but inhale Tommy's magnificence when he stretched, exposing his abdomen. He was a flawless specimen, all five feet nine inches. He had his mother's rich Cherokee features; his straight nose and forest green eyes were gifts from his Irish father. His body was solid, strong arms, toned legs that led to a well-defined abdomen, and Suva's favorite part of his anatomy, a perfectly sculpted posterior. She was distracted by thoughts of why she shouldn't be looking at him like this that it took her a second to notice that he was speaking to her.

"What was that?" she asked as she refocused.

"You should spend more time listening to me and less time looking at my butt." He responded jokingly, her cheeks colored with embarrassment. "What do you want to do now? I'm in the mood for something…" He licked his lips. She knew exactly what he was in the mood for.

"No, not tonight. I'm tired. Plus, I have to call Jason back." Tommy started placing his books into his bookbag, watching her intently. "Your big green eyes don't scare me." She stated dryly. "They are too amazing to bring about fear." Defusing him instantly.

"Not amazing enough, because I am leaving unsatisfied," he said suggestively.

"Get over it, Wohali. It's just ice cream." Suva rose and hugged him good-bye.

"It's not just ice cream. It's strawberry flavored; there's a big difference. Plus, we always hang out after we study." He had a valid point, but Suva needed to put in some quality phone time with Jason. Tommy was halfway out the window, he stopped and walked right up to her, bent until their noses were inches from each other, he inhaled deeply until her essence filled his lungs. He rubbed her right earlobe. "My hair is now shoulder length. I'm serious about not cutting it. You know I could use the truth circle right now and get you to admit to it. But the power is yours" That was the last thing he said before slipping out the window; it took a while for her breathing to normalize.

Suva settled under her favorite sheet, smothered between tons of pillows, and called Jason. They spent the usual time arguing about her hair. Around minute fifteen, Jason said it was time for bed if they were going to be well-rested for school; he was so disciplined, and that's why she loved him so much.

Was she in love with him? That was the question that kept popping into her head; she knew she was too young to understand what it is to be in love. But she knew in her heart of hearts that the feelings she had for Jason were not those of a person who was in love.

She was counting sheep when her T-phone started vibrating. It was a regular cell phone, but because it was Tommy's idea to get matching cell phones that only they knew about, they called it their T-phones. She smiled before it stopped vibrating the first time. She wasn't sure if it was the prospect of hearing his voice that excited her or if it was the fact that they had secret cell phone bills that they paid in cash to avoid a paper trail.

"It's 2 a.m., shouldn't you be sleeping?" she asked her tone heavy with mockery.

"I miss you, and I needed to hear your voice." Suva took deep breaths; his voice electrified her nerve endings. Words failed her. Two hours later, they were still talking; time always seems to go unnoticed when they were on their T-phones. At five, they forced their good-byes because they both knew they had to get up in two hours. Friday came and went very quickly. Before they knew it, they were watching the sunset from the Boughen's cabin; the cabin was by far the group's favorite place to hang out. The outside looked like a tiny two-story wood cabin, but after passing through the narrow hallway where the coats hung, the interior beauty hits you. You walk right into the massive family room with a log fireplace and a sizeable 75-inch television, accompanied by the latest in entertainment and every conceivable video game. To the left of the family room was the very spacious kitchen that had white-tiled counters; the kitchen was perfect because the pool was just a few feet away.

The only drawback to the cabin was that evenly spread out over the two stories were ten bedrooms equipped with Whirlpool and king-sized beds. They weren't allowed to have any unsupervised overnight stays, and their visits were restricted to specific days. Never the less they still enjoyed every moment spent there. After eating, they sat in their usual circle to do a pulse check. To start the pulse check, they held hands and breathed deeply, releasing all the stress of that week. Each person would unload whatever baggage or wins they had that week — getting support and advice from the others.

Tommy had a good week.  He felt a little pressure trying to make the Academic Decathlon team, but he was up for the challenge. Duncan didn't like being teased that he wasn't a true Irishman because he was even-tempered. He detested stereotypes.  "The Irish are some of the sweetest people on the planet" He protested.  Jason had no worries his week was great. Sofia had intense anxiety because her grandmother was sick, and she feared the worse. Ayesha's challenges surrounded not matching up to her mom's expectations of beauty, and she thought only a nose job would fix it.  Suva was about to speak when Ayesha interrupted.

"There's a new rumor going around." The group waited for her to finish as there was always a rumor about them circulating. "They're saying you kissed Tommy." Ayesha stopped laughing when in response Suva said,

"Oh," Ayesha straightened, and in a sober tone she continued.

"Benjamin Toad said it came from his most reliable source. He won't reveal as it would be against his journalistic integrity." Suva stared at her blankly. Jason heard the rumor but ignored it.  It could never be true, Suva would never kiss another, she was dating The Jason Henri V. Ayesha's insecurities urged her to press the matter further.  "Su did you kiss Tommy?" Tommy remained his usual calm and unfazed self.

"Ayesha, I have a lot I want to share, so can we finish up our pulse check, please?" Suva appealed to the others.  Ayesha broke contact, went to the kitchen, returned with a knife and drew a circle in the carpet. "Ayesha, you'll ruin the material."

"I am invoking the Truth Circle." The truth circle was something the group inherited from Suva and Tommy, who started doing it as kids. Once you are in the circle, the outside world doesn't exist.  Social norms do not apply.  There is no judgment; what's said in the circle can never be used against you. There's complete honesty and confidentiality.  Suva and Tommy exchanged quick glances. Suva stood in the circle. Sofia joined her in the circle as the objective third party and asked,

"Suva, have you and Tommy ever kissed." Suva played with the thin silver ring on her right ring finger then responded calmly.

"Can the question be more specific, please?"  While the others were curious Ayesha was getting antsy.

"Suva, have you and Tommy kissed in a non-platonic way, have your lips touched, has his tongue ever been in your mouth…"

"Move it along, Sofia." Jason felt uneasy with the visualization. Ayesha was itching for the answer.

"No, we have not kissed."

"Do you want to kiss Tommy?" Ayesha asked. The question visibly affected Suva, but Jason suddenly pulled her from the circle. His gut told him what the answer would be.

"Ayesha, you know the rules. No questions from outside the circle." Tommy was a little disappointed; he was eager to hear Suva's response. Although he already knew. Suva didn't get to express her challenges or wins from the week. She felt emotionally heavy and needed the release, but her vulnerability retreated after the truth circle. Her woes regarding being called a "halfer" would have to wait.

To break the tension, Duncan suggested pizza and the pool. On the drive home, they were all happily exhausted.

## Chapter 2

Suva woke up excited in anticipation of Saturday Brunch with her parents. Her father, the super busy attorney, and her mother, the on-call head of pediatrics, ensured they had time for and with their daughter. During brunch, they got caught up on each other's week and signed permission slips for the swim team's overnight training sessions and the actual meet. The Lanaghans were incredibly proud parents; their parents struggled to provide for them, so now their focus was on giving Suva all they never had.

"Good afternoon, Mom and Dad." Tommy joined them for brunch. Suva's parents noted the effects of Tommy's voice on Suva's face. Both parents had the same thought: *why aren't they dating yet!*

"I completely forgot about my appointment. Thank goodness for Tommy." Suva was sharing with her childhood hairstylist Mavis. Mavis had convinced her mom that a relaxer wasn't the answer when Suva's curls seemed uncontrollable. None of the ladies heard a word Suva was saying; they were all entranced by Tommy. Being Suva's salon chauffeur he amassed quite a few admirers.

"Tommy dear, I see you haven't had a haircut in a while. You do know that grooming men's hair is one of my specialties," a lady at least three times his age, remarked sexily.

"At your age, I bet you have a long list of other specialties you would like to show poor Thomas," Mavis commented, laughter erupted. "Plus…" she continued, "he only has eyes for Miss Su here." Tommy and Suva exchanged looks in the mirror.
Because Tommy didn't deny the claim, Suva felt compelled to speak.

"Come on, Mavis, we're best friends. Tommy is with someone, and so am I." The room got quiet. Tommy broke the silence,

"Mavis, the deal is, I won't cut my hair until she kisses me." Suva wished she could just crawl into a shampoo bottle. Tommy toyed with the thin silver ring on his right middle finger.
*That ingrate! She was going to kill him!* The ladies hooted, some took out their scissors and puckered up.
Suva replayed that night at the cabin three months earlier when they almost kissed. The moment took place after a spontaneous dip in the pool while they were drying themselves in front of the fireplace.

Kneeling face-to-face as the warmth from the flames permeated their wet bodies; Tommy cupped her face, his lips inches away, Suva pulled back. He boldly stated,

"You can't fight our chemistry forever!"

"Watch me!" He caressed her right earlobe gently,

"Hhhmm, as a tangible sign of my patience, until we kiss, I won't…cut my hair!"
Mavis spun Suva in the styling chair. Tommy gave Mavis instructions,

"Straighten it."

"That's not logical, hon. We have swim meet training all week." Suva refuted, but Tommy persisted.

"Atsila, please, even if it's just for three days."
He added silkily and rubbed her right earlobe.

"Go ahead, Mavis, and do a swoop to the right,
please. Thanks." Tommy waited two hours for Mavis to
straighten Suva's thick mane that now fell to her
midriff.   During the ride home Tommy's fingers conversed with Suva's silky strands.  Suva knew it was going to cause an argument with Jason; he loved her hair curly. Where did her loyalty lie? Later that night, in the theater room of her house, Suva's fears were confirmed by Sofia's reaction to her best friend's straightened hair.

"What were you thinking? Sofia ran her fingers through Suva's hair and went on hyperbolically. "Jason will not be happy!  We will have to sit through yet another pointless argument about your stupid hair."  Suva stared at the screen; of course, she knew it would be an issue, but for some reason, she was weak when it came to Tommy. *Doesn't boyfriend trump best friend?* Suva couldn't wait to be an adult. She was certain men do not have a say in how grown women carry themselves.

"It's a beautiful day. We should chill at the cabin instead." Suva adjusted her tennis outfit. They were on their way to Henri Manor; it hosted the best tennis courts in Mayberry.

"Oh, please! You just want to avoid Jason," Sofia blurted out, seeing through her friend's façade. Sofia was right, Suva didn't want the unnecessary conflict. At the main gate, the guards let them in. Jason drove his golf cart to that side of the property to greet them. The Henri Manor looked more like a country club instead of a family home that had been passed down for generations. Jason and his father were on their way to play a round of Sunday golf with some of Mr. Henri's most valued clients. The importance of the game was lost on Jason; his mind was occupied by one thought, seeing Suva in her cute little tennis get-up.

"Let me give you girls a ride over to the tennis courts, clay, or rough top?" Jason asked en route to the courts. The girls decided on clay. At the courts, Sofia started warming up. Jason led Suva to a nearby changing room. They started kissing even before the door closed. Gently lifting her against the wall he positioned himself between her legs. Feeling a rush of excitement Jason deepened the kiss. Needing his hands free, Jason broke the kiss and released her slowly. Panting, Suva leaned against the wall for support. Desire coursed through her; she grabbed Jason, taking his tongue into her mouth. Jason ran his hand up her inner thigh, inches from her center, Suva stilled his hand.

"Swan..."

"Jason..." Resting his hands on either side of her head. Staring at each other with aggressive undercurrents. "Babe, I'm not losing my virginity in a changing room." Suva broke the silence. Jason eased away from her.

"Swan, give me your location of choice, and I will make it happen. I know it's not the cabin, your room, the backseat of the jeep, a five-star hotel or..." His voice trailed off. He unconsciously turned the thin silver ring on his right middle finger.

"You forgot the tent by the lake." Suva smiled, trying to lighten the mood. It worked. Jason released a long sigh. "Jason, I just need more time." Jason relaxed. Exiting the dressing room Suva hugged him. He smelt so good. Suva couldn't resist licking his neck. Jason felt it to his core.

"Swan, you can't do that shit and not expect me to want sex." Suva rolled her eyes. She signed, "a lick is not sex." Jason smirked and said heatedly, "a finger is not sex either!"

Witnessing their aggressive strides, Sofia chuckled under her breath. "You're mad about the hair, huh?" Sofia remarked to Jason when he got on the golf cart to leave. Jason waited. Suva froze. Jason waited. Conceding, Suva took off the hat releasing her straightened hair.

"Swan? Why?" Suva looked at Sofia seething. "Suva, your curls are what makes the other guys envious of us. With straight hair, you don't look biracial. You doing this is a blatant disregard of my wishes, if I'm not getting sex the least I can get is obedience."

"Obedience, listen nuh, mi a nuh yuh pickney!" Jason kissed her and drove off.

## Chapter 3

Coach Wilson was a very serious man.  Once in Mayberry Academy history, some students caught him on tape smiling, he made the team do laps until he was confident that they would destroy the footage. Despite his demeanor, Coach Wilson was their favorite teacher because he shared their passion for being the best.  The team kept reminding themselves of that as their muscles ached from one of his brutal overnight training sessions. They waited thirty minutes in the dorms for him to fall asleep then assembled in the game room. Ayesha was the exception; she was still in the bathroom styling her hair and redoing her nails.

"Where's Malibu Barbie?" one of the girls from the swim team asked, rolling her eyes.

"Hey, back off, Ayesha es familia!" Sofia came to Ayesha's defense yet another time.

"I mean, I get Sofia and Duncan…" A male continued the conversation, gesturing to the couple sitting on one of the lounge chairs. "Sofia is a goddess inheriting her father's Costa Rican ancestry in the form of that heavenly figure and her mother's Taiwanese grace and…" Duncan gave him a territorial look.  Duncan had grown weary of these conversations. He moved then returned the thin silver ring from the base to the tip of his right middle finger.

"I don't get her place in the group. She's so plastic and superficial." Another teammate pressed on with genuine curiosity.

"Shut up Karen; she superficially outswims your ass all day every day!" Suva wanted to end the conversation before Ayesha returned. Ayesha entered the room, looking pageant ready and in a barely-there Teddy.  The guys hooted.  Tommy sprung to his feet. Suva and Sofia bit their lips; they knew Tommy was furious.  In Ayesha's room, Tommy searched through her duffle for non-lingerie clothing. An unbothered Ayesha applied more ruby rose lipstick.

"Tommy, we've been over this. My momma says I'm ugly, and my beauty can only be found…" She pursed her lips. "…in the cosmetics section.  She popped her gum. Tommy held both her hands.

"Ayesha, you are an amazing young lady. Beautiful inside and out." Ayesha walked away from him and stood before the full-length mirror.

"Tommy, you are so misguided. Momma says that inner beauty is a fallacy.  People notice Sofia and Suva because of their exotic mix. Momma reminds me every day that if I didn't get these double Ds for my fifteenth birthday." She adjusted her breasts in the push-up bra and spoke, almost to herself.  "No one would ever notice me."

"I notice you," Tommy responded genuinely.

"You noticed me out of pity. After the scandal with Aaron, you supported me as a friend. I begged Suva to hook us up, but you weren't into me. You only said we were secretly dating to shut my mom up that night over dinner at my house!" They both smiled, remembering how her mom spilled wine in shock. "You won't even have sex with me…because you don't find me attractive!" Ayesha popped her gum defiantly.

"Ash, after the blowback from the Aaron scandal, do you think that sex is the answer?" Tommy hugged her snuggly. "I see you. You are beautiful inside and out." Tommy cared for her deeply. Rebuilding her confidence was a difficult feat.  He had to contend with her mom, who provides hefty servings of disappointment daily, that feeds Ayesha's feelings of inadequacy.

At the crack of dawn, Coach Wilson woke the team; they had breakfast and headed to class.  This was what they disliked about Mayberry Academy; athletes weren't given preferential treatment. Duncan didn't mind going to class; it was Thursday, his favorite day.

## Chapter 4

On the day of the Meet, the arena was bursting at the seams with competing teams, and their respective diehard supporters. They had competitions from high school juniors to college seniors. The final event was the women's 4×200m freestyle relay, Sofia at the lead, and Suva anchoring. The team was burdened by anxiety as they were second in the rankings. Moments before the race, Suva's chest tightened, and her breathing became labored. Jason tried calming her down; coach went to the officials to get the medic. Panicking team members gathered rubbing her back. Suva grabbed her chest trying to breathe through the terrible wheezing.

"Swan, talk to me, what's wrong?" Jason tried soothing her. Kneeling before Suva, the medic listened to Suva's chest.

"You need oxygen, get the Oxygen, she's having a panic attack!" Tommy spoke calmly,

"Oxygen won't help." He sprinted to his duffle, returning with a small apparatus. He cleared the area around her. "Breathe deeply. In and out." With wide eyes she puffed once, then twice. Releasing some of the tension from her air passage. By the third puff her breathing normalized.

"Tommy, where did you get an inhaler?" Suva was getting air outside.

"Just breathe…" Tommy demanded gently as he played with her right earlobe. "Since your first attack, I always have one handy." Suva was defensive,

"I was twelve. I've only had two…three attacks since!" Tommy chuckled,

"That's why I have to keep renewing YOUR prescription…just breathe." Back inside the arena, the team gathered in concern. Tommy was very vocal with his thoughts. "Coach, I don't think Suva should participate in the race." Coach Wilson could hardly get a word in. "After an attack, her doctors strongly advise against any rigorous activity."

"How do you feel Suva?" Coach asked in earnest; he was just as surprised as the rest of the team to learn of her condition; his students' safety was paramount. Tommy interjected,

"She's unfit, Coach, and it is in her best interest that she sits this one out." He was so passionate, placing her to sit on the chair provided.

"Tommy, I feel fine. I'm okay, Coach, I can do it," she began to stand.

"No, she is not, Coach," Tommy went on, placing her to sit again. He kept on ranting his objections.

"Tommy, Tommy…Tommy," Suva paused. "Wohali!" Tommy stopped and sat quietly. "I'm ready, Coach, let's take this one home for Mayberry Academy!" That got the team excited. They chanted their school's name. "I'll be fine, Wohali. Meet me at the finish line." Tommy watched her every move, looking for any signs of distress.

At the starting shot, Sofia took off in perfect form; by the third leg, they were behind by milliseconds. Suva gave Tommy one last reassuring glance, and she was off; her entrance was spectacular. Excited stumps vibrated the stands as the crowd cheered fanatically. Coaches yelled, and team members concentrated all their energies on their swimmer. On the final turn, Suva was shoulder to shoulder with her archrival, an Australian girl from Riverdale Academy that people swore had fins. They touched the wall together. There was a hush in the arena; anticipation silenced the crowd. You could hear the proverbial pin drop as fingers crossed, and small prayers went up. Tick-tock, tick-tock… explosive screams went off in unison. With one eye closed Suva peeked, Mayberry Academy was at the top of the leaderboard. Before she celebrated, she embraced then exchanged a few words with her archrival.

"Catch you next season, mate," were the last words she heard, Tommy lifted her out of the pool, inhaler in hand. The team was ecstatic! They celebrated all night, but they got crushed by the college teams the next day in the free for all swim-offs. They had bragging rights within the high school circuits, but they were outranked within the college leagues. The team swore revenge next season. The school was buzzing with Tommy's heroics, his quick thinking and protective determination were the top story of that week's Mayberry Academy Tribune. Him being on the cover in his swim trunks was hilarious. Tommy did not like the attention and started bribing students to stop the fanfare. Jason and Ayesha were not impressed with Tommy's little display; this caused slight tension within the group. They were happy Suva was fine, but what was up with the secret mind communication that silenced Tommy.

The Boughens and the Lanaghans took their children out for a celebratory dinner. The hibachi restaurant was the first spot their parents tried when they moved to Mayberry. The waitress came to take their orders. The parents ordered, then Tommy spoke,

"For the appetizer, she'll have the soup of the day extra mushrooms. Entre', the smoked salmon, lobster fried rice with steamed asparagus. For dessert, the strawberry sorbet. Oh, and virgin Pina Colada." Suva closed the menu and ordered,

"He'll have calamari salad, no onions, with sweetened raspberry iced tea, for an appetizer. The main…the spicy tilapia with broccoli. Then dessert, the strawberry sorbet." Melissa felt the need to explain the oddity,

"As kids, they would switch plates. It evolved into them knowing what the other would prefer." The waitress smiled. The meal was superbly entertaining; they had fun with their chef. During dessert, a cake was brought out with "Congratulations to our little goldfishes" written on it. Tommy pointed out that they were being insulted because goldfishes aren't fast swimmers.

"Smartass!" Mr. Lanaghan replied, playfully slapping him on the back of his head.

"Don't hurt my *Ayastigi*; he took good care of me." Suva gently rubbed Tommy's head. He froze. She quickly removed her hand. Suva cleared her throat and raised her glass. "It's my distinct honor to present my *Ayastigi* with this gift. Thank you, Wohali." She placed a box in front of him. Tommy opened it, and it was a gold ring with a miniature orange diamond-encrusted Ferrari. "Hold on to that until you get the real one." Cheers all around. Suva gave him a playful peck on the cheek, the jolt startled them both.

"He is truly your warrior. Inhaler, man!" Atsila added. On the drive home, Tommy and Suva sat in the back as usual. He had his arm around her, and she snuggled close. He whispered something, and she lifted her head for clarity. They were inches apart. Suva was so conflicted; she wanted to bite the forbidden fruit. She took a deep breath to clear her head…dammit! His sweet masculine musk seduced her senses. *No! It wouldn't be honorable.* He moistened his lips, exhaling his desire to lick her honeydew. She felt the warmth of his breath on her lips; she could already taste them. There was a half an inch of separation between them. The lights came on. Melissa announced,

"We're home."

## Chapter 5

Tossing and turning, Suva gave up on sleep. Tommy's sexiness was plaguing her consciousness. The T-phone vibrated, she hesitated. The line was silent, nervousness was unfamiliar terrain for them. A knock drew Suva's attention to her window; she smiled opening it for Tommy. Tommy sat on the ledge, playing with the thin silver circle on his right middle finger, never breaking eye contact. A gush of wind lowered the temperature of the room. She shivered but dared not move, his eyes now a darker shade of green held her captive. Tommy's voice massaged her ears,

"I want nothing more than to hold you in my arms and kiss you…but nothing we share should be tainted with irresolution." He took a deep breath, stood and turned his back to her, and gazed out the window.

"Wohali, I feel the same way, but…" Suva played with her ring. Inches away from his back, her fingers ached to feel his muscles flex beneath them.

"Atsila, it is very simple." He turned and caressed her right earlobe. "I want you, but I'm not going to take you." Suva heard her longing in his voice.

"Wohali, we can't be selfish. We must think about Ayesha and Jason. What we do affect the members of our group." Tommy gave in.

"Buenas Noches, mi amor." He went through the window, a cloud of sadness hanging over his head. Halfway down the balcony, Suva's hands stopped him; she pushed him against the wall with a slight force. He braced himself for the brutal attack. Instead, she tenderly pressed her lips against his. Ignoring her desire to deepen the kiss, she glided her tongue over every contour of his lips with flawless precision. Tommy tried to move his hands, Suva pinned them to the wall on either side of his head. She eased back a little and stuck her tongue out, daring him to get it, her hazel eyes glistening with mischief. Tommy reached for her tongue, and she eased back; after the third try, he freed his hands and pinned her to the wall.

There was no teasing, no flirting, Tommy cupped her face and ravaged her mouth, their tongues met and danced. He deepened the kiss while running his fingers through her hair. Their passion created a heated vortex blocking out the chill. Suva's center permeated with new warmth; she pleasured in it uninhibitedly.

Tommy held her tongue captive. They pushed apart for air. When their breathing stabilized, Tommy, released Suva, she attempted to stand, but her knees buckled. He steadied her, and they both laughed. They didn't expect that kissing each other would have been so electrifying. Suva pulled him in for more.

"Honey, wake up." *That's weird*, Suva thought, she saw Tommy's lips moving but heard Mavis's voice. She woke up.

"That must've been some dream. I haven't seen you smile like that since you got pre-accepted to ManU."

Mavis was already making the bed. Suva walked on air into the bathroom, utterly unaware of Mavis' mockery. At breakfast, Suva was so energized; she grinned from ear to ear. Her parents noted two instances of unconscious humming. She finished her food and danced with an imaginary partner back to her room.

The Boughens and the Lanaghans tried to have joint family game nights at least two Sunday nights out of the month. It was the first time Suva saw Tommy since her steamy dream. They had a hard time keeping Suva focused. She would often get this dazed look in her eyes. After a rousing game of Scrabble, they watched a movie in the theater room. Suva was oblivious to the film. She kept tasting Tommy. She was brought back to reality by Mrs. Boughen's voice over the intercom. "Suva honey, Jason is on the phone for you."

"Thanks, I'll take it in my room," Suva shouted into the receiver. Tommy, knowing it was a group-call, went with her. Tommy was not sure what got into Suva. In her room, she opened the line and put it on speaker.

"Hey, guys, what's up?" They all responded at once; Jason spoke up.

"Okay, let's try this again. I am confirming the colors for tomorrow. Ladies variations of Lavender. Guys shades of blue. All assignments completed. Mañana."

That Friday, since their parents were out of town on one of their overnight couples' retreat, Tommy and Suva decided on an all-night movie mania. The group was invited, but everyone flaked. After the third movie, they took a food break. In the kitchen, they laughed about the stupidity of the last comedy. Tommy was making grilled cheese sandwiches. Suva hopped on the kitchen counter.

"You know your mother doesn't approve of that, young lady," Tommy admonished.

"Well, unless she has hidden cameras, I don't see how she's going to find out." Suva scanned all the walls just in case.

"I don't know what your deal is with counters anyways." Tommy placed the first sandwich on a plate.

"I don't know, Tommy, I just like them. Only the wide ones, though, I think tiny narrow counters should be illegal." They both laughed at her exaggeration. Tommy placed the second sandwich on a plate; he felt the dish wasn't complete, so he retrieved some grapes from the refrigerator. The green ones, those were Suva's favorite. She hopped off the counter, took the two dishes, and made her way back to the theater room. The next morning, the parents came home revived and excited to see their babies. When the results of a preliminary search came up empty, they got a bit worried. Atsila, in true fashion, was about to call the state troopers when Melissa stopped her. As suspected, both teenagers were deep in sleep in the theater room, cuddled tightly. The parents watched them sleep; simultaneously, Melissa and Kyle looked at each other with wry smiles. They slowly backed out of the room, went to the entertainment room, and equipped themselves with the tools needed to execute their idea effectively.

Suva was in dreamland when the blare of the evacuation alarm shook her. Her heart was pounding; she cleared the cobwebs.

"Wohali, get up, honey, we have to get out of here!" She frantically shook Tommy, who was always a little harder to wake up. "Wohali, wake up!" She gave him a very powerful shake, and he was up. They ran speedily from the theater room along the long corridor then down the massive stairs. Halting at the sight of Kyle and Atsila standing at the bottom of the stairs with two mega powered water pistols, looking battle-ready. Kyle ran his index finger horizontally across his throat, and the alarm stopped. For thirty seconds, all you heard was the heavy breathing of the teens. Atsila started singing,

"*Bad boys, bad boys, whatcha gonna do? Whatcha gonna do when they come for you?*" The other two parents emerged from behind the sofa. Tommy whispered something in French, Suva sped off, missed a step, and fell at the base of the stairs. The parents yelped and ran to her aid; she held her ankle.

"Mommy, lawd god! Mommy!" Suva repeated, rocking back and forth in pain. Her mom examined her. When Kyle noted that Tommy wasn't by Suva's side. From the top of the stairs, Tommy whistled, and Suva popped up. The distraction had allowed him to jump over the stairwell and sneak into the entertainment room and retrieve his weapons. When she was a couple of steps from him, he tossed her a red supercharged Smith and Wesson fully loaded with liquid power. Deaglan crouched behind Melissa feeling for his weapon. Suva laughed sinisterly. She pointed to the pile of water guns that Tommy had neatly arranged along the top of the corridor. She got splashed in the face.

"Mommy! Alright. It's on now! Watch mi an yuh." That was the start of the household showdown. The men's attempt to clear a path to the entertainment room for artillery was futile. The kids held them off, Suva blocked entry to the passage, and Tommy held them behind the column. The adults communicated in German as the teens were not yet fluent. Atsila was trying to make her way from the right column to the family-size sofa when both Suva and Tommy fired at her. She slipped under the surge and couldn't get enough traction to raise herself. The teens sprayed her profusely.

Melissa scanned the room for rescue resources, adjusting the French coffee table she lifted her plush Persian carpet that was a birthday gift. Tommy had no time to react. The wounded soldier had disappeared so quickly behind the floating Persian shield. Suva was efficiently holding off the men, then her dad vanished. "Tommy, let's move, our position is compromised!" To win the game, your opponent must be hit with colored water. The teens enthusiastically advanced downstairs, brandishing two tiny squirt guns filled with colored liquid. No parents.

After clearing the entire house, the teens cautiously proceeded outside. There they were met with powerful blasts; they jumped ninja-style behind the bushes to re-strategize. "Tommy, something is wrong. I can't locate Dad," Suva said while reloading with the garden hose.

"Deaglan is probably too out of breath to move. It's time to end this! These old people must go down in flames!" Tommy stated, with way too much exuberance, they both laughed. After scanning the area, Suva whispered,

"I've located three shooters. One's by Mrs. McNally's rose bushes; one's by the white Lexus and, of course, my mom is in the bushes opposite us. Ready? Let's go!" The teens jumped from behind the bushes and shot red liquid at their parents, swiftly eliminating Melissa then Kyle. Atsila was relentlessly bearing down on them with two power-charged shotguns, the pressure stunk. Atsila got hit with the red liquid on her shoulder, so technically she wasn't down.

"Get her legs!" Tommy shouted at Suva, his vision was impaired by Atsila's onslaught. Suva ducked and was able to hit both legs. Standing at the entryway to the house breathing heavily, the teens tasted victory.

"Wait, how did we get here?" Suva shoved Tommy. "Move, shi..." She felt a sting in the back of her neck and saw the blue liquid on Tommy's nape. Deaglan emerged from behind the coat rack smiling. Blowing the tip of his gun he started singing *"Bad Boys"*. The parents joined him, laughing heartily at the teens.

"Come on. You guys thought you could take-me-out? It was a sacrifice for my squad." Atsila stated braggadociously, embracing her weapons.

"In the true tradition of warfare, the losers must clean up," Melissa teased as she squeezed water from her hair.

"I must admit you guys came close this time. You have improved drastically." Kyle bellowed, attempting his best impression of a General. "My battalion was weakened, with our superior firing skills, you guys were outranked." Several hours later, exhausted and hungry, the teens dragged themselves to the mini-gym on the basement floor of the Boughen's house. It was the only place that had stalled showers to wash off the colored liquids that stained tiles; that lesson they learned the hard way. Emerging from the basement, heavenly smells guided them to the balcony. A buffet of burgers, sausages, and vegetable kababs was at end of the scent rainbow.

The group dined and caught up on the week's happenings. They enjoyed these organic family moments. Deep in laughter, no one heard the persistent ring of the phone or the doorbell. Jason was perplexed; he hadn't heard from Tommy and Suva since yesterday. The parents were out of town so what the hell could they be doing undistracted home alone. He tried the door, it opened, he scanned the house and found no one. He followed the sound of Suva's voice, and she was moaning! What! Tommy shouted Suva's name. Jason quickened his pace. The louder the moans, the faster he walked towards the balcony.

"What the fu.." His aggressive interruption startled the group. Focus shifted from the reenactment of Suva's fake fall to a very embarrassed Jason.

"Pickney, what's wrong with you?" Melissa admonished. Jason wanted to disappear; he offered profuse apologies. The group laughed at him for the whole week. They eased up on Friday when Ayesha was bragging about how gorgeous she was, then *wham*! She walked into the glass door at the cabin. It was so hysterical! Ayesha ran squealing, gripping her new nose.

## Chapter 6

Outside of the scope of academia, football and cheerleading were the cornerstone of Mayberry Academy, who were the reigning State Champions. This fanaticism translated to a meeting to prepare for the pre-season meeting that was six months away. The quarterback and head cheerleader are chosen months in advance and then groomed. Ayesha, Suva, and Ashley were head cheerleader nominees. Ashley Winthorpe was not pleased with that lineup. After all, she is a legacy. Her ancestors were Mayberry head cheerleaders. Coincidentally, Jason and Tommy were competing against her equally dissatisfied boyfriend, Avery Hunter, for quarterback.

"Thanks for coming, we have refreshments." Coach Wilson adjourned the meeting and pointed to the far left of the room towards the finger food. Cliques gathered to gossip over the nominees or Mrs. Atkis' botched boob job. Suva and Tommy were organizing all the volunteer sheets for Coach Wilson.

"Hey halfers, kissing Coach's butt won't earn you any extra points," Avery drawled, stopping in front of Suva and Tommy.

"You tell them, baby." Ashley popped her gum. "You halfers belong with your kind."

She popped her gum again, and Avery gave her butt an approving slap.

Coach Wilson started one of his "cheers don't win games, money does" speeches when Avery and Ashley's choking interrupted him. They were turning red. The crowd grew concerned. Jackson, the current running back, called 911 but stopped short when the Operator asked what was wrong with the teens. Duncan shrugged,

"Allergic reaction, maybe." He moved over to Avery. "Same with him." Tommy rushed to his locker and retrieved two pen-like items, simultaneously ramming them into their thighs. After their gasping subsided, everyone turned to Tommy for an explanation.

"It's epinephrine!" he exclaimed, surprised by their ignorance. "Suva is allergic to asparagus." Silence.

"Your boyfriend sure thinks of everything, Suva." Jill, the school's mascot, patted Suva's back. She turned to Jason for a high five. "Tommy, you are awesome!" Moving on to high-five Tommy instead when a red-faced Jason ignored her raised hand. Tommy left her hanging, so she high-fived herself. "Ya'll have no team spirit." She mumbled as she walked away.

Suva thought it best to ride home with Jason.  They drove in silence.  His anger was felt in every turn; he blew a squirrel for being a public nuisance. He cursed the mayor for excessive stop signs. At her door, the floodgates opened.  "I'm irritated by people thinking Tommy is *your* boyfriend and not mine." He paused, Suva's muffled laugh highlighted his slip.  "Swan, it's so not funny." He turned to her, softening his tone. "How would you feel if the entire school thought that Ayesha and I were together?" Bright lights halted the conversation. She breathed a sigh of relief when she saw her dad's car.

"It seemed as if we saved you from something," her mom commented as they ate grapes in the kitchen.

"Yes, honey, you ran out of that car at lightning speed." Her dad laughed and took her off the kitchen counter. She jumped back on the counter and popped a few grapes in her mouth.

"Someone called Tommy, my boyfriend again." The silence urged her to continue. "It was Jill…she even wanted to high-five Jason." Her dad took her off the counter again.

"That's a tough spot for Jason to be in." Suva followed her parents to the plush sofa that not too long ago was a shield. She plopped between them, absorbing comfort. She told them about the nominations and the EpiPen incident. They were surprised that Tommy carried around an EpiPen.

"Tommy is something else, I tell you," Melissa remarked and played with Suva's curls.

"See, that's exactly how girls gush over him. They make those comments all the time, and Jason has to stand there and…" She threw her hands up in defeat. She deliberately omitted Ashley's and Avery's statements. Her father caught the momentary flash of anger.

"Pumpkin, what's wrong?" He cupped her face, continuing before she could fabricate a denial. "Whatever it is, Daddy will try his best to fix it, understand it, pay for it, or kill him." Suva couldn't control her laughter.

"Well, I really can't stand Avery and Ashley. They keep calling us names." Suva huffed. "Mi juss go bax har inna har claat one day." She gestured aggressively.  Melissa rubbed Suva's shoulder.

"Baby, talk to us."

"Yes, honey.  Daddy's here." Deaglan got into protective mode. He knew that when his girls use Jamaican dialect something was good or extremely bad.

"Okay, maybe I'm not going to slap her in her face, but she would deserve it for what she calls us." Suva was pacing. "Mom, Dad, they call us incompletes and halfers." She paused for impact, but her parents were lost.  "They use those words in public, it's in the notes stuffed in our lockers and beneath our slashed tires that they get creative.  They say we are pretending to be the true race, and we don't belong in regular society. We don't have enough white in us to purge out the rest." Hurt took her strength. Suva didn't realize she was sobbing on the ground until her mother wiped away tears.

Deaglan carried Suva to her bedroom while Melissa drew a bath. Melissa sat on the floor in the bathroom while Suva soaked. The air was light and filled with lavender, both from the candles and the soak.  Melissa bit back anger,

"Honey, I'm sorry you have to go through this. Why didn't you tell us it started happening again?" Melissa was at a loss for words. The ridicule she and Deaglan had experienced had caused immeasurable pain. But they thought that society had progressed. When will people look beyond the color of your skin?

"That's why I didn't want to tell you guys. I don't want you regretting being together…regret having me." Memories of Suva in kindergarten hit Melissa hard. Suva would cry every other day because she got teased by a different group of kids. The black children would tease her about her hair that it was too straight and pulled on her back-length braids till her scalp was sore.  She was shunned by the white children because it wasn't fair that she got to wear contacts. Suva wore her *Barbie* shades for a month because her parents refused to change the color of her eyes; she was the only black child with hazel eyes.  Melissa was called to come to Suva's kindergarten class because of a situation. Suva refused to wash the dirt off her skin.  One of the kids told her if she was one color, then maybe someone would play with her.  After negotiating with Suva to wipe the dirt off her face, Melissa talked with the teacher.

"Nice uniform," the teacher commented. "I see why she did that. She wants to be like you. Often, children imitate who they spend most of their time with." Melissa couldn't understand the teacher's logic. Suva spends equal time with each parent. Well, they have been busy for the last three days, doing tag-team parenting.

Deaglan has a big case. That was even why she got there before him.

"Mr. Lanaghan spends a lot of time with Suva. Sure, his job can be hectic, but we try." The teacher stared at Melissa, confused.

"We?"

"Mel? What happened? Is Suva all right? I came as soon as I could." A scared Deaglan hugged and kissed Melissa. The teacher gasped,

"Mr. Lanaghan, this type of behavior is frowned upon!" Deaglan immediately drew back. "You should be ashamed of yourselves." She pointed her finger alternatively. "Imagine, Mr. Lanaghan, we nominated you for the parent of the year because of your bravery in adopting this little girl. Then you publicly flaunt your affair! And you, missy, your agency will hear of this, fraternizing with your employer. I thought you nannies had a code!" Deaglan saw his outrage on Melissa's face, he thought her question was fitting.

"A wah dah gal yah juss say?!" Fire and brimstone were about to rain down; Melissa stepped towards the teacher, just then Suva pulled on Melissa's scrubs.

"Mommy, Daddy, home, please." Melissa lifted a gloomy Suva and cradled her.

"Sure, baby, Mommy will take you home." She turned to the teacher sized her up. "How can you expect the children to behave any better when they have ignorant, narrow-minded buffoons guiding them?" Even after they left, the teacher was dumbfounded, relieved, but dumbfounded. Suva's sobbing brought Melissa back to the present.

"Mom-my, you sa-aid that know…" Suva couldn't get her words out straight. Melissa's hands trembled. She gently washed Suva's back with the sponge and encouraged her to take slow breaths in between words. "You lied to m-e. You to-ld me that know-le-dge was power and per-sons who beh-haved that way were ig-no-rant. But, Mom, the people who ridi-cule me are educ-ated. I'm so confused. I lack the intellectual capacity to solve this riddle. If I'm supposed to 'be with my kind,' who am I supposed to be with? Somebody black or white?" That last statement took a lot out of Suva. She surrendered to her tears and collapsed in the tub. Melissa went in the tub with her fully clothed holding her up from behind.

"Honey, you can love and be with anyone you want. Real love knows no bounds. It doesn't see in black, white, yellow, or orange for that matter." Melissa sang and held Suva until the sobbing subsided.  Singing always made things better.  "Honey, you are so beautiful inside and out, those people need to shut their mouths."  Suva felt a sense of ease.  "Baby, you stand in your truth, writing your narrative; you are self-assured and powerful.  There is greatness within. I am extremely proud of you."  Suva inhaled her mother's encouraging words and exhaled all the negativity.

Tommy used the back of his right hand to wipe the steam from his bathroom mirror and towel-dried his hair with his left. The ride over to Ayesha's house was awkward.  She kept trying to undo his zipper, which led to their usual argument.

"Ayesha, sex is not the only way two people can connect. Sex is not the only way two people show love." Tommy pleaded with her. Ayesha only had one goal, to suck on his lollipop. Every time she tried undoing his zipper, he would thwart her efforts.

"I'm so frustrated! Tommy, virginity is an archaic notion!" She protested, slamming back into her seat.

"All you want to do is talk, talk, talk, and talk some more. Tommy, we already walked in the park, strolled on the sand, and yes, I love watching the sunset with you. I enjoyed that foot rub you gave me that day I wore my Manolos. But come, on, can we get to the good stuff already."

Tommy stared at her, speechless. He twirled his ring.  He moved her hair out of her face, cupped it and spoke very deliberately. "Ayesha, you are a gorgeous and sweet girl, under all that makeup, plastic, and hair dye is a fantastic young lady. You are just too blind to see yourself the way I see you." He gave a long deep kiss and held her. Ayesha had never felt such love and genuine care. She had also never felt such desire. If he could kiss this good, imagine what he can do in bed.

"You can't kiss me like that and not expect me to want to ride you like the prized stallion you are." She licked her lips seductively and made her best cowgirl impression. Tommy couldn't help but smile.

"You are relentless..." Tommy's anger simmered into understanding. Ayesha pulled down the visor and began fixing her makeup in the mirror.  "You know all the girls fantasize about you. They keep saying I'm lucky for having you all to myself." She reapplied her lipstick. "Little do they know that I've never even tasted you." She stopped, pursed her lips, and looked over at him, she had an epiphany.

"Wait, Tommy are you intimidated by my experience?" She turned back to the mirror and applied blush. "You don't have to be; I'm willing to teach you."

Tommy smirked. "We all know how experienced you are, Ayesha, and no one is intimidated. You realize you've never once said 'make love,' you always say, 'have sex.'" Feeling satisfied with her face, she closed the visor.

"What's the difference? As long as you are inside me, giving me hours of pleasure, I'm good."

Tommy turned off his car. "Therein lies our biggest problem." He got out and opened the passenger door for her. At her front door, he kissed her on the cheek. "Goodnight, Ayesha."

Tommy stared at his reflection. He needed to see Suva. He wanted to punch Avery so severely. That punk was a bully. He didn't mind being called a half-breed, mixed breed, or whatever derogatory term people would use. All that never daunted the Cherokee in him. But Suva didn't deserve that. She was such a delicate flower. It was a chilly night, so he grabbed sweatpants instead of his usual underpants. He saw Suva through the window, sitting on her bed in her nightgown.

"Atsila, I've had the strangest night. Ayesha practically fought me to suck my d—" He stopped abruptly when he saw her parents. "Mom, dad. I didn't see you there." He adjusted his sweats.

"Continue," Melissa teased.

"Umm, well, she, ahh, practically fought me to suck on my d-elicious ice cream. We stopped and got dessert on the way over to her house."

"Do you want some chamomile tea?" Melissa offered and handed Suva a cup.

"Sure." Tommy sat on the bed beside Suva. They discussed Tommy's nomination and the events of the night. Tommy expressed his anger toward the dumb-As.

"I think something is off about those two. They have the same rare allergies. Who the heck is allergic to fish essence?" Suva asked. "Mrs. Blake, the nice lady that baked the cookies. She said she made fish for Mr. Blake's dinner on the stovetop. The fish was nowhere near the oven." Suva stood up to top off her tea. "I'm telling you they are related. Only siblings can have as much in common as they do."

"Suva! Don't be mean." Deaglan chuckled.

Suva looked at her dad and locked her lips and threw away the invisible key. Then she unlocked them and said, "Just one last thing. Mom, you need to test them. They have the same shaped eyes and their hands, Mom, their hands!" She relocked her mouth and threw away the key. Tommy rolled his eyes.

"Are you sure you threw it far enough?" Deaglan asked between chuckles. Suva signed yes.

Ayesha was getting restless. She was all alone in her room, looking pretty, with no one to admire her. She walked to her window and saw Travis Bent. He was sneaking into his house way past curfew. She recognized a kindred spirit. He was the one she tried pot with for the first time. Her parents caught them, and she was grounded forever. When his room light came on, she called.

"Hello, Ayesha. I don't have any more weed." Travis always a kidder. Ayesha twirled the phone cord.

"You have something else that I want." Travis perked up.

"I certainly do, meet me by the pool in 10, no, make that five minutes. I need to take a quick shower." He was about to hang up.

"You are not coming to my room?" Ayesha asked sheepishly.

His response was sharp, "Come on, seriously?" The line went dead. Four minutes later, he had her against the side of the pool house, his hand in her panties and mouth ravishing her neck. She tried kissing him on the lips several times. Annoyed, he stopped her. "Ayesha, this is just sex, not romance." He shifted positions, with his back against the wall he guided her head to his midriff. Ayesha paused for a moment and looked up at him. *What the hell am I doing here,* she thought. *Oh well, at least he's begging for it.*

Ayesha devoured him; she pulled out all the stops, ensuring that he would never forget how good she was. She had a point to prove all he had to do was let her, and she knew he would enjoy it. She was so deep in thought about Tommy that she didn't notice Travis's moans and tightening fist. Travis had to pull her off millisecond before he exploded. Travis had difficulty speaking, "Damn, girl, you are really good at that. I almost plastered your face." He grabbed her off her knees and pushed her face-first against the wall and pulled her panties down. Ayesha felt him inside her, but the pleasure she was expecting to feel literally wouldn't come. When it was over, Travis retrieved a small transparent sachet of herbs.

"This is for you being such a good girl. Until next time." He handed it to her and left. Ayesha took a long hot shower. No matter how much she bathed, she still felt dirty. At least, he was pleased enough to want a next time, unlike Tommy, who valued her too much to sleep with her. What a load of crock! She doesn't even know why she is with him anyways. He would rather they cook together than go to La`Shores, the hottest restaurant in town. There is a two-week waiting list, two weeks, but with her dad's connections, they would have gotten a table. What's the sense of having it all if you can't have it *all*? Some people didn't know how to appreciate their privilege.

In bed, she was restless. It seemed she had an itch that only Tommy could scratch. As soon as it was scratched, she would break up with him. She would do it publicly, too; she wanted him to feel the same humiliation she has been feeling for all these months. Making her wait for sex, such a load of crock! Before she fell asleep, an idea came to her; the Academic Decathlon was in two weeks. That's where she would make her move. It was a brilliant idea, her best yet.

## Chapter 7

"This dress is awesome. I have to get it." Ayesha was going crazy over an orange Gucci strapless dress. The group was at their favorite boutique, shopping for decathlon outfits. The Academic Decathlon was a meeting of the minds, an annual high school competition that brought out the most astute of scholars. Schools competed in ten categories: Science, Mathematics, World History, Global Languages, Geography, Lexicology, Technology, Sports, Music, and Politics. The girls were in the dress section, and the guys were looking at the store's sports memorabilia. Suva preferred the memorabilia section. "I don't see why we can't just wear something from our closets." She was looking at a lavender sundress, knowing she already owned something similar. Sofia chimed in.

"I understand what you are saying, Suva. However, this Versace dress is screaming *mi nombre*." Sofia took it off the rack. Ayesha chimed in,

"Suva, we have to look good. We must make a statement. We are hot nerds. No longer are we subjected to thick glasses, high-waisted pants, and pocket protectors." Ayesha shuddered at the image. "It's our time to shine, and we have to sparkle." Suva had to give her an A for consistency. Ayesha always had that flare and will probably have rhinestone crutches when she's a hundred.

"How do I look?" Sofia asked twirling.

"Te ves muy caliente, mami. Spicy!" Suva commented, snapping her fingers to the right, then left then right again. Sofia blushed at the confirmation of her very thoughts.

"I'm getting it." Ayesha dragged the girls to the lingerie section.

"Do you think this is sexy?" Ayesha held up a thong, and the tag was the largest part of it. "Wait, no, this one is perf!" She held up a crotchless panty and matching nipple less bra.

"Ayesha, what are those for?" Sofia asked, blinking rapidly. Ayesha had a wry smile on her face.

"No, not what, but who are they for." Ayesha kept searching through the racks, commenting on the items under her breath. Suva wanted to get back to training, besides Ayesha is always dramatic, why should today's antics be any different.

"Well…" Ayesha turned to Sofia.

"I'm just trying to keep the fire burning. Don't want my man to get bored. What do you think of this nurse's outfit?" Suva was still unbothered.

"Wait, wait…" Sofia grabbed Ayesha's hand. "Keep the fire burning; when did it get ignited?" Ayesha walked off, stopped, and came back to where Sofia was.

"A girl never kisses and tell." Suva's head snapped up. Sofia was just as shocked, so she pressed on.

"Ayesha, when did it happen, where, how, when?" Ayesha casually continued sifting through the bras, allowing time to pass building intrigue.

"At least now, I know he's straight." The ride back to the dorms was quiet. The guys didn't know what transpired while the girls were shopping, but they knew better than to ask. Except for Ayesha, who was unusually chipper, Suva and Sofia looked shock. Tommy tried making eye contact with Suva, but she never looked his way, he sensed deliberate avoidance.

Dr. Theopolus was the head of Mayberry Academy's Science department and head coach of the decathlon team. He is a no-nonsense educator who believes in hard work, lengthy study sessions, and active training. His idea of "active" training was the team practicing with new questions before studying the material. This, he said, causes you to rely on your brain, not memory. Surprisingly, his method works. Mayberry was enjoying its 12th year as champions.
Each team member was assigned specific categories to study. Suva: Global Languages and Lexicology; Duncan: Mathematics and Science; Sofia World History; Tommy Technology; Ayesha and Jason: Politics and Geography; Avery and Ashley: Sports and Music. Immense pressure was on the alternates, for they had to study everything. After three hours of training, the teens wondered wearily into the playroom. Dr. T had ordered pizza.

"Can someone please tell me why the dumb-As are on the team again." Sofia voiced what everyone was thinking. The six teens glared across the room with annoyance. Suva explained.

"To be fair, they are both musical prodigies. And oddly enough, they both have a knack for sports trivia."

She paused and raised her brows and her right index finger. "You know who else was a musical prodigy back in his day? Mayor Hunter." Laughter irrupted. They decided to regroup after they showered. There was a knock-on Suva's door, she ignored it.

"Atsila, open the door. I know you are standing behind the door, trying to hold your breath." She exhaled, took a step back, and opened the door.

"Tommy, what are you doing here? Mi a go bade." She raised her toiletry pouch.

"Why are you ignoring me? You haven't made eye contact with me since we left the boutique. What's wrong?" Tommy furrowed his brows. He approached her, and she circumvented him. She rushed into the bathroom and locked the door.

"Tommy, everything is fine. I need to shower."

"I'm going, but I'll be back soon for you to fess up." Tommy showered quickly. Giving Suva a little more time, he sat on the bean bag in the room for five minutes. On his way to Suva's room, he saw Duncan. He asked him to tell the group to start without them. Locking Suva's door, Tommy paused. She was lying on her tummy in just her robe. Her rear was plump and curvy, begging to be touched; thick, majestic hair flowed down her back. She turned to look at him, and her robe shifted exposing delicate skin. His pants suddenly felt tight. The looks in their eyes spoke volumes.

Tommy moved over her, his body aligned with hers perfectly, her sexy posterior providing the perfect cushion for his pelvis. She smelt like cherry blossoms. He rubbed his nose over the curve of her neck. Suva moaned and leaned into his caress. Her reaction awoken his groin pressuring his zipper. He slowly tasted her skin, licking and sucking. The sensation of his tongue evoked varied moans. He was pleased. She started moving provocatively against him, his pulse quickened. Suva gripped the sheet as their movements got feverish. Tommy eased up, placed her on her back, Suva's robe fell open. Her breasts were more glorious than he had imagined. His seductive air disappeared; he couldn't restrain himself; she awoken his primal beasts.

Suva moaned, "Wohali, Tho-mm, Tho…"

Tommy opened his eyes to see Ms. Spence standing over him.

"You have to turn your lights out. Dr. T. canceled tonight's training session. We'll start at 5 a.m. instead of 7 a.m."

Tommy was happy he was still sitting, or else Ms. Spence would have gotten an eyeful. He was sweating; he took a very long, freezing shower.

## Chapter 8

After the early morning practice, the team gathered in the cafeteria for breakfast. Tommy found himself avoiding Suva. She got a problematic question correct and high-fived him, and it triggered him. Her smell, her taste, the sweet sound of her moans, were all too vivid.

"Earth to Tommy," Ayesha called out to him. "You haven't touched your food. Tommy, what's going on? You've been a little off today." Ayesha gave up on the conversation. Tommy blankly ate his food, another downfall to avoiding Suva, deciding what to eat. Tommy had been peripherally stalking Suva. But now, her body language merited his focus; she was sitting with Jason. They were having a very heated conversation, but you wouldn't know unless you knew Suva's "I'm extremely annoyed, piss the hell off" face. Jason got up. Suva pushed her tray away, bit an apple, then tossed it. She looked up, and they made eye contact. Suva rolled her eyes and looked away. Tommy was confused.

The decathlon team was drained. When Ms. Baker called Duncan's name for roll, he answered, "What is Indonesia?" Ms. Baker commented,

"Dr. T is pushing you too hard. Gifted yes, but teenagers nonetheless."

"Thanks for your concern, Ms. B, in a few days it will all be over," Jason assured Ms. Baker as he fought back a yawn. An announcement came over the PA system. There was an emergency meeting of all student body representatives in the library. Suva asked to be

excused and made her way to the library. She was not in the mood to utilize her interpersonal skills. Where the hell was Tommy? He never made it to class, probably off somewhere having sex with Ayesha. Suva gagged at the thought of their bodily fluids co-mingling. In the meeting room in the library, she found herself alone.

"A weh dem people yah deh," she cursed to herself.

"I sent them away." Tommy came up behind her. "I needed to speak to you alone. Silly, but this was the only thing I could think of." He ushered her to sit. She sat three chairs away from him.

"You can give me the courtesy of eye contact," Tommy stated with more attitude than expected. That dream threw him. Now being this close to her, all he wanted to do was make her scream his name. Suva saw the glint in his eyes and the smile on his face.

"Listen. If you want to have a discussion with me, at least be present." She got up and walked to the window, staring out at nothing.

"Suva, why are you so mad at me? You never get upset. Does this have something to do with why you've been avoiding me?" Tommy finger-combed his hair and waited for her to answer.

"Thomas, I have not been avoiding you. You've just been too busy getting your freak on." She didn't turn to face him. She couldn't bear to see the desire on his face.

"Suva, what are you talking about, which freak am I getting on?" Tommy mocked. Suva got to her boiling point. It's one thing to have Ayesha throw it in their faces but for him to blatantly deny it. She turned sharply,

"Mi cyah believe yu! Liad!" She got angrier with each word. "Mentiras. Usted debe estar avergonzado de sí mismo!" He couldn't get a word in. Suva glared at him and pointed an accusatory index finger in his chest, poking him with every word. "Mensonges mensonges. Je pourrais juste te tuer tout de suite!" Tommy took a deep breath. Held her finger and spoke in his most soothing voice.

"Atsila, Patois, Spanish and French, really? I am not a liar. I have done nothing to be ashamed of and what!" Tommy rubbed her right earlobe. He couldn't help but smile; she was hella sexy when she was angry. "Atsila, just talk to mi nuh, in English, please." He guided her to a chair and sat right next to her, keeping his hand on the small of her back.

"Well, Ayesha keeps bragging about how great you are in bed. Buying sexy lingerie for AD to keep the fire burning. Hablar acerca de demasiada información." Suva's anger started resurfacing.

"Atsila, breathe…finish." Tommy's voice was calm, but his neck was fire red.

"I know you guys are together, and it's your business. You have all right to have as much steamy sex with her as you want. I just thought you and I were closer than that. I would have preferred if I heard it from you first. Yuh nuh?" She twirled her ring. "Then you started avoiding me. Tommy, you never avoid me. I couldn't fathom…then this morning at breakfast, you guys ate by yourself, and I couldn't even decide on what to eat." She sighed, twirling the ring again. "Then the idiat boy Jason was on me again about my eating habits."

Tommy's anger went from 10 to 60. Jason was always getting on her about her weight. "What issue did the body police have this time? You ate more than a grain of rice?"

"He said that I should watch what I eat because there is going to be a pool party in AD, and we want to look good. Then reminded me that I was predisposed to chunkiness. Not only are blacks traditionally heavier, but Jamaican women tend to wear their fat around the stomachs and thighs." Tommy got up and went to the window.

"How can you stay with that narcissistic borderline racist? You are curvy size 6. Your body is perfect." His tone softened with his last sentence; he turned and cupped her face. "Your body is perfect. Your curves drive me crazy. I can't sleep without dreaming of caressing every inch of you. My senses go into overdrive when you are near me. Your gluteus maximus causes me to walk into walls."

Suva's heart melted. He does tend to walk into walls a lot. But he blames it on needing new glasses. She chuckled at the thought of Mr. Coordination, walking into a wall because of her. She found it secretly flattering.

"Suva, Ayesha, and I have not had sex. If I had any such intentions, you would be the first to know." Suva felt so relieved. "The reason I was avoiding you…I had one of my erotic dreams about you, and I couldn't focus around you. I know I am wrong for saying this. But I want you…my heart, my body, and my soul. I'm yours yesterday, today, forever. I don't need a Truth Circle to admit it." They stood there silently. It was the first time Tommy had verbalized his feelings in such a raw manner.

"Well, your body better inform Ayesha because she is certainly gearing up for you at AD," Suva said jokingly, but it fell flat. They both wished things were different.

"I want to talk with Jason; he needs to lay off. He is so used to size negative 2, plastic girls that lipo their stomachs, throw up their food that he cannot appreciate a real woman. I just don't get it, in what world is woman's beauty indicative of her size!"

"Tommy, I'm a big girl. I can take care of myself. I wouldn't give up this," she slapped her rear; it made a smacking sound. "for anything." His body reacted. He took her hand and placed it on his erection.

"In case you ever have any doubts about your amazing body." She blushed but left her hand there. It was her first time touching him there. Tommy's breath stopped; he kept praying it wasn't another dream. Suva's curiosity moved her hand just a smidge; when he moaned, she licked her lips. Tommy didn't know what to do with himself. The blare of the school bell broke the trance.

## Chapter 9

The long-awaited decathlon weekend had come. The teens were thrilled to be at the hotel finally. It was breathtaking, all twenty stories with an Olympic-sized pool. The exterior and interior décor was white with gold trimmings. The rooms had sliding doors but no balconies except on the twentieth floor, which housed the suites. The junior suites were on the nineteenth floor, the rooms between the eighteenth and third floors ranged from king to standard size. The large banqueting rooms on the second floor doubled as conference areas or competition ground. The first floor houses the gym to the right of the reception area, then to the left, beyond the lounge, is the expansive dining hall. The courteous staff was sharply dressed in their full white uniforms with gold name tags.

There was a sea of teenagers and their coaches in the lobby, everyone trying to get checked in as quickly as possible without getting trampled. The manager announced, "Sorry but the hotel is completely booked, so, unfortunately, there are no rooms available for upgrade. We apologize for any inconvenience."

Mayberry Academy's Decathlon Committee pre-registered for the competition, and as returning champions, they got complimentary accommodations and in-room check-in. The exhausted teens were stoked about bypassing the crowd. As they piled into the elevator, a petite blonde eyed Jason, then waved at him right before the doors closed. Jason never waved back. The teenagers were fidgety in the elevator, mumbling about staying at a lame no-balcony hotel. The adults smiled. Ashley stopped popping her gum.

"Where is this room anyway!" Elevators made her uncomfortable. The others got excited as the floors climbed. In unison, they counted cheerfully "16…17…18…19…20!" They jumped, stopping abruptly when the elevator shifted. Realizing how childish they were acting as if they didn't have trust funds. The door opened; they exited the elevator in a calm, civilized manner. Ms. Spence opened the Presidential Suite. Ashley popped her gum again and pointed to the room to their left. "Ms. Spence, is it because of the halfers why we couldn't get the Honeymoon Suite? Hotel can't risk such massive inbreeding, huh?" Ms. Spence ignored her and ushered the group inside. The suite was the standard layout kitchen, dining area, a mini office, a sitting room and three bedrooms with baths. The balcony wrapped around the expanse of the suite and was furnished with two small tables with large umbrellas extending from their centers presumably to block the elements.  Dr. Theopolus sat quietly on the tan couch in the sitting room and placed his papers on the large coffee table in the center of the room. He was deep in thought, he preferred to go straight to quizzing, but there were several mundane activities to get out of the way first.

The opening ceremony later that night, it was a formal affair that he didn't care for. It wasn't the pageantry that annoyed him but the fact that he had to wear a tie. The general breakfast on Friday morning and a college fair all day in the lobby, then the preliminary rounds in the afternoon. Preliminaries, his students could defeat those tyros while sleeping. Then on Saturday morning, after all, the cognitively deficient teams have been weeded out, there'll be four quarterfinal matches, one semifinal match, and then the battle royal. He already saw them on the podium Sunday as the winners.  Ms. Spence called out the room assignments.

"Four girls in room A, the remaining two girls will be with me in room B, and the boys will be in room C. The group turned and looked at Dr. T. without looking up, he rubbed the couch on which he was sitting.

"This converts into a bed."  Ayesha, Suva, and Sofia quickly grabbed Meg, one of the alternates, and rushed to room A.  They couldn't stand the thought of rooming with Ashley. Meg was grateful because she detested Ashley, and she didn't mind the company of the cheerleaders.  The Mayberry gang got ready for the evening's event.

Atypically, the males were waiting on the ladies.  Avery thought he was killing it in his black pantsuit and bow tie.  Tommy entered the room in a full black Armani suit with gold necktie and cufflinks, and Avery's balloon deflated. Even Ms. Spence stared.  Ten minutes later, the girls scampered out.

"This dress looks good, but I can't breathe."  Ayesha agonized, the others agreed.

"Speak for yourself, ladies."  Suva twirled her black dress with gold-beaded embellishments. "My dress is so airy."  The annoyance on Jason's face gave her pause. *Dammit!* She and Tommy had on coordinated outfits.  Tommy was also looking at Suva with intensity. To escape, Suva walked away. Tommy and Duncan made audible groans.  On the second floor, Jason held Suva's hand and walked toward a small group of people gathered at the ballroom's north entrance.   Jason announced Suva as the captain of the Mayberry decathletes. He shook hands with all the executives and excused himself.

"Excuse me, Ms. Mayberry, Maxwell Thunder." Suva laughed and took the outstretched hand of the person she was paired with.

"I'm Suva. Seriously, Maxwell, what's your real last name. I'm sure your parents are not Mr. and Mrs. Thunder. Plus, Maxwell is Scottish, not French, alluding to his accent." Suva kept laughing until Maxwell answered,

"Actually, no. My parents are now divorced. It's Mr. Thunder and Ms. Storm." Maxwell had a straight face, and he held on to Suva's hand without her even taking note. Suva looked at him in disbelief.

"I do not believe that you have the misfortune of going through life as either Mr. Thunder or Maxwell Storm?" Suva's laughter died down when she read his name tag. It said Maxwell Thunder. She cleared her throat and searched for an apology.

"No apologies necessary. I find you intoxicating, so I would never take offense to anything you could ever have to say." The chairman signaled, and they marched in.  Suva struggled to keep a straight face throughout the ceremony. The speeches were long, so Maxwell's shenanigans were a welcomed distraction. He had her laughing so hard, her cheeks hurt. Suva couldn't understand why she found this arrogant, egotist so entertaining, was it his French accent?

"Let me apologize in advance." After the dessert plates were cleared, Maxwell held Suva's hand yet again and stroked it and spoke in his very superior tone. "A beautiful face like yours should not have to be subjected to any form of anguish" He paused, attempting empathy. Suva became slightly alarmed; if this heartless beast can show compassion, something must be wrong.

"Maxwell?" She leaned in, moved with concern.

"As I said before, I do want to apologize in advance because when my team annihilates, nay, slaughters your puny team,
your pretty little face shall and will be in...*comment dites-vous*, shambles." Suva smiled, kept the proximity, used her left hand to hold his tie, and pulled him close.  Maxwell inhaled; with all his messing around, he never stopped to appreciate how heavenly she smelt and how sexy her lips were. Suva spoke softly.

"Maxwell, you are so hot, let me cool you down." Suva poured a glass of ice water all over his crotch. She got up and sashayed away. Sofia and Ayesha ambushed Suva in the restroom. Sofia retouched her makeup, and Ayesha adjusted her cleavage. When Suva wouldn't dish, Sofia, with lipstick in hand, pushed her.

"So, Ms. Elation, we all saw you laughing your ass off, what's..." Before Sofia could finish, Ayesha interjected,

"Yes, Su, what's up with that?" Sofia continued,

"Don't get me wrong, he is muy caliente, but only Tommy has ever made you laugh like that. Even Jason commented on it." Ayesha chimed in.

"Agreed, only my man has ever made you grin like that. Ironic, huh?" She finished with an attitude.

"Let me finish," Sofia snapped.

"No, let me conclude this ridiculous conversation." Suva had had enough of the yapping. Suva exited the bathroom only to slam right into Jason. "Lawd unuh caan lef mi alone," Suva hissed. Jason held her hands and led her to the dance floor.

"I missed you tonight. I had no arm candy to show off," Jason whispered. Suva didn't answer. Instead, she buried her face in his chest.

"You smell amazing, Jason." Jason smiled,

"Enough for you to taste me?" Suva pulled up from his chest, leaned in, and kissed him. The kiss lingered.

"You taste even better than you smell." Jason forgot about what transpired at dinner and kissed her again, this time deeper and longer. Alone in her room, Suva read her Global Languages book. She was reviewing indigenous languages, prepping for the written exam. Jason popped in,

"Swan, there's a sick party by the pool. I'm the odd man out. I need some arm candy." Suva agreed. Jason was excited; he left her to get ready; he wanted to be the envy of the boys when she made her sexy entrance.

Suva's hands were tired. She'd gotten up early to wash her hair; now it was hell to dry. The girls gave up, citing shoulder pains. Suva was perplexed, the pool party was a disaster. Jason argued with her over her lackluster outfit, Tommy and Ayesha were mad at her for reasons. Suva was relieved when Maxwell pushed them into the pool, breaking the tension. Tommy stuck his head into their room.

"We are leaving for breakfast in 30." He walked over to the bundle of madness atop Suva's head. Took the comb from her, he divided it into four sections and went to work with the dryer. The brush hair dryer combination left her hair straight and bouncy. They made eye contact in the mirror.

"Thomas, why the silent treatment?" He stared blankly, Suva breathed deeply. "Listen, not certain what's in the hotel's cool-aide, but everyone just needs to chill!" Her brush strokes got slightly intense, "Jason's mad about none revealing swimwear, and Ayesha is giving me attitude!" Tommy retrieved the brush.

"Last night my smoking-hot, cleavage-baring girlfriend was in a string bikini dancing on me, and that didn't get a rise out of me.

But the sight of you exiting the elevator got me hard. That's why Ayesha is mad."

He rubbed her right earlobe. "I'm mad because we have to play out this stupid teenage melodrama only to end up together." He walked away, then shouted back. "Maybe you should give Jason what he wants." Suva was pensive, then styled her hair with vigor.

Suva sat at the table calmly, crossing her legs, the low-cut figure-hugging fuchsia dress rode higher on her thighs. The few strategic curls danced airily when she moved. Eating paused. Tommy pushed a tray pass Jason's wide-open mouth, resting it before Suva. "Aren't you cold, Swan?" Jason asked timidly. He couldn't avert his eyes from her bountiful bosom. After the meal, Suva carried her tray to the bin. Jason walked briskly behind, shielding her sexy behind. Over the bin, Jason whispered, "Swan, what are you wearing? People are gawking." His mouth watered for her gorgeous mounds.

"You wanted eye candy." She ran her hands from her breast to her hips. "Don't I look sweet?" Suva left him there speechless.

"Mil a fhéachann tú go hiontach!" Duncan got very Irish. A young man walked up to the table and handed Suva a piece of paper with his telephone and room number on it. They enjoyed watching Jason squirm. In the elevator, Jason pushed Suva against the wall and kissed her deeply. All those guys can watch, but she was his property.

Ms. Spence stayed on the competition floor until all first-round matches were finished. She returned to the suite, armed with new insights and the schedule for the following day.

Dr. Theopolus was already drilling the team. An hour later, while the team snacked and enjoyed a brief break, she debriefed.

"Great job on winning your matches today! You were focused and played cohesively." The youngsters smiled, feeling pleased. "Ashley, you need to reduce your response time by five seconds. You burn valuable time when you use the entire fifteen seconds to think after you've pressed the buzzer." Ashley popped her gum nonchalantly to mask her fear. While music was a part of her, when she sees the crowd, she forgets how to breathe. Ms. Spence flipped the page. "So far, I'm only concerned about three teams and one player. Hartford, Westwind, and Huff. Huff's captain is brilliant! He doesn't show any nerves, and his response time is two seconds." She flipped the page searching for his name.

"Maxwell Thunder!" The teens shouted in disdain. Ms. Spence smiled at the team's unified infuriation. She wrapped up her debriefing with match times.

"Who are we playing in the quarterfinal?" Avery asked nonchalantly. Suva and Tommy answered together,

"Doesn't matter, we don't see opponents, just victory!" Avery pressed on.

"What if we lose a match?" The teens laughed and, in a chorus, shouted,

"Victory is the only option!" He opened his mouth but was silenced by several thrown cushions.

"Rookie!" Jason laughed and tossed another cushion on him. "Avery, that trophy is ours, but every year, we are kind enough to allow these intellectually inferior teams to try and borrow it." The teens cheered. Dr. T liked rewarded their team spirit with an additional ten minutes of free time. The six quarterfinal matches took place concurrently. Mayberry's game was in a room that seated fifty; on the platform, ten judges faced the two teams. The judges' backs were to the audience while the two sides stood around their respective semicircular tables with a buzzer in the center. Each team had a clear view of the quizmaster's small podium. The group said a little prayer, placed their hands in the center, and raised it, shouting, "Mayberry!" Duncan tested their buzzer; it buzzed, the judges looked up sharply.

"Just making sure," Sofia said with a forced smile. The team won the first two matches with ease. The semifinal match presented them with a well-needed challenge. Even so they moved like one organism; each player understood their role and executed it efficiently. During the last round of the match, the lightning round, each team is given three minutes to answer as many questions as possible from all ten categories. Huddled over the buzzer the teens waited anxiously. Suva was at the end of a pep talk.

"They are just ten points behind us, so focus!" Jason was distracted by the petite blonde in the front row. She winked at him. *"What the hell is Molly doing here?"* Suva's stern voice got him to refocus. "Let's get it done!"

Dr. T noted that Westwind answered fifteen questions during their three minutes. He mouthed fifteen to Duncan, who informed the team that they needed sixteen to win. They attacked the buzzer answering with their heads down. When the bell rung, signaling the end of the round, they all looked at Dr. T, who mouthed twenty. They shook the hands of the Westwind team and marched to the suite. The teens were scattered over the sitting room, eating, eagerly awaiting Ms. Spence's arrival. Meg took a swig of her juice,

"I hope we get to play Huff because they are an excellent team." Sofia nodded in agreement, and Duncan raised a potato chip. Ms. Spence entered the room, she got right to business, pacing as she spoke,

"We are playing Huff, and watching their matches, they are just as efficient as we are. With that, the team pushed their food aside and turned to Dr. T. He pushed his glasses up on his face and clapped his hands enthusiastically.

"Team, we've been waiting for this challenge. We have four hours before the match. I will practice with Suva, Ms. Spence, you are with Duncan. The rest of the team practice with the alternates. We will reconvene here in three hours." Dr. T and Suva stayed in the sitting area and went over the Global Languages book cover to cover. Duncan and Ms. Spence went into room B and the others into room C. After three hours, they all gathered in the sitting room. Books closed, Dr. T wanted them to use the hour to relax. The phone rang, Ms. Spence answered, after a moment, she replaced the receiver.

"Duncan and Suva, get ready, we have to be in the testing area in ten minutes. That was an AD official. They want to do the written section at 6:30 p.m. so that the match can start promptly at 7 p.m." Suva, Duncan, and Ms. Spence hurriedly made their way to the competition floor. Maxwell eyed Suva when she walked onto the platform, *"no, she will not distract me from this Global Languages paper."* Standing before their respective tables, the teens were instructed to begin. They had twenty minutes to answer one hundred questions when Maxwell heard, "Time! Pens down," he was delighted. He answered eighty-eight questions, that was a personal best. He was surprised by the disappointing look on Suva's face. At 6:55 p.m., both teams, the ten judges, and all audience members were seated; the only person absent was the quizmaster.

"So, how was the written test?" Tommy asked, the group listened intently. Duncan spoke first,

"I answered them all." Suva inhaled deeply,

"Well, …it was nowhere near my personal best." At precisely 7pm the quizmaster walked to the podium.

"Let the massacre begin!" Duncan's deep voice set the mood for battle; adrenaline kicked nervousness out of the way. At the end of round 2, the teams were performing at optimal levels. The audience was rapt by the spectacle: if Mayberry got two questions correct, Huff would get the following two. They had speed, precision, and accuracy; it was astounding. After Huff's lightning round, Duncan and only Duncan held his head up, and Dr. T mouthed twenty-five. "Guys, we need twenty-two to tie, so let's get twenty-six for good measure." They took a collective breath. Suva spoke in a firm but comforting tone,

"Per aspera ad astra!" The audience was silent with anticipation, and the Huff team held their breaths. Three minutes felt like fifteen. When the final bell rang, Duncan nervously raised his head, and Dr. T mouthed twenty-five. The team de-huddled and waited for the quizmaster to say the final score. The quizmaster was not in his place; he was having a deep conversation at the judge's table. The audience started to mumble as their curiosity grew. One of the judges hurriedly exited the room. The quizmaster returned to the podium,

"Ladies and gentlemen, these two teams have made history tonight. After such a cognitively stimulating match in which all questions were answered correctly, we now have a tie." The audience gasped collectively, and the coaches started walking toward the judges' table. The quizmaster continued, "Coaches, please remain seated. We have contingencies. The results of the written test will be the deciding factor."

The judge returned to the platform with four large envelopes; the quizmaster returned to the judges' table, and they all scrutinized the contents thoroughly.  Suva felt her chest tightening; she knew she didn't answer all her questions. Now she was going to cost the team victory.  How could she show her face in Mayberry again?  The Tribune was going to eat her alive.

"Breathe, Atsila, you didn't let the team down, and you won't be banished from Mayberry." Tommy's soothing words took her out of her head. The quizmaster returned to the microphone.

"Ladies and gentlemen, based on the results of the Mathematics paper we have." He didn't pause, but to everyone, that was the most prolonged breath ever. "We have another tie. The Global Languages score is the decider." He went back to the judges' table. Suva's stomach dropped; her head started spinning.  She kept blinking, trying to focus on the judges' table, even attempting to read their lips.  The room went silent except for the sounds of hearts beating heavily.  "This has been a truly thrilling competition!" The quizmaster was so excited. He kept yapping on, utterly oblivious of the twenty teens behind him, simultaneously screaming at him to shut up and announce the winner. "Teams should feel proud of the superb job—" He was interrupted by the audience's collective shout "Who's the winner?"

"Mayberry Academy!"

The room became chaotic; people were either screaming with joy or anger. The Huff's head coach was enraged; he immediately attacked the judges' table, demanding a recount and full disclosure of the scores. Celebrations halted, and the room was at a standstill. Suva felt someone watching her; Maxwell was staring intently at her, looking calm and relaxed as always. He mouthed, "Congrats; you deserve it." He winked, she smiled.  All attention went back to the quizmaster.

"These are the results of the requested recount. The Math scores tied at 100 percent, Global Languages, Huff has a score of 88 percent and Mayberry with a record-breaking 93 percent." The celebrations resumed drowning out his voice.  Jason hugged Suva, flushed with relief, Suva leaned into the embrace.

"How about we skip the pool party and have our celebration?" Suva agreed. He was excited about spending alone time with Suva, with the benefit of hiding from Molly.  Tommy wanted desperately not to be bothered by Jason and Suva's public displays.

He needed a distraction.  So, when Ayesha asked him to come to her room instead of going to the pool party, he quickly agreed.  The teens made their way to the pool except for Suva, Tommy, Jason, and Ayesha.  Suva was about to knock on the door to room B when Tommy opened it.  He awkwardly passed her and walked across the suite to room A.  Suva could only imagine what Ayesha had in store for Tommy armed with sexy lingerie.  Jason wasted no time kissing and caressing her.  Then Suva announced that she's going to get a sweet surprise for him in the lobby.  He winked and suggested strawberry.  In the hall, Suva whispered her request to the concierge; he winked, "I see we are having a party."

Entering the room, Tommy smelled roses.  He was instructed to close his eyes and stand in place.  When permitted he opened his eyes to a dimly lit room, with two candles and heart-shaped rose petals arranged on the bed.  His pulse accelerated, Ayesha was breathtaking in black see-through lingerie that hugged her like a second skin.  Her hair fell perfectly; her natural skin looked so beautiful.  She approached him slowly, kissing him gently.  The lack of aggression touched him, and he kissed her unguardedly.

Over in room B, Jason was busy preparing for Suva's return.  He lit three red candles and placed them strategically around the room.  Jason knew AD would do the trick.  Her willingness to get flavored condoms excited him.  He was going to rock her world!

Tommy got lost in the tenderness of Ayesha's kisses, she licked and tasted his neck, his chest, his torso.  When she unfastened his belt, he stopped her.  He needed to catch his breath.  "Ayesha let's talk."  Standing up, Ayesha gripped his erection,

"I think he has something else in mind."  She ran her hands along his shaft.  Tommy's breath caught.  Ayesha led him to the rose petal bubble-filled tub in the bathroom.  Inside the tub Tommy cradled Ayesha's back against his chest.  Kissing her neck, his hands tantalized each nipple, awakening them.  Encouraged by her moans his hands explored further, she welcomed its arrival at her center by spreading her legs.  He teasingly stroked her delicate folds, while sucking on her neck and caressing her nipple, matching the intensity of her moans.  Holding her tightly as she climaxed.  Closing their eyes, they marinated in the moment.  "Tommy, that was…that was great!"

Smiling and stroking her hair Tommy didn't open his eyes.  He was completely relaxed.  He didn't know that pleasuring someone could be so…pleasurable.  Resting even deeper he pulled her closer.

"Yeah, Suva, it was…" Tommy exhaled soothingly. The aggression with which Ayesha pulled out of his arms caused water to splash from the tub. "Are you ok?" Asked a frantic Tommy. Him not realizing what he said made Ayesha even more furious, she stormed out of the bathroom. Wrapping a towel around his mid-drift a clueless Tommy pursued her. "What happened?" Ayesha tossed his clothes on him. Noticing the mark on her neck, Tommy probed further. "I didn't realize I was sucking your neck that hard."

"Get out!" Ayesha held the door open just long enough for him to pull his pants up. She started removing the thin silver ring from her right middle finger. Suva gasped at the sight of a shirtless, open-pants, Tommy. Suva stomped to door B. Conflicted about who to console Tommy stood in place. Ayesha slammed the door hard. Tommy was flabbergasted. *What the hell just happened?* Jason opened the door in a robe.

"Dude, nice!" He bellowed supportively to a half-naked unresponsive Tommy. An excited Jason pulled Suva into the room and started kissing her.

"Jason, what are you doing! Why are you in a robe?"

"It's too much, I know." He dropped the robe. Suva couldn't think; Jason kept advancing, trying to kiss her.

"Jason, please stop and put on some clothes. I can't think…when did the suite become a nudist colony dammit!" Jason put on his robe and paced angrily.

"I don't get you. Why did you volunteer to get the flavored condoms?" Suva choked in shock. "Condoms! What condoms? I went to get ice cream." She threw the ice cream at his chest. "Cho, bum cho, which damn condom, nuh greeve mi!" Suva exited the suite. Jason put the ice cream in the refrigerator and got dressed. In the elevator, he looked at his reflection. This was not how he envisioned the night ending.

On the sixteenth floor, the door opened, and there was Molly, looking stunning in a pink bikini. Inside her room he flung her against the wall, kissing her aggressively. "I thought you had forgotten about all the fun we had last year," Molly said in between kisses. Jason placed his right index finger over her mouth. Molly switched places with him and began kissing his neck; she started to run her hand down his torso when he exploded. Jason spewed profanities; he went into the bathroom, cleaned himself up, and went back to the suite.

# YESTERDAY

On the flight back, Dr. T was mystified by his history-making team. They were grunting and dragging along as if they suffered defeat. Not even the thrill of collecting the championship trophy earlier that day was enough to make them smile, he can solve complex theorems, but to him, teenagers would always be a conundrum.

## Chapter 10

The teens had no time to dwell on AD's unfortunate occurrences because they went into the long gruesome process of preparing for and sitting their final examinations. At a post-exam movie night, hosted by Suva, the teens destressed. "So, are we going to the senior prom?" Munching on caramel popcorn, Sofia looked at her friends for a response. The reaction was that of non-interest. Tommy spoke up.

"We are not Seniors, so no." Ayesha looked at them, puzzled.

"Come on, guys, we have to go to prom. We are the social elite, the Secret Six. We have fashion statements to make and booties to shake." She did an offbeat dance.

"You have a great point, girl, as a matter of fact, that should be our slogan." Suva laughed hysterically and repeated, "We have fashion statements to make and booties to shake." It was settled with a vote; they were going. When the boys left the room to get more food, Suva pressed Ayesha about Tommy's birthday. Ayesha played with her overly bleached blonde tresses. *Tommy does not deserve a celebration. Since he loves you so much SUVA, why don't you deal with it!* Out loud she said,

"Haven't finalized things yet," Suva suggested an intimate dinner with family and close friends. Ayesha objected, stating that she'd prefer booking a hotel for the night; even though it was his birthday, she wanted to have fun too. Suva dropped it.

The prom was held in an immaculately decorated ballroom at one of Mayberry's finest hotels. The six teens were exquisitely dressed. They had fun dancing and just being teenagers. Afterward, they hung out at the local diner. Over entrées, Suva reminded them to review their travel documents for the upcoming trip to Jamaica. It was tradition for her family to do yearly destination vacations. After such a hectic school year, a summer vacation in Jamaica was precisely what was needed. The teens were excited to hit the beach and drink actual coconut water.

On the morning of June 29, Suva rose at the crack of dawn, made breakfast for Tommy, and served it to him in bed. The parents came in singing, happy birthday. "We are doing our part early." Dancing like a giddy-headed child, he blew out the massive 18 candle. Mavis removed it and cut him a slice. They left him with his gifts.

Tommy stopped chewing when he saw Suva's gift. It was the catalogue of the latest Formula 1 drivers and their cars with specifications. Scanning through each driver autographed their picture along with personalized birthday wishes. He flipped searching. "No way! What! Noooo!" There beside his favorite racer ever, Andre "Precision" Subryan was his custom-made burnt orange Ferrari with the words, "Happy Birthday, Wohali" written across its side. Tommy screamed, shouted, jumped through his window, ran across the balcony, shouting Suva's name. When she wasn't in her room, he ran down the giant stairs, still screaming. He found her in the kitchen washing dishes. Tommy lifted Suva and spun her around.

"Thank you, thank you! That's why I love you." Suva was delighted that he liked his gift. In fairness to the other gifts Tommy didn't open them. Outside Tommy's house, Ayesha honked the horn. He kissed his mom, hugged his dad, and jumped into the car. Ayesha and Tommy spent the day at the same hotel where the prom was held. Tommy appreciated how calm and relaxing the day was. They lounged by the pool and participated in various water sports. Later that night, Tommy got dressed for dinner while Ayesha was in the bathroom. His gift was on the bed. He tore the wrapper eagerly. There was an aftershave mist; he never shaves on account that he doesn't have facial hair. There was a thong that smelled like fruit and his and her erotic gels. He closed the box.

Tommy was very quiet at dinner. They were having a wonderful four-course Italian meal. When he spoke, he spoke from the heart, "I think we should break up...we want different things. You enjoy sex...I crave intimacy." Ayesha was relieved, but her ego lashed out. If anyone was ending this miserable sexless relationship, where she was subjected to modest dressing, it should be her. She adjusted her ring.

"Tommy, don't give up just yet. The JA trip will be tots cool. Surely we can find intimacy there." That appeased him, he ended the night early so they could meet up with the others. Ayesha grit her teeth; they were wasting a perfectly good room and goodies.

Two weeks before the trip to Jamaica, Sofia pulled out, her family was spending the summer in Costa Rica. The night before the trip, Jason and Ayesha explained to Suva and Tommy respectively that they wouldn't be flying down until Suva's birthday. Plus, Duncan's family decided to vacation in Ireland. Suva was crushed.

At the Mayberry International Airport, bittersweet good-byes were exchanged. Suva, Tommy, and their parents were getting ready to board their flight.  Suva's sad countenance inspired Duncan to extend his left hand. The six teens took off their rings, interlocking the thin silver grooves, forming one thick circle in Duncan's outstretched palm.  "No matter our location we are one, connected, Yesterday, Today, Forever." Returning each ring, they embraced warmly, with promises of daily phone calls. Their chatter was cut short by the announcement that flight R818 was boarding. Jason pulled Suva in for a deep prolonged kiss, whispering in her ear,

"I'm going to miss you, can't wait for your birthday. I love you deeply." Suva blushed and floated away. She was still on cloud nine as they settled in first class. She gazed out the window as the plane took off. She always loved looking at the landscape, Mayberry's vast library, stable concrete structures, the different-sized pools in the backyards, and the beautiful parks.  Mayberry was a beautiful place that had the right amount of nature.

Midway through the flight, feeling restless, she put her mystery novel down.  She couldn't get that kiss with Jason off her mind. She felt guilty having him wait so long for sex.  She sighed because she wasn't ready for sex.  One she didn't see what the big deal was and two, she didn't feel as if she was mature enough for it. The thing is if she didn't give in, how much longer would he wait?

## Chapter 11

The pilot announced that they would be landing soon. The sight of lush greenery and clear blue waters washed away Suva's nervousness.  She poked Tommy while doing her happy dance. Descending the stairs from the plane, they were greeted by the crisp air and warm sun of the Tropics.

"Sangster has changed since the last time I was here," Melissa commented. Deaglan, holding her hand on the descent, agreed.  Tommy, who was assisting Suva, ran his hand through his hair and adjusted his shades, "Tell me again why we had to fly into Montego Bay as opposed to Kings-town isn't Kings-town the capital city?" Suva chuckled at his pronunciations.

"Tommy, you are such a tourist, they are going to eat you alive.  Montego Bay is the tourist capital, plus the estate is closer to Montego Bay than Kingston."

After clearing immigration and Customs, they exited the airport, giving the baggage handlers a lovely tip.  Melissa got around the steering wheel and scanned the passengers in the rental vehicle. The Boughens were ecstatic. They loved coming to Jamaica; it was where they got married and honeymooned. Atsila nudged Melissa on her shoulders, and in her best Jamaican accent said, "Come, man, mi hungry, to the nearest KFC!" The van vibrated with laughter. Melissa had everything covered. They could always count on her; she was their organizer, party planner, and chauffeur. At KFC, Suva swiveled back and forth on the red and white chair, giggling with anticipation. Melissa and Kyle were standing at the back of the very long line.

"Is today a national holiday?" Deaglan commented, marveling at the long line.

"No, Daddy, Jamaicans love KFC, the line is always long," Suva remarked, stopping the chair in his face. She twirled to the right and then back in his face, laughed, and said with much expression, "Afta all, nobady does it better!"

Tommy couldn't help himself; he gazed at Suva. Her hair was up, and she had on shades to complete her relaxed vacation look, she was radiant. He smiled to himself at the idea of seeing her in a two-piece, her hair all wet. They left KFC with two buckets of chicken, fries, corn, and biscuits. Suva's mouth watered, she grabbed the bag and sat in the back of the vehicle. She unabashedly searched through the box until she found the barbequed treasure. She raised the breast high.

"Yuh know how long mi a wait paan yuh." She bit a large chunk out of it. She chewed slowly, savoring all the juices. A shouting, Melissa blasted the horn.

"Stupid taxi driver, he just stopped in the middle of the road." She kept honking. "Come out of di road; a mus buy yuh buy yu license, cho." They chuckled at her understandable road rage. Suva looked; they were driving past Walter Flecther's Beach.

"Mom, why are you passing the beach?" Her mom pointed ahead of them. They drove by what looked like a diner to their right. It had a picture of a pelican in the sign. When they passed the Doctors Cave Beach, Suva knew they were going to Cornwall Beach. She was correct; her mom took a sharp left and entered the Cornwall Beach parking lot. They paid the entrance fee and noted a large sign, *"Only food purchased on the property should be consumed here."* The radiance of the sun partnered with the cool breeze to cloak them with serenity. Silky white sand guided them to the splendor of the ocean. Tommy patiently waited for Suva outside the changing room.

"That's what you are wearing?" He walked off.
Suva ran to catch up with him.

"What's wrong with my swimsuit?" He kept on walking. She grabbed his hand.

"I don't like it." He continued walking.

"It was my mom's. It's vintage. Classic black one piece."

"Some things are just old, not vintage!" Suva was taken off guard, and it was the first time he expressed dislike for her clothing choice. Pointing her finger at his chest, she said,

"Well, I like it so you can go sit on a cactus." She sashayed away. She really had a sexy backside. Irony slapped him in the chest, Ayesha was always stripping for him, yet here he was desiring to see Suva in a two-piece. He dropped his stuff at their spot under some low hanging trees and wandered into the ocean. The water was fantastic; he floated and looked at the clear blue skies. *So beautiful!*

"We are doing that!" Tommy shouted to his companions, pointing at the Jet Skis that rode up. They were busy hiding and eating their contraband food. Two hours passed and Tommy and Suva said nothing to each other. Tommy had to plate his food. Suva and her dad were the last pair to go out on the Jet Skis after negotiating a better price because they felt they were being charged the "tourist" rate. Tommy wanted to punch the man operating the Jet Ski when he directed some comments at Suva.

"Empress, yuh can go free, caue yuh pretty like money!" Tommy wanted to punch him in the face. He had to apologize to Suva because her being mad at him had him feeling off-kilter. The group sat quietly and watched as the orange hue of the sun slowly became one with the dark blue of the ocean. Tommy took a picture of it. It was a day well spent; they enjoyed the water, ate good food, and shared lots of laughs. There was still tension between the two teens; the parents proposed beach volleyball. Suva suggested playing guys versus girls.

The game was going great; the guys were leading 14–13. Twice, Suva had spiked at Tommy, and twice, he had deflected. Deaglan served, Melissa responded, Kyle, countered, sending the ball over to Suva's side of the net. She looked at Tommy with fire in her eyes. He, in turn, readied himself to deflect. Suva jumped, groaning when she gave the ball a power hit. Tommy didn't react in time, and the ball connected with his groin. Tommy fell to the ground releasing a guttural moan, trying to hold but not touch his penis. The parents surrounded him; Melissa wanted to help him.

Suva was frozen in the spot she landed in, tears running down her face. When Tommy allowed someone to touch him, Kyle carried him to the van. A sobbing Suva sat beside him on the back seat. "I'm sor-ry, Wohali. So-s-or-ry," she tried speaking in between sobs. Tommy held her against his chest with his right hand and cushioned the icepack against his crotch with his left. Seeing her cry was more painful than the hit. Suva's tears subsided as her mom passed the airport then the community of Ironshore. The last thing Suva saw before she fell asleep was the Rose Hall Great House.
When Suva opened her eyes, the only light she saw was the brightness of the headlights. She eased off Tommy's chest, being careful not to wake him, smiling a little because his hand was still on his groin. She was sorry to have hurt him. She realized where she was, on the long stretch of unpaved road leading up to the estate.

The estate was originally a sugar plantation. She wasn't sure of the exact story, but her lineage began when the original owner's son fell in love with his house slave. They got married when slavery was abolished and raised their family on the plantation. His parents disowned him; he never returned to Spain, so much wasn't known of that side of the family tree. Sugarcane was now a small part of what was planted on the property. Fruits and ground provisions were farmed for sale on the local market. Melissa had plans to expand into exporting. The house had been restored time and time to preserve the unique design; utilities and bathrooms were the only upgrades allowed. With the house in sight, Suva smiled.

Seeing the white eighteen-bedroom house brought back so many fond memories. Her relatives, at one point, wanted to change the color, but her grandma would not have it. She said her house was not a rainbow. There was a long deliberation before a compromise was reached. They could paint all the panels, window panes, and the outside steps a light shade of blue.

The house was three stories with an impressive porch on the first floor that wrapped around the house. The porch had four chairs that hung on reliable chains from the roof. There were two unnecessary fans in the ceiling because the breeze was always cool. Two chairs were on either side of the door; each chair had a small round antique table in front of it for serving. Suva loved swinging on the chair watching her grandmother knit; it was always so calming. The floors of the house, including the porch, were all wood and were always shined to perfection. The large door at the main entrance of the house was white, with four blue squares evenly spaced on it.

Entering, you stepped into a large waiting area where shoes were kept. To the immediate left, there's a sitting room with a black Grand Piano surrounded by a large sofa. When Grandma Hazel entertains, she plays for hours. A few feet from the sitting room were the four guest bedrooms. To the right of the waiting area is the first dining room that seated ten people. That room is separated by a door that leads you to the formal dining room that seats twenty and is always adorned with fine china and candles. It was only used for special occasions. The best thing about that room was its proximity to the kitchen, which was only a door swing away.

The kitchen was the family's crown jewel. They all loved to cook. The beautifully restored brick oven was the centerpiece of the kitchen. It masterfully birthed several delicious breads, puddings, and Carrot Cakes. The modern eight burner stove could not compete. Suva recognized Mr. Egburt, who was waiting to receive them. He was the groundskeeper and is married to the housekeeper. As a gift to them, Suva's great- grandfather built them a cottage on the property, so they didn't have to journey home every night. They eventually took up permanent residence in the cottage, raising three children there. The youngest is now a freshman at a top university. The Egburts wanted their eldest son Tony to work on the property, but Suva's grandfather opposed, emphasizing that children should be reading books, not working the yard. Tony is now the community's doctor. The Egburts were family.

Before the vehicle could come to a complete stop, a bundle of back-length wavy hair sprinted from the house, colliding with the van. Tommy jumped out of his sleep, startled by a screaming Suva. She almost trampled him, trying to get out of the van. The two girls continued their hysterical screams until the vehicle stopped, and Suva was free. The two screaming girls embraced for what seemed like an eternity rocking each other back and forth and squeezing tighter and tighter. Jay Suva's aunt came out the house to help Mr. Egburt with the bags. The party greeted each other and shouted pleasantries over the two screaming teenagers.

"Where's Grandma!" Suva inquired, still holding KG's hand, both girls jumping on the spot.

"She's on her—" Before Jay could finish the sentence, both girls took off almost hitting KG's dad as he was coming out the house. Suva stopped long enough to give him a hug. "Hi, Uncle Ronnie. Bye, Uncle Ronnie."

"She's asleep!" Ronnie shouted to the girls as they charged up the stairs and made a left heading for one of the four master bedrooms on the second floor. They slowed down as they approached the door, not wanting to startle their grandma. They slowly opened the door; the room was precisely as Suva remembered. Wooden floors, large closet, king-size bed with a million pillows all cloaked in hand-knitted pillowcases. To the left of the room beside the closet, there was a large antique dresser. It had two oil lamps, and the shades had Home Sweet Home painted on them. The furniture and walls of the room were plastered with framed pictures. Their grandma was asleep in her rocking chair on the balcony. Suva took her time walking up behind the chair.

"My double scoops are back together," Grandma Hazel

spoke before she opened her eyes. Suva fell on her, squeezing her tight. "Look at how tall you've grown." Hazel spun her around and cupped her bottom and hips. "You even have a bum-bum and shape." Suva blushed and hugged her grandma again. KG jumped on the bed still charged with excitement. Hazel held Suva's hand, and they walked back to the room together.

"Grandma, are you going to make pudding tomorrow?" Suva's eyes danced under the lamp light.

"I sure did. Yuh luv your belly too much!" Hazel teased.

"Grandma, I flew thousands of miles just for your pudding." Suva licked her fingers and rubbed her tummy. KG and Hazel exchanged glances and giggled. Suva jumped in the air. "Wait, wait, wait, have you already made some?" When Hazel slowly nodded yes, Suva started pulling her toward the door. "No sah mi go dead, I love it!" Suva couldn't contain herself.

"Calm down, child, I have to get my robe, a lady is always proper." Hazel disappeared into the closet. Suva loved her Grandma; she was so sophisticated and graceful. She had the air of a strong African Queen. She was always polished and ready to take on the day. She was a firm believer in education, and she was well read. While she believed in gender equality, she trained all her children to be fully domesticated. Looking at her grandmother's golden skin and long dark curly hair, Suva felt at home. That was what she enjoyed most about being with her extended family. She wasn't black, white, or mixed-race around them; she was just Suva.

Hazel donned a plush black robe and twirled her thigh-length hair until it was a neat bun at the back of her head. While Hazel was in the powder room freshening up, Suva and KG were chanting, "Pudding, pudding, pudding," giggling hysterically. The three ladies exited the room together as the two teens pulled on their grandmother's arms.

"Pudding, pudding, pudding!" Hazel tried to silence them, then thought, *What the heck?* so she joined in the chant as they descended the stairs.

"Pudding, pudding, pudding!" The other family members gathered in the waiting area. Mr. Egburt was parking the van, so they chatted while they waited on him. They were used to Hazel carrying on with her double scoops; it keeps her young. They watched as the threesome disappeared into the dining room.

In the kitchen, Suva laid out three plates and glasses. She got milk out of the refrigerator and poured it into the three glasses. Hazel used a dishcloth to open the brick oven. With her hand still on the handle, she turned and asked the girls if they wanted potato or bread pudding. "Both" was the concerted response. She placed two respective slices on each dish. Suva dug in with her fingers and took large bites.

"Thanks, Grandma!" She was still chewing as she spoke. Out of habit, she hopped on the counter. KG knew what was coming; she smiled and continued cutting her pudding with the fork into bite-sized pieces her elbows off the counter.

"Young lady!" Hazel's tone was very stern. Suva swiftly jumped off the counter, went to the sink, washed her hands, retrieved a fork, sat down, her legs crossed at the ankles, and duplicated what KG did. "Good girl!" Hazel leaned in and hugged her from behind and kissed Suva's hair.

"My two beautiful granddaughters. I love you. You have blossomed into amazing young ladies." Hazel held her chest and smiled. "You have made your grandmother proud." When she got quiet and stared off, they knew she was thinking of Grandpa Steve. He died three years earlier, and it was still difficult for the family to talk about. That's why this trip was so special. It was the first time Melissa had been back since the funeral.

"Mom Mom I need pudding inna mi gut!" Melissa broke the silence; the clan followed her.

"Grandma Hazel, you are a miracle worker." Deaglan grabbed Suva's fork and took a bite. "This is delicious, but more importantly, Suva is sitting at a counter and not on it." An annoyed Suva tried taking back her fork, but he kept biting as he spoke.

"Not only that..." Melissa took KG's fork and ate a few bites herself. "Suva is eating with a fork and not her hands."

Suva made a face when her grandmother wasn't looking. Hazel plated pudding for everyone. "Thomas baby, which type would you like?" Tommy, looking at Hazel, opened his mouth to answer but honestly didn't know which one he preferred.

"I'll share it for him, Grandma." Suva took the knife and cut a large slice of the Bread Pudding and placed it on a dish with a fork in front of Tommy. She then poured him some lemonade. Kyle stated optimistically,

"I guess that's a truce." Suva responded with defiance,

"No, it's not." Uncle Ronnie and Aunt Jay stated in unison.

"We're lost," Suva stood beside Hazel and hugged her. Then stated dryly,

"Tommy was very rude today; he insulted my *vintage* swimsuit." Jay turned to Tommy and extended both his hands, balancing them like scales. Tommy wanted so badly to be somewhere else.

"No, I do not care to weigh in. Grandma Hazel, this pudding is great!" Suva continued speaking,

"He said my one-piece was just old, not vintage!" Hazel laughed.

"Is it the same black one-piece I gave you, Melissa?" Melissa laughed too.

"Yes, Mom, Mom." Hazel ran her fingers through Suva's hair. "Honey, in all fairness, that swimsuit is old." The group laughed. "Vintage, yes, but it's too old for young hot stuff like you." Hazel kissed her forehead. "Tell you what, Grandma is going to make you a more age-appropriate swimsuit, okay, dear." Suva pouted her lips and nodded yes. Kyle stood and patted Suva's head.

"And look how youh damaged mee one son." Suva cleared the dishes, she washed, and KG rinsed. Atsila was puzzled,

"Girls, you don't have to wash the dishes, it's so late." The room fell silent, and everyone looked at Hazel.

"Of course, they have to wash them. We don't sleep comfortably with dirty dishes in the sink." Hazel kissed the girls. "Plus, there's no maid here." Hazel, seeing the confusion on Atsila's face, explained further. "Mrs. Egburt is not a maid; she's the housekeeper."

## Chapter 12

Later in KG's room, Suva unpacked while KG brushed her teeth.

"KG, I can't believe you got one of the master bedrooms." Suva was putting her clothes in drawers that were cleared out for her. KG answered her from inside the large walk-in closet that led to the bathroom.

"Suv, I am an only child in this unnecessarily large house..." She came back into the room and held a pink cotton dress in her hand. "Suv, this is nice, mi go want a wear. Plus, no one else was using it, so why not." She laughed and disappeared into the closet. After unpacking, Suva showered. They were lying side by side on a rug on the balcony, staring up at the stars. Suva breathed the refreshing Jamaican air.

"Bet the stars aren't this bright in Mayberry." KG always had a tone when she said, Mayberry. She almost said it with a British accent.

"Yea, yea, enough about that." Suva blurted out. "I'm thinking of going all the way with Jason." KG choked on air; she coughed and cleared her throat several times. She sat up.

"All the way to Africa, you mean? When did you decide that?"

When Suva shrugged, KG pulled on her hands until they were facing each other. When Suva didn't answer, KG pressed on. "Gabe and I aren't even thinking of that. I thought we were going to lose it at the same time. We made a pact, didn't we?" The gravity of the conversation weighed on Suva. She stood and walked to the edge of the balcony and gazed over at the papaya trees. "Hello? Earth to Suv. You can't just drop a bomb like that on me and not explain yourself. Pickney!" Suva turned and faced KG.

"I decided on the plane. He loves me, and he has been so patient, he looks so disappointed every time I say no." Suva exhaled, sat on the balcony wall, and twirled her ring. "Plus, he is coming down just to spend time with me; he deserves something, right?" KG pulled her off the wall,

"Then, get him a damn plaque!" KG started pacing.
"Cous; you can't have sex with him out of obligation, yuh know dat, right? Aren't you supposed to be gifted?"

When it seemed like her questions weren't getting through, KG walked right up to Suva and shook her hard. "Yuh a idiat? I haven't heard one thing about you and how you feel about all of this." Suva laughed at KG's question, but she didn't overlook the seriousness of the matter. KG spent the remainder of the night lambasting Suva's plan.

During the days that followed, the teens explored the vast expanse of the property. Suva got reacquainted with all her favorite fruit trees. She tried to no avail to get in contact with Jason and Ayesha; they were not ill, just unavailable. Jason's mom had a nasty attitude every time she called; that lady needed a lesson in deportment. So much money but no class. Suva and KG were in their own world, forcing Tommy and Gabe to bond. The guys soon realized that they were kindred spirits. The girls stayed under an Otaheite apple tree while the guys climbed it, placing them in a satchel. The breeze was cool, and the aura was relaxing.

"Are you sure you're ready? Why Jason? A mean he's not even all that." KG grilled Suva yet again about her virginity-losing plans. Suva laid flat on her back as Tommy dropped apples between the girls. Suva took it up, bit off the top, and used it to rub the remaining skin. That's how they washed apples when water wasn't available. The girls threw the seeds at the boys who returned fire with rotten apples. Suva caught one and clocked Gabe in the back, leaving a large red stain. After their battle, they walked a forbidden path, under some fences, and through a distant neighbor's yard. They ignored the signs, Beware of Dogs; then they got to a set of train tracks.

"Welcome to my neighborhood; I am literally from the other side of the tracks." Gabe extended his arms in a welcoming gesture.

"So, I know I shouldn't be the one to talk about it but," Tommy spoke very carefully, "is it because you have a dark complexion why KG's parents are against the relationship? Or is it because you live on the other side of the tracks?"

The mood changed; KG and Gabe reflexively held hands. They stopped in the middle of the dirt road.

"Well, it's Gabe's parents who are against the relationship." Suva felt the need to fill the silence.

"Gabe's mom, to be exact." KG's tone was lifeless. They walked for another three minutes and entered a house that was painted in the same shade of blue as KG's. It was a quaint, comfortable three-bedroom house; except for the concrete foundation, the entire structure was made from wood. KG put some space between herself and Gabe. She introduced Suva and Tommy to Gabe's mother who was sitting on the intimate veranda. Suva didn't go on the tour of the house; she stayed on the terrace, so she could talk to Mrs. Ranjeet.

"Mrs. R., How are you? Can I call you Mrs. R? You have a lovely home." Suva was eager to get to the meat of the matter but decided on being gingerly.

"Thank you." Suva sat on an ottoman that was to the right of Mrs. R. both ladies took in the scenery. There were several trees spread out around the yard. Banana shrubs formed a square fence around the parameter of the property, there were two Ackee trees in the mix and one grand Almond tree in the center of the yard, it was often used as a cool escape on a hot day. Suva got straight to the point,

"Mrs. R., why don't you want Gabe and KG to be together? My family is cool with it."

"They are from two different worlds, they just don't fit well together, people will reject them." Suva was even more confused.

"I don't get it. Mrs. R., I would understand if they were in the States, but in Jamdung, couples aren't ostracized because of skin color." Mrs. R. stopped knitting and glared at Suva.

"Child, skin color is not the issue, class is. I've been washing and cleaning the houses of persons that run in the same circle as your family. They regard me like the help. They will never accept my Gabe." Suva stood up, hands on her hips with nostrils flared.

"Well, they can just kiss your—" She stopped remembering her manners. "I'm sorry, Mrs. R." She sat back down, straightened her back, and crossed her ankles. "When I hear bull—I mean such absurdity, deportment goes out the window. Let me get this straight, not only is Gabe attending the same school as their kids, and he is number one in the class, yet they still have an issue? Cho!" Suva hissed her teeth.  Mrs. R. knitted a few more rings then commented,

"My Gabe is on a full scholarship, and I clean their floors. He will never be good enough." Suva held up her hands, interrupting Mrs. R. "Wait, wait, suh him brighta dan dem but because his brain has allowed him certain privileges, he's looked down on? Ridiculous! Same crap, different geography!" Mrs. R smiled; this girl was a firecracker. Suva sobered up and rested her hands-on Mrs. R.

"I understand exactly how you feel and can relate to your stance on the matter. I am a constant target of such discrimination. I know you don't want Gabe to get hurt, but by preventing him from enjoying the wonders of teenage love." Suva squeezed even tighter.

"You are hurting him even more. You are teaching him that when life's challenges come, he shouldn't face them head-on, instead he should avoid them altogether."

Suva leaned in and whispered, "Not to mention, in his teenage brain, KG is the love of his life and dem go deh fieva, College will dent that plan." Suva looked her square in the eyes and softened her tone. "Plus, he is the boy you raised. He loves with his heart, not his station in life. Mrs. R., let him be the boy you raised." Mrs. R. gave Suva a long tight hug.

"How old are you again?" Both ladies laughed. From inside, KG and Gabe watched in amazement at the two strangers operating as longtime friends. KG commented that Suva had that way about her. Her personality was intoxicating. People couldn't help but be drawn to her. She firmly believed that everything could be resolved with a mature conversation. KG laughed; Suva was the light touch to her brute force. That's why they worked well together; they balanced each other.

"That's why I fell in love with her." Tommy's verbal admittance just stayed there; the teens dared not touch it. Later that night, KG got a call from Gabe. His mother was allowing him to go with them on their vacation excursions. He said she decided to let him be the boy she raised.

"Girl, what did you say to Gabe's mom?" The girls were lying side by side in KG's bed. They were exhausted and excited about the next few days. Melissa's itinerary was intense.

"KG, I said nothing special. I just spoke from my heart." KG reached over and hugged Suva.

"Thanksssss!"

"No thanks necessary. Your happiness is all the tanks I need." Suva squeezed her equally as tight. KG was about to ask a question. "Don't even say it!" She pushed a cushion in KG's face. "No, I've never thought about life without you, and yes, they would have to bury me with you. Now shut up and go to sleep."

At the crack of dawn, the family caravan hit the road; all passengers were in high spirits. The teens were in the second van with Hazel, driven by Ronnie. The adults felt guilt and slight relief when the teens commandeered their grandma. After all, she wanted grandkids, so she should have to deal with their noise and constant questions. The foursome was able to enjoy adult married conversation as they journeyed. "Quiet down, guys, please!" That was Ronnie's millionth plea for silence. Hazel was the ring leader. She was even louder than the teens. They kept singing louder than the songs playing on the radio and teasing Ronnie that he was driving so slowly a baby just crept past him.

They were playing a game called PP in which players get a point if they are the first to identify a red license plate that had PP on it. Jamaica had different-colored plates, for example, red, green, and the most popular of all white. Depending on the road you are on, red plates aren't so standard, so players had to be alert. "PP!" Ronnie pointed at a minibus that passed the van; they all cheered and rubbed his head. It was a beautiful day, the ride was bumpy at times due to the potholes on the roads, but the lush greenery to their right and calm ocean to their left made up for it. At specific points, when they had a clear view of the sea, they would pull over and take pictures. Gabe couldn't believe that these people were so crazy. He was in the presence of doctors, lawyers, and professors, yet all they cared about was how Grandma Hazel would be driving faster than Uncle Ronnie. Back on the road, Ronnie decided to challenge Melissa; he drove really close to her van and kept honking.

"Not fair, Uncle Ronnie, that's very distracting," Suva spoke up, poking her uncle playfully.

"Decide where your allegiance lies, or we will let yuh aff right yah suh," Hazel teased Suva. Everyone glared at Suva.

"Okay, fine. Wait for a stoplight, then to you can pass her. She always waits too long after the light turns green." Suva got cheers for her show of loyalty.

Their first activity was White River Rafting on the Martha Brae. The water was cold, the river got rough at specific points, but to Tommy's surprise, the bamboo rafts were very sturdy, and the man with the dreads was quite skillful in navigating the rapids from start to finish. KG and Suva were hand in hand continually talking, so he and Gabe stayed at a protective distance. They were getting upset by how men reacted to the girls, always staring at their bottoms, making deflating tire sounds. Them relating to the fascination of the outstanding view did nothing to alleviate their anger.

At a stoplight between Martha Brae and their next destination, the Green Grotto Cave, Ronnie saw his chance. His passengers encouraged him, giving him the all-clear that there were no vehicles behind them. He eased out to the right, ensuring the road was clear and pressed on the gas. Realizing his attempt, Melissa put the van in gear and sped off. They were neck and neck on the road, maneuvering around potholes. Not wanting to be outdone by the teens, the adults started shouting encouragements to Melissa. Kyle held Melissa's hair out of her face because the wind was blowing her long tresses in her eyes. There was a corner up ahead, so someone had to either pull forward or drawback. Ronnie slowed down and shook his head, accepting defeat; Melissa eased off the gas, laughed, and pointed. In that moment of comfort, Ronnie sunk the clutch put the van in first and sped ahead. Ronnie's victory was the central topic during the Green Grotto Cave tour.

The girls continued their relentless chatter, Gabe longing for attention expected that the bats would scare them silent. Tommy laughed at him, reminding him of how fearless the girls were. Suva has killed roaches with her bare hands. The girls did stop talking when the guide informed them that a scene from a *James Bond* movie was shot in the cave. They were obsessed with the British movie franchise. Those words magically changed the mood; Suva looped her hands within Tommy's, and KG and Gabe interlocked their fingers. After the caves, they hit the road again.

Suva recognized the red dirt and old ships immediately; they were passing Kaiser Bauxite in St. Ann, Dunns River Falls was a few minutes away. She started doing her happy dance as they drove up the steep winding road that took them from the main road to the Dunn's River Falls parking lot. They unpacked the vehicles and approached the entrance. There were two lines, one for locals and the other for tourists. Melissa did a final tally, four teens, Hazel, Ronnie, Jay, the Boughens, Mr. Lanaghan, the Egburts, then paid for the group. They got their armbands but declined a tour guide for the facilities and to climb the falls. Inside, Atsila headed straight for the craft display tables that were to the left of the entrance. She scanned over wooden sculptures of very shapely women and some very amply blessed naked men with dreads. Kyle took up a naked man.

"Honey, I think I've found your next anniversary gift." He dangled it back and forth.

"Put that down, so inappropriate." She pushed his hand down; they both laughed at his silliness. Suva tried the bead necklaces.  Tommy was drawn to the black, green, and yellow Jamaica inscribed armbands.  They continued walking after making their respective purchases. The teens dropped their bags and ran toward an older man and a donkey. The donkey was draped in a colorful blanket with a sombrero on his head.  The entire group took turns taking pictures with the donkey. Gabe kept calling it Burt and asked the man if Burt's family didn't miss him when he was at work all day. On the long way down to the bottom of the falls, Tommy commented, "Let, let me get this straight, we have to walk down five hundred steps.  Only to climb up the falls? Then walk down these same steps again?" There was a resounding yes from everyone at the party to all his questions. The group laughed at him. Suva and KG patted him on his shoulders.

"It's going to be worth it, trust me," Suva said teasingly. KG chimed in. "Just be happy you don't have to carry Suva's bags up the falls."  Tommy adjusted the weighty bags in agreement. Midway through the descent, they rested on a bench at the base of an enormous tree. They took some more pictures. It was a glorious place to be. The air was refreshing; the sound of the water cascading off the rocks was so relaxing.  They continued their journey through a mini tunnel, which had ocean-themed painted walls. When Tommy saw the light at the end, he sighed in relief.

"Are you kidding me!" He lamented at the fact that several steps were remaining.  "This is ridi—"

The view silenced him. The group stood still at the top of the stairs taking in the aerial view of their destination.  Soft waves encouraged the crystal-clear water to kiss the pearly white shore. There were water and sand as far as the eye could see. The trees were tall providing shade from the bright warm sun. Tommy's hair danced in the breeze. He looked to his left and saw how powerful the water was flowing down the rocks. He started doing his happy dance.

"Wohali, wasn't it worth it?" Suva was pleased that he was excited about it.

"Baby, it was so worth it! The last one down is a loser!"  He and Gabe took the bags and sprinted down the stairs. Suva didn't rush with them. She held her grandmother, savoring each step they shared. At the base of the stairs, Suva maneuvered around happy patrons; she passed a shack advertising the rental of lounge chairs, climbing shoes, and scuba diving gear. The family was lucky to find a spot to the right of a small man-made pond home to tiny fishes. After changing, Tommy wanted to climb the falls immediately. Suva advised him to take a dip in the ocean first. He ignored her and headed for the falls. The family followed him, cameras in hand. At the bottom of the falls where the spring water flowed into the ocean, without hesitation, Tommy jumped under the gush.  Tommy sprang from the flow, screaming.  Suva and KG fell to the ground, laughing. Atsila recorded the whole thing. A shivering Tommy glared at the group,

"You...could...have...warned me!" Mrs. Egburt gave him a towel. "Suva did tell yuh, yuh ears too hard." Tommy dropped the towel and lifted a laughing Suva, tossing her into the ocean.  She resurfaced quickly, fighting to catch her breath because she was still laughing.  Splitting into two random teams, the group played no-net water volleyball, swimming, and sandwich eating contest. The parents climbed the falls first while the teens secured the bags. Suva and KG were making sandcastles while the boys Jet Ski-ed.  Suva watched Tommy as he dismounted the Jet Ski. His chest was bare, his swim trunks were riding low on his hips. His abdomen was spectacular, and you could count the six defined bulges. She couldn't get over the V curve between his lower abdomen and his thighs. She bit her lips unconsciously.

"He sure looks delicious." KG teased a dazed Suva. Suva blinked once, twice, ensuring she didn't say her thoughts out loud.

"Yes, the view is spectacular." Suva pretended she was looking out at the ocean all along.

"Cous, stop pretending you weren't lusting after Tommy. I saw you." They both giggled. "I've never seen you look at Jason like that." KG casually stated. Suva couldn't find a single instance to reference, so she remained silent. KG could always see right through her. The jubilant teens climbed the falls three times. By the third ascension, Tommy was accustomed to the heavy flow of the water and the slippery rocks. They didn't use the style of climbing that Suva dubbed as the "Tourist Way" of forming a human chain all the way to the top. Gabe loved watching KG climb; she was such a petite petal that climbed with the precision of a ninja.

Tucked discreetly at the halfway point was a little concealed nook.  KG and Gabe fought the heavily cascading water to access it. The space was large enough to fit two adults intimately.

Tommy and Suva sat on the rocks waiting for them to no doubt make out. Gabe emerged with a huge grin on his face.

"It's your turn," he announced. Suva waved her hand,

"That's negatory." Tommy held her hands.

"Atsila."

Inside the nook, to be comfortable Suva had to sit between Tommy's legs. It was surprisingly peaceful, and Suva rested her head on his chest and exhaled. He rubbed his nose on the top of her right earlobe. She pulled away. Tommy gently eased her back into him. "Atsila, just relax and enjoy the moment, nuh." Suva closed her eyes and got lost in the comfort of his warmth. They both inhaled deeply. It was too much for Suva. She pushed off the rock exiting the nook. Before Gabe and KG could ask, she held her hand up.

"Nothing happened!" and kept on moving.

To end the day properly, the gang got food from a nearby KFC. Suva stuffed her face with barbeque breast, hot wings, biscuits, and corn on the cob. The teens were so full they fell asleep immediately and slept the entire ride back to the estate.

## Chapter 13

During the weeks that followed, Suva was delightfully exhausted. Spending her days with Mrs. R. and Hazel, her evening with the extended family then staying up all night galivanting with KG, Gabe, and Tommy. The four were inseparable. It was July 30, and the teens wanted to go to the nearby Spring before the girls got their hairs shampooed for the Emancipation and Independence Day celebrations.

At the Spring, Suva was relentless; she swung from the old rope hanging from the highest tree, bellowing the Tarzan roar before splashing into the water. She won the underwater breath-holding game. She backflipped and swan-dived off the highest rocks. The fun had to end; it was time for the girls' hair appointment. The hair salon was a cozy little wooden shack with one sink and one hairdryer. Suva sat in one of the four chairs. Each chair had its mirror. The hairdresser called in reinforcements when both girls let their hair down. Tommy took out his book to settle in for a long wait.

"My yout yuh normally read? Nope, come on." Gabe pointed to a building a few blocks over. The boys said their good-byes and walked toward the building. For the next five hours, the boys played dominoes and cards. Suva loved her hair. The twists were neat but not tight. It was expertly done and flowed down to the middle of her back. It smelled great and looked shiny, Tommy left a big tip. Tommy kept twirling the rope-like twists on their walk home. Gabe did the same with KG's except hers rested on her rear, and his hand kept slipping. At dinner that night, the family, along with the Egburts, were eating in the grand dining room. Suva's eyes started watering. She assured a concerned Tommy that all the laughter was the source.

"Grandma Hazel, this rice and peas is so good, I could eat it by itself." Suva chewed while she spoke.

"Is that why half your plate is covered with curried mutton?" Hazel scanned the table as she spoke; she was filled with such joy. Watching her family eat and having everyone together over the past few weeks brought on a rush of emotions.

"Look at my double scoops, looking so beautiful. Tisha outdid herself. I hope you left her a good tip."

"We did," Gabe and Tommy responded in unison. During dessert, Tommy got up, held Suva's face, and examined her eyes. They were still running, and she started rubbing her nose.

"Wohali, I'm fine. I guess I was in the water for too long."

"Has he always been this overprotective?" Gabe whispered to KG. She nodded yes and whispered back, "I'll tell you why later." Suva excused herself from the family room and retired to bed early; she had a slight headache and didn't want to distract the family from their rousing card games. KG went to bed with her. In the morning, Suva woke up feeling revived; she had a healthy serving of ackee and saltfish with yam, boiled dumplings, and green bananas. After breakfast, they were sent to do some errands. They decided to go fruit picking before starting the list. At noon, they were lounging under the Nesberry tree. Suva was laughing hard at something Gabe said, then her breath caught. Tommy was by her side immediately,

"Are you okay? Is your chest tightening?"

Suva took a deep breath, then another.

"Yes, I'm fine, false alarm."

They joked about Tommy's superman overreactions while walking to the apple trees.

"Tommy has alwa—" Suva didn't finish her sentence; the group heard a thud. She was on her side on the ground. They rushed to her aid. Tommy held her up, opened her mouth, and used his finger to remove the small piece of Nesberry she was chewing. Suva was unresponsive. Tommy laid her flat on the ground, ran his hand along her rib cage, feeling for the xiphoid process, but mouth to mouth wasn't necessary as Suva jumped up wheezing heavily. She kept motioning with her hand for her pump. She squeezed Gabe's hands, he held on, comforting her.

"We have to get back to the house," KG kept shouting over and over. KG's was panicking intensely on the inside. Tommy lifted Suva, and they all started running. Damn, the house was far. When he got tired, Gabe took her and carried her on his back. They had to stop twice when she got unresponsive again, stopping their hearts. Tommy almost ran Mr. Egburt over; without stopping, he dashed to his room, retrieved her pump from his nightstand, rushing back downstairs. He started panicking when he didn't see her.

"Atsila!" he yelled at the top of his lungs.

"We're in Kay's room!" Gabe yelled back.

Tommy administered the pump, and she calmed down, and her breathing seemed settled. But every time she inhaled deeply, she started wheezing again. Her eyes were running, and she kept rubbing her nose. Tommy was convinced she was turning light purple. Mrs. Egburt rushed into the room and picked up the landline.

"It's Melissa."

KG took the receiver and explained everything. Auntie said to give her the pump in three consecutive doses. It started working until she inhaled deeply. The room got silent; no one moved. Suva's eyes closed, and her limbs became lifeless.

"Remain calm and call Mom, Mom, she will know what to do. I'm on my way."

Everyone started panicking, and Mrs. Egburt started crying.

"Unuh shut up; I need to think." Tommy calmly checked her pulse; it was slow but steady. He retraced her every move. Then he yelled, "Shit, take off all clothes, get her into the shower." The three teens got her up and headed for the bathroom. "Remove those sheets and bring fresh linens," Tommy yelled orders before they disappeared into the bathroom. They stripped her down to her underwear, Gabe held her steady. KG washed her hair and face; Tommy washed everywhere else. "We have to get rid of all our clothes too." Gabe was thinking of how they would accomplish that while holding Suva. By this, Suva was alert but still struggling to breathe. That instance, Hazel and Jay came in.

"We'll take it from here."

Tommy didn't want to let go.

Hazel patted his back reassuringly, and he released his grip. The teens all sped off to separate bathrooms, not caring that they were half-naked in the hallways.

"It's going to be all right, honey, Grandma Hazel and Auntie Jay are here now."

The ladies took off her remaining clothes, rewashed her hair, and bathed her properly. The three teens returned to find Suva with a nebulizer mask over her face, breathing steadily. Tommy rushed to her side and held her right hand, and Gabe held her left. KG rubbed her feet to ensure that they were warm enough. Tommy looked at Hazel.

"You just happened to have one lying around?"

Hazel pulled the drapes to let in sunlight and fresh air.

"Yes, because my granddaughter has asthma."

Tommy moved some hair out of Suva's face.

"The attack was caused by an allergic reaction. At first, I thought it was the laundry detergent. But Suva has worn that shirt three times since we've been here." Hazel nodded in agreement and added,

"Then I thought it was something she ate, but let's face it, she's eaten everything on the table last night at least five times since she's been here." Gabe was quite intrigued at how deductive Tommy and Grandma Hazel sounded. Tommy continued,

"Then it came to me, the only new and unknown variable she was introduced to was at the hair salon." He pointed to Hazel to finish up.

"Exactly, that's why we had to get rid of anything your hairs"—she pointed at KG—"came in contact with."

Suva removed the mask and sang the Matlock theme song, laughed, coughed, and Tommy put it back on her face. Melissa ran into the room. They erupted in laughter. Her hair was incomplete. The back was twisted, but the front looked like she was electrocuted. "Get out!" Everyone screamed.

"Come on, guys, I know it looks awful, but it's not that bad."

Hazel guided her outside and explained, Melissa showered. The teens were glued to Suva's side even after dinner was brought up. No one touched their food. Suva was on her third and final dose; she was exhausted. The last thing she remembered before falling asleep was Tommy feeding her water.

## Chapter 15

Mrs. Ranjeet entered Suva's room and walked toward Suva. Gabe jumped off the bed and stood at attention.

"Mommy, nuh kill mi! There's a reasonable explanation for me not coming home and not calling. Sorry, sorry, sorry! I don't think I'm a man." Gabe was hyperventilating. His mom eased him out of the way.

"This is the calmest I've seen her. She is quite the firecracker." Hazel smiled in proud agreement. For the first time, the two ladies spent time together and didn't argue. Hazel had phoned Gabe's parents and informed them of the day's happenings, so they came to the estate at dawn. Gabe took the toiletries from Jay and went to Tommy's room to shower. KG was asleep at the foot of the bed. Tommy was half on the bed and the chair, still holding Suva's hand. Hazel woke them and sent them to shower before breakfast. Tommy didn't budge.

"I'm not hungry." His stomach growled in protest.

"Wohali, go and eat something. I'll be here when you get back." Tommy stood but didn't loosen his grip.

"Promise." Suva signed promise. He walked away, reluctantly.

"Let's get you cleaned up. Dr. Egburt is here, and we know you had a crush on him." Suva shushed her grandmother, checking to see if Tommy heard her statement. Suva was ordered to stay in bed for a few days. She was given a prescription to take twice daily with meals, no dairy. He would check on her in a few days. Fingers were crossed that she would be well enough to enjoy her birthday. Tommy was not comfortable with how the doctor made Suva giggle like a little school girl. He kept the stethoscope a little too long on her chest. A doctor shouldn't be telling a patient that she's developed into a beautiful young lady. He could swear Suva was blushing. He had to clear his throat twice to remind her he was still in the room.

Suva kept trying to get either Jason or Ayesha to confirm that they were coming for her birthday. She missed Jason; he was missing everything. Suva convinced herself that he must be training hard and sprained all his fingers that's why he wasn't able to pick up the phone to call her. She grew restless and called his house again.

His brother answered and flirted with her as usual. Reminding her that Jason was a boy and didn't know how to truly appreciate a woman with her "assets."

He said the strangest thing, "Honey, do me a favor and throw away your inhibitions while you're in Jamaica. Have all the unlimited fun you want." He hung up before Suva could probe. Suva turned to her right side and hugged the pillows. It was a beautiful day, and the sun was bright, the room had a mellow ambiance. The medication started working; she could finally breathe freely. What could Jason be doing? He would be on the next flight if he knew she was ready. She was surprisingly excited about it now. Her near-death experience ignited something in her. The room she selected had a king-size bed. She'd been secretly putting candles, additional pillows, and chocolates in there when KG wasn't with her. Speaking of KG needs to get on board and cover for her when she disappears on her birthday. There was a tightening pain in Suva's abdomen. She curled into the fetal position, trying to recall the date of her last period. This cannot be happening; her birthday was in eight days. "You are going to ruin everything, just go away."

Tommy stood at the door with Suva's lunch tray, watching her talk to her stomach. "Do we need to adjust your meds, hon?" Tommy placed the tray over her after she sat up. Gabe and KG placed their trays on the bed too. Suva's throat was still tender, so she drank soup. The others ate white rice and mackerel in tomato sauce with steamed vegetables.

"Suva, Tommy said you were talking to your belly, what's up with that?" Gabe gulped his Coconut water and waited for Suva to answer. Suva pushed the tray away,

"I'm full." Tommy slid the tray back in front of her, filled the spoon with soup, and held it to her mouth. Suva rolled her eyes and crossed her arms. They had a back and forth conversation with their eyes. Suva rolled her eyes saying no; Tommy widened his saying yes. Finally, Tommy said,

"Atsila!" Suva opened her mouth. He fed her until the bowl was empty. He gave her a large glass of water, placed the pills in her mouth, and she drank half the glass, grit her teeth, and said thank you.

"To answer your question, Gabe. My tummy started tightening up this morning." KG swallowed.

"Prolly your time of the month soon." Suva exhaled hard.

"That's just going to ruin everything, cho man, cho." Tommy got up, took Suva's tray, and headed for the door. He stopped and turned.

"First of all, your period is due on the sixteenth; secondly that tightening is a side effect of the medication. Yes, I read the fine print. Thirdly, please stop acting like a grump, it's very unbecoming and far from being ladylike." He walked away, shaking his head. The reprimand left a bad taste in Suva's mouth. KG laughed and pointed at her cousin.

"He sure told you." KG sobered up. "Suv, please don't tell me you are still thinking of going through with that ludicrous idea!" KG shouted as quietly as she could. Suva grabbed her.

"Shut up, shut up, shut up!" Gabe stood.

"Obviously, my services are no longer required here." He walked to the door, rushed back, kissed KG, and turned to Suva. "I will go distract Tommy, so he doesn't overhear your stupid idea to have sex with Jason." Suva gasped in shock and slapped KG on the arm.

"Yuh chat too much!" KG was just as shocked as Suva.

"She didn't tell me. You've been sneaking things into that room when she is not around." Gabe pointed at KG. "So clearly, it's something you didn't want her to know. By the way, mi nyam off di chocolate dem, de-li-cious!" Suva couldn't help but smile. Gabe was truly perfect for KG. "Jason doesn't deserve an icy mint much less your virginity! But, if you want to give it to him then it should be because..." Gabe cupped KG's face. "Her smile peps you up. Her sexiness drives you mad. You have permanent blue balls, but you respect her enough to wait, because anything good is worth waiting for." He kissed KG slowly. When he released her face, she and Suva high-fived and said in unison,

"My, my!" Gabe smiled and left the room.

"No sah mi cah manage your man, him full a lyrics!" KG, still on a cloud, nodded in agreement with Suva's statement.

"Su, Su, does Jason make you feel that way?" Suva curled up in her cousin's lap.

"I'm so confused, K." KG played with Suva's twists, patting her on the head,

"Suva, you're putting too much pressure on yourself. No man not worth that, especially egotistical Jason!" Suva closed her eyes, replaying Gabe's words, only one person came to mind.

"Tommy, are you a cat burglar? We didn't even hear you coming." Suva opened her eyes to see Tommy standing by the bed.

"KG, Grandma Hazel says Suva needs to get some rest. Gabe and I are gonna raid the Nesberry tree, you coming?" KG waved no. She and Suva fell asleep talking. She hoped she had gotten through to her cousin.

On August 1, Suva was still on bed rest while everyone went into town to participate in the Emancipation Day celebrations. She didn't mind the alone time. It gave her a chance to organize the secret room. Going back and forth to the general linen closet proved more strenuous than she had anticipated. Her chest tightened, trying to retrieve the comforter from the top shelf. She was overcome with dizziness. She fell hard, hitting her head on the floor. She was disoriented from the fall, and her vision was blurry, no, it was the comforter over her face.

"Atsila!" Tommy tried helping her, Suva shrugged him off.

"Low mi nuh man!" She angrily tried getting up. It took her three attempts, but she refused his help. Tommy started taking the comforter off the floor.

"Thomas, just move! Cho!" Tommy froze, the harshness of her tone reverberated through his body.

"Suva, I was only trying to help. We heard a thud from downstairs and…" He breathed deeply, looked her in the eyes. "You need to get it together. Because whoever this is." He gestured up and down the periphery of her body. "I don't recognize her."

Tommy's statements resonated with Suva; she just stood there silently, looking at KG and Gabe, who had joined them. KG motioned Gabe to follow Tommy. She snatched the comforter from Suva and threw it on the ground.

"Wha rong wid yuh gyal?" She paced off her anger. "What's-so-special-about-this-damn…" She paused. She calmed down. "Su, you are angry at the wrong person. You are angry because you almost killed yourself trying to set up the stupid secret room." KG lowered her tone. "For a boy who has treated you all summer the way you just treated T." KG picked up the linen, took it to the room, and organized it. When she got back to the hallway, Suva was sitting on the ground. Her back braced against the wall. "Just know for the first time ever, I don't have your back. You were so wrong!"

The adults couldn't figure out what went wrong. All four teens were somber. They picked at their breakfasts, they missed lunch, and they were silent lambs at dinner. Even though Suva was strong enough to come down for meals, she ate alone in her room. All inquiries got brushed aside.

On August 5, the estate was buzzing about the Independence Day soiree. A few staff members began speaking in hushed tones when Suva was around. Suva felt lower than dirt. They must've heard about how awful she was to Tommy. In the kitchen, watching her grandmother make a carrot cake, Suva asked, "Mommy, why is it that the staff is always whispering when I am near them?"

Hazel wiped her hands on her apron and patted her granddaughter's head.

"Suvvy, no one is whispering, dear." Suva hugged her grandmother and squeezed her tight.

Tears ran down her face. "It's going to be fine. Suvvy, everything will be just fine." Hazel felt uneasy. She comforted her granddaughter as best she could, by baking six Puddings. Suva thought she was going to explode from all her guilt. What made it worse was she missed Jason. She knew something must've gone wrong for him not to show up or even call her. He must be in a coma. She went to the only person she knew could make sense of everything and turn her world right side up again. Deaglan and Kyle were swinging in one of the chairs on the verandah, watching the sunset.

"Daddddy?" Both men knew what that tone meant. Kyle kissed Suva on the forehead.

"Chin up, lass," he said, then gave Deaglan a good luck glance. They walked silently hand in hand. Deaglan knew it had something to do with that lad Jason. He always allowed her to speak on her terms. She motioned toward the large Ackee tree with the swing. She sat, and he pushed her gently. Deaglan felt conflicted as Suva tearfully relayed her plans that led up to the big comforter debacle. His fatherly instincts wanted to castrate that Jason lad and express disappointment in Suva's premature decision, but logic dictated differently.

"Suva, honey, let's analyze the facts of the case, setting emotions aside first." Suva wiped her tears and adjusted her posture. Her dad continued, "What are the problems that we need to resolve?" Suva got pensive.

"Well, Dad, there are three matters at hand: my apology to Tommy, my decision to have sex with Jason, and making things right with KG and Gabe." Deaglan was amused; she always unconsciously prioritized Tommy. He decided to poke the bear.

"Suva, I'm sure you were equally rude to KG, Gabe, and Tommy, so why do you need to apologize to Tommy separately?" Suva stood and paced back and forth.

"Daddyyyy. You may not know this." She turned to him and checked if anyone was near. The last bit of sun was dipping behind the mountains. "We may specially care about each other. But I'm obligated to Jason. Lanaghans honor their word." He admired his daughter's loyalty to Jason. He wanted to tell her that Jason was an entitled little punk that didn't deserve her; instead, he said,

"Pumpkin, this is where we interject emotions. Love at its core is about following your heart while being guided by your intellect." He pressed his finger against her heart and then her head. "Where was the decision made to have sex with Jason, your affective, or your cognitive?" Without hesitation, Suva stated, "With my mind. I didn't want him to suffer anymore. Daddy, you should see the disappointed look on his face when he expects more than kissing, and then there's nothing."

Deaglan scratched his head. "Suva, you are not Santa Claus, and it sure as hell isn't Christmas, yuh don't owe him a goddamn thing!" Standing in front of her, he straightened her shoulders, used his hand to raise her head, and focused on her eyes. "What has Daddy taught you?"

Resting her head in his palm, she recalled what he always drilled into her. "My mind and body are my greatest assets, and they are not to be traded but gifted to a worthy partner. One who is kind, understanding, respectful, and most importantly, patient. For if he cannot be patient, then he shall forever be relegated to the friend zone." They both laughed that last part was a new addition. Suva buried her face in her father's chest. He hugged her snugly and rubbed her head.

"When I visualize my future, I never see myself waking up with Jason. I always see Tommy making me coffee and having small talk over breakfast."

Deaglan smiled inwardly. "Have you told him that?" Suva shook her head no against his chest.

"Dad, I will never admit how I may or may not feel about Tommy." Her dad spun her out for a surprise twirl. She maintained her form.

"Suva, are you sure you don't want to be a professional dancer? Look at how poised you are."

"Daddy, hear mi, noooo!" He kept twirling her when she was about to speak, he dipped her. They were laughing hysterically when the dinner bell rang. Walking back, Suva hugged him around his waist, and his arm was over her shoulder. "Daddy, plan of action, apologize to Tommy, KG, and Gabe. Not have sex with Jason." Deaglan's heart got lighter. He was not ready for his almost seventeen-year-old daughter to be having sex, especially with a boy who didn't appreciate her. "One final thing, Dad. Grandma says I am paranoid, but I am positive that the staff is talking about me. I even think Uncle Ronnie and Auntie Jay are doing it too."

Deaglan laughed. "Suva, the guilt was making you see things."

Suva felt much better; her dad could always fix everything. From her dream Barbie house, her eighth-grade science project, and even her ninth-grade cupcakes that got burned right before the bake sale. After washing her hands in the downstairs powder room, Suva happily strolled into the grand dining room. Tommy, KG, and Gabe were all absent. Hazel answered her question before she asked.

"They're not hungry. No, I don't know where they have disappeared to." Suva excused herself. She checked KG's room first, empty. There was no light in Tommy's room, but the balcony door was open. He was sitting on the balcony wall, gazing out into the darkness, the wind animating his shoulder-length hair. Suva was nervous; her last apology was in elementary school when she didn't save him a seat on the bus for the museum field trip.

"Thomas, may I speak with you?" He didn't acknowledge her presence. That stung, but she guessed she deserved it. She pressed on, "I wanted to apologize for my unsavory behavior towards you; it was unwarranted and unladylike. I am truly sorry I hurt you." Tommy still didn't respond. Suva started walking away, tears running down her face, then she walked up to Tommy and wrapped her arms around him.

"Mon amour. Je suis vraiment désolé." She cried harder. "Tu es mon meilleur ami et je ne suis pas tout sans vous. Je ne suis pas ensemble." Tommy felt more horrid hearing her cry than when she had yelled at him. He turned and embraced her.

"You are my best friend and I am not whole without you either." He played with her right earlobe, leant in, and kissed her eyes even as the tears flowed. That moved something in Suva. It sent shivers down her spine. Suddenly, they realized the intimacy of their position. Suva was between his legs. He kissed her other eye, tasting her tears.

"Estás perdonado." Suva felt relieved hearing those words. She was about to point out that technically, her apology was in French so the forgiveness shouldn't be in Spanish. But the beauty of his eyes silenced her thoughts. She took Tommy's hand and led him to the bed.

"Lay with me." Suva laid on her side, she felt emotionally drained and physically exhausted. Tommy held her close; Suva pulled him closer till there was no space between them. Automatically, their fingers interlocked. The moment wasn't sexual. It was just intimate, two friends comforting each other. KG and Gabe let out a concerted

"Aaawwwww" when they found Suva and Tommy all cuddled up sleeping. KG jumped on the bed. "*Reunited and it feels so good!*" Suva grabbed a pillow and smacked her with it. Tommy shielded his groin when she started jumping on them. Gabe sat quietly at the edge of the bed. Suva pulled him into the mix. The four collapsed onto each other, laughing.

"Great, now that we are good, I can eat some food. Mi a dead!" Suva jumped up and dashed off running thunderously to the kitchen. That annoyed and delighted the adults. The noise meant that peace was restored. By 8 a.m on August 6 all the adults and estate staff were already in town for the soiree. The teens didn't have a traditional breakfast; instead, they raided the many fruit trees on the estate. The teens were excited; they were going to the town's square to watch a live play that chronicled the town's interpretation of how Jamaica gained its independence. In KG's room. She swapped Suva's Jamaican flag–themed outfit with a lavender mini dress.

"Wear this instead. I even have a headband to match it." KG ignored the perplexed look on Suva's face, went to the vanity and retrieved a lavender headband, and placed it on the bed beside the dress. Suva rubbed her hands together in anticipation.

"I can't wait to see the costumes and laugh when they butcher the British accent." Both girls giggled. KG teased,

"You just like anything British because our favorite book is set in London. Who am I kidding." KG jumped in the bathroom, and in unison at the top of their lungs, "*The First Castle, The Third Castle,* and *The Final Castle* are the best books ever! Queen Ada, the warrior goddess, is all that and some banana chips."

They high-fived, did the happy dance, and said, "My, my." KG pushed a razor behind the shower curtain.

"Smooth it out, cus." Suva pulled the curtain and tossed the razor at KG.

"I am a champion swimmer, and I stay smooth *all* over."

By 4 pm, everyone except KG was ready; she decided at the very last minute to change her outfit. Gabe was growing impatient. He didn't want to miss the start of the play. The house phone kept ringing, but no one was on the line. While waiting on the verandah, the phone rang again. Suva stopped Tommy from going to answer it.

"Someone is messing with us; it is ringing in a pattern." The boys poked fun at her.

"Boy, Suva, that brain of yours." Gabe patted her head and walked away. At exactly 4:50 p.m., Mr. Egburt drove up to collect the teens.

"What happened to the fun of walking to town?" Mr. Egburt responded,

"Hazel says no walking; dust will flare up yuh asthma." Tommy placed his arm around Suva and nestled her head on his shoulders. She fell asleep quickly. When the vehicle stopped, Suva opened her eyes; she didn't recognize where she was. She smelled the ocean, heard waves crashing against the shore, saw a banner hung on two coconut trees. Exiting the van, she noted unlit tiki torches scattered across the sand; there was a contraption that looked like it was set up for *Limbo*. She swore she saw an area that had leaves over it like when pigs are roasted in the sand at a luau.

"Tommy, we are at the wrong place." Suva slowed her pace. She nervously followed KG's lead, when she got to the banner, people jumped out of bushes, and she swore even out of the sea and yelled, "Surprise! Happy birthday!" Suva held her chest and started wheezing; the crowd grew silent, and Tommy searched for her inhaler. Suva laughed.

"Kidding! Serves you all for tricking me." The group

laughed, and there were hugs all around. Suva poked Auntie Jay for being in on it and gave the Egburts disapproving looks. She punched her dad, "Guilty conscience, huh!". She was about to attack the staff members when Tommy pulled her away. They walked to the right of the gathering for about two minutes, then sat side by side on a large towel.

"This…" Tommy motioned at the beautiful sunset. "This is why everything had to be perfectly timed." It was breathtaking; they sat in silence and watched the sun disappear. The island breeze encouraged them to relax with soft caresses on their cheeks. Before ducking out, the sun, turned a majestic burnt orange hue. Not wanting to be outdone the waves offered their salutations by gently brushing against their feet. Suva got lost in the moment. Not knowing what to say next, she said the first thing that came to her mind.

"Jason and Ayesha missed a good time. That was a romantic sunset." Tommy looked at Suva in disbelief. He got up extremely irritated. He paced back and forth, disappearing beneath some trees, returning with a small piece of stick.

"Atsila, really, though!" He drew a large circle in the sand. Tommy stood in the ring and extended his hand; she looked behind her, hoping someone from the party would rescue her. They were all too busy lighting the tiki torches to hear her silent cry for help. Suva took his hand and stepped inside the circle. The world faded away; it was just her racing heartbeat and his piercing green eyes. Tommy spoke,

"Are you fully recovered, or are you putting on a show for Grandma Hazel?" Suva didn't expect that.

"That's what yuh using the Circle for? Yes, I am fully recovered. The medication and the rest did wonders…thanks for being there." Tommy touched her right earlobe.

"Suva, that's what you do when you love someone. Being there for you is as natural as breathing." He paused. "Are you stupid to give it up to Jason!"

"What? Who told? Wait, did you call me stupid?"

"Atsila just cut the crap and tell me what you feel for me in here!" He placed his hand over her heart and felt its rapid beats. Suva stood there, silent. Tommy waited. He didn't show exasperation, he just waited. Suva closed her eyes and mustered up some courage.

She channeled her favorite character from the Castle trilogy focusing on how brave Ada was when she defeated the gores and took back her city.

"Wohali, I love you." She held his hand on her heart. Tommy's heart melted. He reached into his pocket and took out a box. Now was a perfect time. He started bending on one knee. Suva dragged him up.

"Yow, stop playing, Thomas!" They both laughed at his silliness. He handed her the box, she opened it, and warmth rushed through her body. It was a beautiful thin gold diamond-encrusted necklace with a pendant of some sort on it. Tommy took it from the box, placing it around her neck, he whispered close to her ears.

"On your seventeenth birthday, accept this as a vow of friendship. I pledge to be your best friend yesterday, today, and forever." Suva touched the gold pendant that resembled a crocked L. Tommy continued, "Much like this pendant, where we are right now doesn't make much sense, but every year on your birthday, I will add another piece until it becomes what it was meant to be." Suva hugged him; the longevity of his gift moved her. She pulled back.

"Wohali, this is amazing. Thank you so much." She got on her tippy toes and kissed him on his forehead.

"Is that really where you want to kiss me?" Tommy held her gaze.

"Respecting the truth circle, no. I want to hold you close, lick your lips, suck on your tongue, and nibble on your earlobes." With every word, Tommy adjusted his shorts. Suva licked her lips slowly. "Wohali, even though I want all those things, I will have to settle for a forehead kiss because we are with Jason and Ayesha, and it would devastate them if we kissed. We must honor our relationships, even if they ditched us for the summer. Even if they would never know that we had one little tiny kiss." Suva stopped talking; she didn't like where her mind was heading. Tommy leaned in closer.

"Last question with all your righteous indignation, if I kissed you right now, would you slap me in the face, or would you deepen the kiss?" A speechless Suva smiled, her pulse raced. Tommy edged closer.

"Guys, the sun done set." KG pulled their hands, dragging them out of the truth circle. Suva mouthed "Thank you" to KG.

Suva took pictures with all the guests, mingled a bit, then she was pulled into a tent to change. Hazel and Mrs. R. gave her a box. Suva put on its contents and asked for the rest. All the ladies gushed at her outfit. Atsila and Melissa commented that neither Deaglan nor Kyle would approve but agreed with Hazel that it was more age-appropriate. Tommy and Gabe tossed a soccer ball around with some of the male guests, including a young and fit Dr. Egburt. Tommy was surprised that he was a decent soccer player. He was too easily distracted, though. He missed a ball because he was gazing and confirming with his team that the age of consent in Jamaica was, in fact sixteen. Tommy had control of the ball, and when he saw where the men were gazing, he kicked the ball forcefully at them.

It was Suva; she was standing at the front of the tent in a bright-orange knitted barely-there two-piece bikini. The strings tied around her neck and at her mid-back didn't look strong enough to hold her full C cups that were filling out the top like double Ds. He was happy for the two patches that covered her areolas. Moving down from her perfect cleavage, her flat toned tummy had a cute, hardly visible navel. His heart stopped. The bottom was held together by two strings at the side. The strings hugged her curvy hips, leaving her long toned legs bare.

"Tek a walk," Gabe admonished Tommy. Tommy motioned that everything was fine.

"Not because yuh kick afta Dr. Touchy Feely, but because yuh pitch a tent." Tommy looked down; he didn't realize the obvious bulge. He walked away quickly; he sat on the sand; it was the trees dancing to the sweet rhythm of the wind that calmed him down. The guests sat around a long rectangular table adorned with food. Curried mutton, curried chicken, fried and jerk chicken, roast beef, steamed and fried fish, and Suva's favorite, a whole pig. Suva and Deaglan loved pork. Accompanying all that meat were: fried dumpling, fried plantain, festival, rice and peas, potato salad, coleslaw, and roasted breadfruit. Tommy came back right as Hazel was about to say grace. He sat as far away from Suva as possible and avoided eye contact. People were laughing and chowing down. Hazel signaled Deaglan to get the cake. The group sang happy birthday, and Suva blew out the seventeen candles without making a wish.

"I don't need to wish. I have everything I need. Well, almost, someone's missing." Her parents exchanged weary looks; was she still thinking about that Jason kid?

"My Mavis isn't here." Just then, Mavis popped out.

"Surprise!" Suva ran to her for a long embrace. Hazel interrupted, "That's enough; it's time to cut the cake." KG mouthed, "Pick Grandma," but Suva couldn't understand. Suva told everyone to eat as she needed a bathroom break. In front of the restroom, KG explained in hushed conspiratory tones that Mavis and Hazel were involved in a "who loved Suva more competition."

"It was so heated, but Mavis kind of won with her backhanded comment about teens not remembering who changed their nappies but who explained to them how to use a pad." Suva made a grossed-out face. KG gagged in agreement. "This happened in front of the staff and the boys." Both girls laughed at the horrified looks that the boys must have had. "Aunt Mel caused it when she requested that Mavis do *Macreal Rundung*." Suva clapped in anticipation at the thought of Mavis's *Rundung*.

"KG, Mavis makes the best..." KG covered Suva's mouth.

"That's what Aunt Mel said, and Grandma Hazel went off." Back at the table, knife in hand, Suva asked Hazel to cut the cake with her. After the cutting, Suva thanked everyone for coming and felt vindicated after they admitted the phone ringing was a signal.

"Let's *Limbo* and dance, people!"

Suva was first in line at the stick. Tommy kept his distance; he couldn't handle seeing her bend under the stick, the lower it got, the lower Suva got, showing off her flexibility. It was hard for him to admit, but he missed the one piece. He wanted to punch the doctor right in the nose; he kept making Suva giggle. After all the food was cleared and most of the guests were gone, the DJ slowed the music. Suva's parents drew close, dancing slowly. The Boughens and the Egburts soon followed. Not wanting to be grossed out by their parents, Suva and Tommy helped with the removal of the decorations; no surprise, the good doctor gave them a hand. When he asked Suva for a dance, Tommy wanted to strangle him. "Suva needs to change first. This cold night air cannot be good for her asthma."

Tommy signaled KG and shuffled Suva off to change. Suva hurriedly changed because the DJ was playing dancehall; she went crazy for dancehall music. She and KG always talked about going to *Suns Splash* in Montego-Bay when they were old enough. She put on the Jamaican-colored blouse and black skin-tight cotton pants she had taken out that morning. KG was already all up on Gabe, and everyone was having a good time. Suva politely turned the doctor down, stating that her boyfriend wouldn't approve of her gyrating on another man. Suva still got her groove on, moving to the beat, swinging her hips in slow and steady circles, her tiny waist remaining steady. KG kept urging Tommy to dance with Suva, but they both refused.

On Suva's birthday, the family had brunch under the ackee tree at the front of the property. Suva was delighted to pause the devouring of her fourth slice of fruitcake to accept an overseas call. She expected Jason with an apology and birthday wishes; instead, it was the Dean of Mayberry Academy apologizing for disrupting her summer vacation to inform her of an urgent on-campus issue. The school board had to reschedule the yearly planning meeting with the student government because of Suva and Tommy's absence. Suva was Head Cheerleader, Captain of the Foreign Languages and Mathematics Club, President of the Future Leaders Association, and Captain of the award-winning Academic Decathlon team. Tommy was her Vice-captain on all teams except cheerleading. He was the Student Body President and the student liaison for the Scholarship Committee. In short, they both needed to be at the meeting the following Monday. Just like that, their island getaway was brought to a premature end.

Suva bitterly informed her family that she and Tommy would be flying out that Sunday, accompanied by Mavis. Suva made the best of her final two days in paradise. She brought heaven to earth with Hazel in the form of Carrot cakes. Connected with earth's elements by swan diving off the rocks after hiking to the river. Commemorated her friendship with Mrs. R. by knitting her a doily. Desirous of making every second count, the teens ignored sleep that Saturday night. Instead, games, laughter and Christmas holiday plans got their undivided attention. Gabe fell silent on the topic of spending Christmas in Mayberry; his parents would never release him unsupervised.

Agonizing goodbyes were exchanged. Suva left a trail of tears from the Estate to the Airport. On the flight, Suva lost the battle to exhaustion, this allowed Tommy's wet shirt a brief reprieve; the left chest and shoulder were soaked. It pained him to see Suva cry. Gazing at her slumberous beauty, Suva was clutching her birthday necklace. Butterflies fluttered in his tummy, setting off an earthquake of hope throughout his body. *Someday she will be my wife.*

## Chapter 16

At Mayberry Academy, the meeting was super dull, as expected! Per usual relative to the others' the football team's budget was extremely excessive. Suva postulated that if championships and top academic performance where the deciding factors in budget allocation, the football team would get nothing. All that passion and words resulted in a 5 percent reallocation of funds from the football budget to the arts. After that torture, Suva rushed home. She retrieved a cake box from the fridge. Suva, with precious cargo in hand, reluctantly stopped with Tommy at Ayesha's house. Ayesha was not home, and the housekeeper was unaware of a return time.

In the town car en route to Henri Manor, Suva checked on the cake for the millionth time. Excitement kissed her skin giving her goose pimples. He was going to love the succulent masterpiece she created just for him. At the Manor, Suva dashed from the car ringing the door earnestly, cradling the box as if it was the Hope Diamond. Tommy smiled to himself; he was happy to see her so excited. He hoped Jason would appreciate and reciprocate her dedication. Suva rushed past the housekeeper, shouting "Jason" repeatedly.

"Must you defile my home with your ghetto antics?" Jason's mom glided effortlessly down the stairs, looking much like the refined Southern belle she keeps reminding everyone she was. Virgina Henri was the lady of the house. Traditional employment was beneath her. She believed that being a wife is a full-time commitment. "My son is not here, you crossed-raced hussy." Jason's mother pressed on, her Southern accent thickening to match her annoyance level. Suva didn't budge, so Virginia gave in. "Jason is at the yacht club. He has been going there every day all summer." Virginia checked the time. "Suva, darling, you should hurry and get on down there and surprise him. He should be in the locker room by this." Suva's haste to the town car was interrupted by JR, Jason's eldest brother.

"Suva, Jason is probably all sweaty, wait on him at your house instead." Suva's determination was undeterred.

"Tony, the Yacht Club, please." JR persisted,

"I'll get him, and you hide in the guest house, that would be an even greater surprise." Suva ignored him and closed the car door.

At the yacht club, Suva hurried to the locker rooms. As she got closer to the door, she heard faint sounds of people working out. Tommy held the door open for her while she held on to the cake box for dear life.

"Sur-pr—"

Shock slammed into her like a freight train, leaving numbness behind. The cake box slid from her hands, mirroring the state of her heart, it shattered. Back in the car, the silence was deafening. Tony's insides churned, witnessing the ordeal he was overcome with helplessness. He drove slowly, his way of showing care his emotionally distraught passengers. Tommy was reeling from his turmoil, but he held her hand all the way home. The increasing level of Suva's anger could be heard in the slamming of her bedroom door, the aggressive clicking of the lock on her window, the intense pulling of the blinds, then the smashing of her vanity. Storming into the bathroom, she turned on the lights then immediately turned them off. Seeing herself would be an acknowledgment of her anguish.

Lava like pain was burning her insides, yet the arctic chill of her anger fueled her frantic pacing. She gaged at the memory of the locker room, and she felt dirty just smelling them. Unconsciously she turned on the shower, sitting under the flow fully clothed, hoping the gushing hot water would be an amnesiac elixir. Three hours later, the hot water turned cold, waking her from her catatonic state. On her way to the bed, she left a trail of wet clothes behind. She pulled the covers in one swift motion and buried herself underneath the cotton. Returning to her catatonic state: her clammy hands, sniffling nose, Mavis' persistent knocks on the door, and Tommy's multiple attempts to open her window went unnoticed.

An emergency family conference call was underway, Jamaica and Mayberry were on high alert; the primary objective is getting proof of life, second was to ascertain exactly what caused Suva to turn into an angry zombie. Tommy was tasked with getting a visual of the room. Mavis was the chief liaison responsible for relaying the grave concerns of the family. Regardless of the tactics, Suva didn't budge. Tommy's investigations proved fruitful when he heard a faint sneeze by way of a stethoscope pressed to the room door.

The family in Jamaica was all huddled over receivers at different locations in the house: the kitchen, Hazel's bedroom, and the main dining room. Both stations rotated their concerns as sleep was needed, and chores beckoned. On the dawn of day 2,

Hazel suggested Mavis make an egg and bacon blueberry bagel sandwich with black Colombian coffee. Suva wouldn't be able to resist. Hazel was correct; Suva snatched the tray and slammed the door. Tommy stayed on guard by the door looking wounded. Mavis kept asking what happened, but all Tommy did was shrug and repeated.

"Bullshit, *one bag a* bullshit." That evening a relieved Mavis welcomed reinforcements.   At the site of KG & Gabe, Mavis rejoiced,

"Yes! You guys brought the big guns."  Then she removed the perfectly cooked meatballs from the skillet. KG hugged Mavis and stated boldly to the group,

"We got this!" Gabe reaffirmed her statement, grabbing the second tray of food from the counter.

"Baby girl," KG spoke gently; no movement.  "Suva, uummmm are you ok?" Still no change. KG banged on the door. "Gyal open di door ah stop form fool a yuhself!" No movement. "Oi, I will kick down this backside enuh!" There was shuffling; then, the door sprung open.  Suva gripped her, and the volcano erupted. Suva, KG, Gabe, Tommy, and the two trays disappeared inside the room. Suva couldn't stop crying, so Tommy had to describe the gory details of what transpired. Downstairs, the adults speculated as to who the source of all this drama was. It was unanimously decided that Jason Henri was the culprit; they didn't have any evidence to substantiate their claims. "Just give it time." Melissa was extremely furious, her baby girl was hurting, and she felt useless.

By day 4, Suva allowed visitors, she would play games and have long conversations, but she wouldn't leave her room. Her hair looked like an electrocuted poodle, and her skin was a black robe that Mavis had to wash secretly. The family felt defeated, would Suva ever leave her cave. Hazel reminded them that there was still one weapon left in the arsenal. Walking purposefully to the kitchen, the troops running anxiously behind her.  Hazel stood tall and gave orders, "Apron, flour, potatoes, brown sugar." They all cheered, celebrating their victory before the oven was even pre-heated.

The alluring aroma of Potato Pudding filled the house.
When her signals to Mavis over the intercom were ignored, Suva switched to a manual interface, shouting Mavis's name. No response. After moments that felt like hours, there was a slight turn of Suva's knob. Atsila's breath caught, and she was going to stand for a closer

but Kyle signaled to her to remain in position. Slowly, Suva emerged in her second skin, hair looking like she was in a fight with three ninja squirrels, and she wasn't victorious. While she made her way to the kitchen, no one gave her a passing glance. In the kitchen, she was face-to-face with Hazel, who had a fresh still-steaming slice of potato pudding in front of her. They made eye contact. Hazel slid the plate over to her. The slice was devoured in two bites.

Suva smiled widely,

"That was awesome, Grandma, may I have another slice please." In response, Hazel pointed at the robe. Suva pleaded with her eyes. Hazel started taking up the container that held the pudding. "Okay, okay, take it easy." Suva slowly removed the robe, placing it on the counter. Hazel pointed to the floor. Suva reluctantly complied and tossed it to the floor. Hazel plated a slice of pudding, licked her lips, then walked up to Suva, and handed her a comb and a hair clip. Suva breathed deep and stood firm. Hazel, pudding in hand, calmly walked over to the bin, pressed on the lever, and the lid flew open.

"Wait…uno momento! Mommy, fi real, though?" Suva ran to the mirror at the side of the kitchen, attempted to comb her hair, but the comb wouldn't budge. She ran to the sink, filled a cup with water, ran back to the mirror, and emptied the cup on her head. That did the trick; she was able to pull her hair back in a ponytail.

"Now this looks like my baby." Handing her the plate, Hazel kissed her on her forehead. Loud cheers could be heard as the family rushed in and hugged Suva. Hazel gloated. "Now that's how a professional gets it done." Eating directly from the container, Suva giggled when Mavis threw the robe into the bin. After Suva showered, the family gathered in the theater for an all-night marathon. Chilling poolside, KG was relieved and delighted at the progress Suva had made. Suva was actually in a bathing suit instead of her second skin, the awful robe that she secretly dug out of the garbage.

In the pool, Gabe and Tommy were engaged in a fierce stamina competition. KG thought the activity was juvenile, but the boys just kept doing laps. KG's contentment was suddenly eclipsed by anger, her mood darkened. Mavis announced Jason, and she realized why. The boys were too busy with their contest to see the poolside happenings. Suva's heart rate quickened; she had often wondered what their first meeting would be like. He was looking overly tanned, wearing skin-tight designer jeans and shades.

His hair was noticeably black. Before Jason could open his mouth, KG defensively stood between them. Jason paused and took off his glasses.

"Suva, call off your guard dog."

KG maintained her stance; their noses were almost touching. Suva tugged on KG's right index finger. KG stepped away and stood behind Suva's chair. Jason sat in the chair adjacent to Suva's. With disdain in his voice, he looked at Suva but directed his comments to KG. "I'm very disappointed with immigration for allowing mongrels into the country." He began cleaning his shades with his shirt then looked KG in the eyes. "My apologies, that's not fair of me tossing around insults like that. I mean, what have mongrels ever done to me? Relative to KG, mongrels are a high-class breed."

He smiled, pleased with himself when KG retreated to a chair on the other side of the pool. Jason, being satisfied with KG's distance, focused entirely on Suva. "Sorry I haven't called you in the last two weeks. Things have been hectic at the Manor with all the prep for the end of summer dinner." Suva felt hurt rise to her throat like bile. He was so blasé about everything. She was here withering away from depression, and he was busy choosing centerpieces for the Henri's annual end of summer soiree.

"Why are you here, Jason?" Suva just wanted his visit to be over. She kept glancing at the pool. The boys were still busy splashing back and forth. She wasn't sure what they would do to Jason if they saw him.

"Well, our senior year is starting, and I wanted to discuss our strategy for prom king and queen." He got up and knelt before Suva. "Look, no one has to know about the breakup until after I get my crown." She pushed back her chair and glared at him in disbelief. He didn't even have the decency to apologize for what he did; all he cared about was being prom king.

"Jason, has all that suntan lotion seeped into your brain?" Suva scanned the room. "Where are the cameras because this must be a part of some elaborate apology scheme. A scuba gear–wearing cameraman better jump out of the pool soon." Suva walked to the edge of the pool, searching. Jason looked mystified.

"Suva, you should be apologizing to me. Having me suffer for all those months. My testicles weren't blue; they were damn near purple." Jason's angry tone caught the attention of the boys.

He got louder and louder with each sentence. "I am a Henri, Mayberry royalty, yet I had to negotiate with you to touch your ass. I know your people are used to long-suffering, well, at least half of your people, but I am not." Suva couldn't explain why tears were running down her cheeks. She allowed them to flow, knowing that it was the last time she would cry over this invalid.

"Jason, I waited for you—"

He interrupted her, "You waited for me for three weeks, there's no comparison to me waiting on you for months. Besides, I can hardly stomach that." He motioned to a calmly sitting KG. "Can you imagine how painful it would've been to meet the entire motley crew!" Suva started laughing through her tears. How could she have been so blind, so naive, she didn't recognize this arrogant ignoramus polluting the air in front of her. Tommy couldn't comprehend what he was witnessing. Overexposure to the chlorine was causing him to hallucinate. Jason was shouting at a crying and laughing Suva. He and Gabe jumped out of the pool and headed straight over there. Suva motioned to them to stay there.

"Suva, this is what is going to happen." Jason's tone was laced with finality. He ignored everyone else and spoke only to Suva. "Being the prom king is my legacy. My father and my older brothers were prom king with the head cheerleader being prom queen." He waved his hand over her when he said, head cheerleader. "And if I feel gracious, I will tell the Tribune that we had sex so that the entire school won't pity you for the half-breed virgin that you are!" He walked away, leaving her in silence. The boys rushed to Suva's side to console her. As Jason passed KG, he raised his shoulders and asked, "Nothing to say mongrel?"

KG got up slowly, winked at Suva, and in one swift, precise movement, punched Jason twice in the nose, twice in his right shoulder plexus, then she dropped, split, and power punched him in his groin. Jason yelped! KG got up, looked down at a bloody screaming Jason and said, "Woof, woof, mother..."

"KG!" Mavis pulled her away from Jason before she could finish her statement. Mavis marveled at how fast KG was, her movements were reminiscent of one of those kung fu masters in the old karate movies. She thought he deserved a slap, but KG really put a hurting on him. Her fist connecting with his nose was audible. Mavis wanted to call Melissa but was afraid to leave Jason alone with an unremorseful KG.

## Chapter 17

The Lanaghans and the Henris were face-to-face on either side of the living room. An anguishing Jason laid between them; ice packs were on his swollen: face, shoulder, and groin. Suva was eating grapes on the counter in the kitchen completely unconcerned. KG, Tommy, Gabe, and Mavis were eavesdropping behind the wall near the living room. Mrs. Henri's Southern drawl was palpable. KG mimicked her exaggerated gestures and misuse of words.

"I am pressing charges, that little hussy must be hanged!" She sat on the edge of the sofa to avoid the germs, she was positive, were festering in the fabric. Melissa didn't speak; she vigorously finger-combed her thigh-length hair. Virginia continued, "I know your kind is not used to civilization, but there is a hierarchy in Mayberry, the Henris, we are royalty, an example must be made. She must be taken out back and shot!" Deaglan's neck and cheeks were fiery red; he spoke calmly,

"Virginia this is not Jim Crow's South…" He paused, "This was a misunderstanding amongst teenagers. I am sure they can work it out." Melissa nodded in agreement. Virginia wasn't having it. She stood up to emphasize her point.

"Deaglan, I know your brain has been verbalized by a severe case of jungle fever." She gave Melissa a once-over. "But in the real world, when an animal does something wrong, you punish it." Melissa got up in rage and headed toward her.

"Listen, lickle mawga dry up gyal. Refer to my child as an animal again, and I will slap you so hard, your ancestors will bleed!" Deaglan held her hands and called out for Mavis. Mavis rushed to Melissa's side and pulled her away. Virgina was thrilled about Melissa leaving the room.

"Great! Now that the half-breeds have left the room, us purebloods can truly annihilate the situation." Jason Senior spoke up; he was weary of Virginia's rudeness and embarrassed by her constant misuse of words in her attempt at sounding intelligent.

"Virginia dear, go wait in the car." She huffed and puffed, but her dramatics didn't faze him. "Go-wait-in-the-car!" The men sat and had a long discussion. Jason Senior saw the care in Deaglan's eyes as he relayed the events that led up to the beat-down. Mr. Henri asked to speak with Suva. Deaglan sat protectively close to Suva.

Involuntary tears ran down Jason Senior's face when he heard the words his son used and the way he behaved. Mr. Henri agreed to let the teens work it out on their own. Jason was placed in the town car while the head of the families exchanged final words privately. KG brought Virginia her scarf and pocketbook; she was about to apologize for hitting Jason because violence is never the answer.

"Well, well, at least one of you is aware of your purpose in life." Virginia adjusted her scarf with KG standing there, still holding the pocketbook.

Virginia rummaged through the bag, retrieving her lipstick. "Fetching and serving are what your kind was put on earth to do." KG counted to ten in her head. Virginia focused on her size -2 frame and ensured the pins were neatly tucked in her overly bleached blonde hair. She loved an excellent French roll; it made her her look so sophisticated.

"Mrs. Henri, did you send Suva to the yacht club, having prior knowledge of what she would encounter there?" KG asked in her most polite tone.

"But of course, I was being helpful. Life comes with hard truths. Surely, your kind understands hardship." KG took a long deep breath.

"Mrs. Henri, do you know that Suva cared deeply for your son? It broke her heart to see some girl doing the spread eagle on Jason."

Virginia interrupted KG, "Child, where are your manners? Her name is Mary Beth. Even her name is regal. I told Suva that he went there every day, sometimes twice per day. I'm not to be blamed if Suva didn't know I was referring to Mary Beth's secret garden." For some reason, KG was slightly shocked.

"How can you call yourself a mother and deliberately allow a young lady to walk in on her boyfriend having animalistic sex with another girl?"

Virginia smiled proudly. "I am particularly proud of that fact. I am a good mother, and I am ridding my son's life of all the influenza." KG had just one more question.

"Did you know that Ayesha and her boy toy were also having sex in that locker room?" Virginia headed for the door while answering, "That was unplanned, but breaking that green-eyed fire dancer's heart was just icing on the cake." KG watched silently as Mrs. Henri and her high-heeled toothpick legs went to the town car.

She secretly wished that her heel would break. That lady was pure evil. KG apologized to Mr. Henri for breaking his son's face. She explained that when Suva hurts, she hurts. She asked him to relay her apologies to Mrs. Henri. Virginia was not pleased with the outcome. Her husband was a weak, soft-hearted, half-breed–loving fool. Virginia gasped when she was told that KG was the one who injured Jason. She was worse than being a half-breed; she was a Jamaican. She stormed out of the car, her heels clicking and clacking underneath her. She pushed past Mavis, shouting for KG.

"Where is she? Where is that no-class, field slave nigg..."

KG power slapped her in the face. The impact unraveled Virginia's French roll and broke the right heel of her very high stilettos. KG stood there, daring her to speak, but Virginia was speechless. She was blinking profusely, her vision slightly blurry, and for a millisecond she forgot where she was. Mavis came to her aid and guided her back to the car.

"There, there, the room will stop spinning soon...your vision may take a little longer to come back."

Later that night, over dinner, Hazel was pleased to see Suva smiling and eating again. She couldn't fathom what took place in her absence. Gabe was retelling the story yet again. "KG was like a super ninja, Jason didn't know what hit him before he could grab his Nose, her fist was demolishing his groin!" Tommy took over with matched enthusiasm.

"Yes, but did you see how Mrs. Henri's feet lifted off the floor? She was shocked speechless!" Hazel looked over at KG. "That's a gross misuse of a black belt; sensei would disapprove." KG rubbed Suva's back. They exchanged soft smiles. Gabe let out a roar of laughter.

"I guess her ancestors are bleeding!" The family was on guard, Mrs. Henri was the suing type. Two days later, Mrs. Henri's lawyers called Deaglan to confirm a meeting. Deaglan cut KG's trip short. It was best if he argued that the threat had been removed. They departed later that night. Hazel left an emergency pudding in the freezer, just in case Suva had any setbacks.

"Suva, do you have a minute?" For the first time, Tommy felt nervous having a conversation with Suva. Ever since the locker room incident, she had been giving him the cold shoulder. She was in her library, reading the encyclopedia. Tommy sat directly beside her. Their thighs brushed; she got up, creating distance between them.

"Sure thing, Thomas, may I help you?" Tommy clenched his jaw and exited the library. Suva threw the book at him, almost hitting her mother.

"Baby, why are you trying to damage poor Tommy?" Melissa played with Suva's curls. Suva banged her head on the table, groaning in frustration. "What's wrong, honey? Let Mommy fix it." Suva played with her mom's hair, using it to cover her face. Melissa gently pulled her hair back. "Speak up, pumpkin." Suva stood up.

"Mami, quiero besarlo tanto." Suva pulled the ribbon from her hair, releasing the tendrils. "Pero, sigo viendo a Jason en ese estúpido vestuario!" Melissa held her daughter from behind.

"Stop punishing Tommy; your healing has been his main focus." Melissa spun Suva around. "Remember, Ayesha was on that gym bench too. He was hurt just as much as you." Guilt weighed Suva down. Melissa continued, "Honra tu amistad primero, el resto estará en su lugar." Suva knew her mother was right; Tommy did set aside his pain for her.

"I hate being a teenager. Too much goddamn hormones," Suva lamented. Melissa pulled Suva's bottom lip.

"Watch yuh mout pickney."

"Sorry, Mommy."

"Suva honey, you have one week before school starts. You haven't even gone shopping yet." Suva started banging her head on the table again. "Mommy will take care of it." A few hours later, Suva was called to the den. She stopped short at the door.

"Suva, come on, just have a seat."

Duncan's request halted her exit. Suva reluctantly sat as far away from the group as possible. The six teens sat in silence. Suva was usually the one in charge of mediation. Sofia signaled to Tommy to speak up. He looked away. Jason still wasn't sure why he was summoned to this place. His nose wasn't healed, and he kept feeling the need to guard his groin. Ayesha popped her gum and freshened her makeup. She could care less about this stupid meeting. When no one said anything, Duncan spoke up, "Let me get straight to the point. We are all here to decide if we are going to be friends still. Amidst all that has happened." Ayesha popped her gum again. Duncan continued, growing impatience thickened his Irish accent. "Quit it, Ayesha. After all, it is your indiscretion that necessitates this meeting." Silence. "Well then, Truth Circle, it is."

Jason spoke up, "That won't be needed. We are all familiar with the code. We remain, friends, no matter what. What happens in the group stays in the group." His statement went unrefuted. Duncan paced, looking at Jason and Ayesha,

"Since these two rabbits won't behave themselves, let's establish some ground rules, eh." Ayesha popped her gum again. Suva interrupted Duncan,

"Hear dis, mi a settle dis. Sticking to the code of the Truth Circle. We are still friends. You guys can date whoever the hell you want." Suva spoke slowly, never making eye contact with anyone. Before a response could be aired, two men unloaded heavy suitcases, spreading them across the room. The last entrants to the room were two tall blondes in stilettos, pulling four clothes racks.

"Wait! We aren't going shopping at the mall?" A semi frantic Sofia chimed in. "We won't be wearing similar outfits?" She was on her feet, cutting off the introductions. "Listen, without our coordination; I never know what to wear. Over the summer I had severe difficulties in the wardrobe department." Sammy and Bridget represented the mall conducting home visits for their high-end clientele.

"We can still coordinate, but there will be freedom to deviate at will." Suva offered, already viewing the racks. The teens spent several hours trying on various outfits, making multiple selections. Suva and Tommy happily fell into their usual groove. By the end of the exercise, forty out of the sixty pieces she bought were selected by him.

## Chapter 18

The first day of school was standard, Suva made a face when she was paged over the PA system by Benjamin Toad. His name alone gave her the creeps. Benjamin Toad was a chauvinistic, racist aristocrat with a killer IQ who thought himself superior to all. His face was decorated with an assortment of pimples. Suva hated having to knock on the door to his "office." She rolled her eyes at the sign that read "Benjamin Toad, Editor, and Chief, Mayberry Tribune." The *Tribune* is the school's official newspaper, but under Benjamin's leadership, it's nothing more than a gossip rag, specializing in the humiliation of persons who are not in his good graces.

"Have a seat, Suva; you look delicious as always. So, why has Benjamin invited you to his sanctum?" Before Suva could respond, he held up his hand and continued speaking, "Benjamin has brought you into his kingdom to give you a chance to get on record about the horrific locker room experience that took place over the summer." Suva blinked off her astonishment, ignored his arrogant tone, and spoke softly,

"Benjamin, you do realize this is the janitor's supply closet." Benjamin sat on the edge of the small table inches away from Suva.

"What this place was is irrelevant. Now it is a symbol of power, a kingdom spoken of throughout all of Mayberry. Benjamin's greatness is unmatched."

"While I find your monologue to be prolific, why the hell am I here?" Suva's frustration was evident.

"Your sarcasm is most welcomed. Benjamin is intrigued. But I will get to the juicy stuff." He sat back down at his table. "Benjamin has a confession; he has been stalling so that his servants would have time to distribute the copies of this week's *Tribune*. The entire issue is focused on you and your "meltdown." Do you care to comment?"

Suva stood up and loosened her ponytail. Her hair was straight thanks to a three-hour trip to Mavis. She quickly removed her jacket, revealing blue-fitted high-waist pants that emphasized her small waist and firm behind, the white blouse clung to her breast. Benjamin was speechless at how good she looked; she certainly did resemble any of the featured pictures. The school was buzzing with the story. The students assumed Suva was in Benjamin's office, begging for mercy, as he intended. Suva sashayed through the pitiful stares, her stilettos echoing confidence drowning out the muffled chuckles and judgmental whispers.

"We are having a lunch meeting in the library." Suva was surprisingly calm; she pushed away the salad Sofia brought her.

"A nuh time fi salad now!" At that moment, Tommy placed a cheeseburger with curly fries before her. She attacked the food with earnest. They were in the archives, way in the back of the Library away from prying eyes. They spent the entire forty-five minutes analyzing the *Tribune*. The story was very detailed and well written. The pictures were clear, the vast array of shots showcased Suva in her black robe and *Don King* hairstyle. If those weren't embarrassing enough, the center spread was one of Suva's worst days; she was on the floor in her room, a full tray of food resting beside her. Her face was swollen, and her eyes were blotchy. They couldn't figure out how those pictures where taken.

"Let me stress this again. We are not going to retaliate. I am fine!" Suva walked away, not entirely convinced that she was, in fact, "fine."

The weeks that followed were fierce. Benjamin released pamphlets of the story. He called them collectibles. Around week 5, the momentum slowed, students began to lose interest. There was one positive that came out of her complete humiliation. The student body was now fascinated with her, which resulted in a 50 percent increase in all the clubs that she was involved in. The members of the Sign Language Club were much displeased; they took pride in the small "intimate" numbers. Beth, the president, approached her in the locker room while they were getting ready for gym class. Beth waved her hand in front of Suva's face to get her attention.

Suva signed, "May I help you?" Beth was taken off guard by the aggression in her expression. Suva was usually so friendly. Beth signed back,

"What's your problem?" Suva didn't respond; she sat on a nearby bench. Tears flowed heavily. Suva signed an incoherent apology for her rudeness and additional bodies in the club. Beth sat in front of her and started signing an "it will get better" speech but stopped when she saw the latest copy of the *Tribune* in Suva's hand. ***"This Is How All Animals Should Coexist."*** Beneath the headline was the same picture of Suva on the floor in her room, but Tommy was now in it. He was attempting to feed her something from the abandoned tray a few inches from her. This picture was even worse; Suva's face was red and unrecognizable. Her hair was out of control, and her robe looked like it smelled. Beth held her close. Suva's sadness vibrated through Beth's body. Beth got worried because Suva had something stuck in her throat.

She started signing frantically, "What should I do?" but Suva's eyes were closed. Beth tried pulling away, but Suva held her tightly, her breathing becoming labored. A panicking Beth pushed off from Suva and ran through the door. Suva held her chest. Her inhaler was in her locker, but she couldn't remember her combination. Tommy ran into the room and handed Suva an inhaler. She puffed, breathing deeply. By the third breath, she got calm and opened her eyes. Tommy and Beth were in an intense conversation. Suva didn't interrupt. They were discussing how intimate the photographs were and that it was an inside job. Some vengeful person with a vendetta against Suva who was close to family leaked the pictures. Suva waved to get their attention.

"Hey, *Hardy Boy* and *Nancy Drew*, can we go to gym class now?" The three teens laughed. Brandon, Beth's boyfriend, who was also hearing impaired, entered the locker room and informed them that coach was asking for them. They helped Suva up and wiped her face and straightened her clothes. Even though the school was fascinated by the summer heartbreak and Suva was constantly bombarded with unwanted questions, the group followed the standard operating procedures, they attended all classes, all assignments were submitted on time, their extracurricular activities were maintained, they ate lunch together every day.

Everyone seemed annoyed by all the attention except for Jason, who relished it. The stories painted him as a stud that could have had any girl in Mayberry but chose Suva, a cold, distant virgin. The stories used the word *virgin* as if it were a virus. Jason got several phone numbers and sexy underwear stuffed into his locker. He was the big man on campus. Suva took comfort in her newfound friendship with Beth. Sofia disapproved; being seen with a "mute" as she termed it was not good for their reputation. It was bad enough they had to endure scrutiny because Suva was rigid and cold.

Suva didn't have to respond because Tommy dealt with it. Even though she wouldn't allow him to hug her or hold her hands, he still defended and supported her at every turn. Her favorite was when he slammed John Keller, the captain of the wrestling team, against the Dean's office because he asked Suva to autograph his *Tribune*. She secretly thought that was badass and sexy! The only two persons that he wanted to deck but couldn't were Avery and Ashley.

They made Suva's life a living hell. They decorated the exteriors of their side by side lockers with enlarged versions of all the photos published in the *Tribune*. At a general assembly held in the auditorium, the school was treated to a billboard-sized projection of Suva refusing food from Tommy. Ashley and Avery started chanting, "Half-breed animals," until Dean Shaw put a stop to it. At the door, they shouted in Suva's face. Suva looked at them with gentle eyes,

"You know, if you guys were at the center of a scandal, I would never treat you like this." They kissed as a sign of pride over their stunt and continued chanting,

"Half-breed animals!"

Suva and Beth had a lot in common. They liked the same foods and movies. Beth made it a little easier to get through the rough time without Tommy or KG. Suva's signing went from good to proficient. She was now able to keep up with all of Beth's friends. They were so warm, caring, and nonjudgmental. Interacting with them was a welcomed break from all the drama. Speaking of drama, Suva had to brace herself. It was National Academic Decathlon week, which meant that the committee would have meetings at the school of the reigning champion. It also meant that the championship team had to play host to the remaining top five schools.

Suva heard the screams before she saw him. No one else could induce such fanfare. She waited by the auditorium door for him to come around the corner as the *Tribune* photographer captured all the festivities. Being the prospective captain of the football team, Jason was standing to Suva's left. Maxwell greeted everyone except for Jason and Suva.

"To have lost to such a beautiful Amazonian goddess was an honor." Instead of shaking Suva's outstretched hand, he gave her a bear hug, lifting her off the ground. The student body cheered, Tommy, clenched his jaw. He couldn't stand Maxwell Thunder. His stupid French accent, he was such an as – Tommy's thoughts were interrupted by what Maxwell did next.  After putting Suva on the floor, Maxwell kneed Jason in the groin, and boldly stated, "Imbécile" Momentary silence. *Click click click* The *Tribune* photographer captured it all.  Tommy's disgust turned into temporary respect, he gave Maxwell a firm handshake then stepped over a moaning Jason.  The school was electric with talk of the French stud defending Suva's honor.

The girls were putty in Maxwell's hands. He, however, spent the entire week trying to convince Suva that he could be monogamous for her.  Suva viewed his declarations with much indifference.  The teens had a hectic week. They effectively balanced their class loads, assignments with the mandatory attendance to the many many Decathlon meetings.  Maxwell delivered flowers to Suva's classes, posted love notes on her windscreen, wrote poems on her locker.  She finally gave in when he threatened to have the Glee Club serenade her in the cafeteria.

Suva didn't know what to expect on a date with Maxwell but, she kept an open mind.  Sitting at a coveted balcony table, they ate a scrumptious four course meal at Mayberry's most exquisite French restaurant.  Maxwell shared insights about his life and culture with brilliant comedic timing, Suva's sides pleasantly ached from all the laughter.  The time flew by. Saying good-bye at her door, he wasn't thwarted by her extended hand when he went in to kiss her. *Patience is critical with this one.*

A brooding Tommy sitting on her window, snatched the smile off Suva's face.  They sat on the balcony together. Tommy expressed his disapproval of her frolicking with Maxwell. His disappointment in how she had been treating him as if he was responsible for Jason's actions. But he assured her that he would not cut his hair until she kissed him and admits that she loved him. The next day in the parking lot after the final decathlon meeting, Maxwell thanked Suva for her hospitality and for indulging him with that date. Suva kept glancing across the parking lot. Tommy was due any minute now for them to ride home together.

"Suva, je t'ai compris. Vous avez besoin d'un homme pour prendre en charge." Then Maxwell kissed her. She was astonished but maintained the kiss.  When he released her she knew she was completely smitten.

"But clearly, I am not that man, he is." Maxwell gestured toward the other end of the parking lot where Tommy was standing observing them. Suva gave Maxwell a hug and thanked him. As Suva walked away, Maxwell shouted after her, "Si jamais il briser votre coeur, je serai ici pour réparer les pièces."

Suva smiled back. "Merci Maxwell, le monde mérite de voir le vous que je vois."

They both laughed. Driving away, he whispered, *Not a chance.* The ride home was quiet. Tommy was fuming; *how could she kiss him after the serious conversation they had last night? What was she thinking?* At a traffic light, she glanced over at him. She was mouthing something. He put the Mercedes in park.

"I hope that's my apology you are rehearsing." Suva looked over at him.

"You are the most phenomenal person I have ever met. Ich liebe dich." Tommy was surprised. His face was immediately flushed.

"I won't apologize for kissing Maxwell because it confirmed that I only want you." Tommy closed his eyes, allowing the words to wash over him. Despite his best attempts, he couldn't formulate a single word. "Wohali, one day we are going to kiss, and it will be magical, beautiful and blah blah blah me me me, but yow let it happen naturally." Warmth ran through Tommy's body; it had been so long since she called him that. On the green he paused; if it were a dream, he would be awake by now.

Maxwell's shenanigans helped Suva's social life. The student body was no longer interested in her summer heartbreak. Benjamin did send her a thank-you card as her story was the longest-running highest-selling the *Tribune* had experienced in years. He urged that he should have exclusive rights to her next social crisis.

## Chapter 19

It was Thanksgiving, Suva's usual excitement around the food and family was tainted by how much she missed KG. Unlike Suva, who wished it would just be Christmas already, Tommy was thrilled! Tommy loved Thanksgiving because of all the food and football. Every Thanksgiving, there was a ruthless grudge match between the Mayberry Academy Alumni and varsity team. While the varsity had speed and agility, the alumni used their burly bodies and experience to brutalize the youngsters.

Per tradition, the night before Thanksgiving was friends and family game night at Suva's house. Duncan's and Sofia's parents were present; Mavis, her husband, two daughters, and son were in attendance as well. Ayesha's and Jason's parents sent wine and their apologies. The doorbell rang, Suva hopped off the kitchen counter, grapes in hand and ran past Mavis.

"I'll get it." Suva excitedly welcomed Beth and Brandon. The teens teamed up against the adults in a riveting game of *Charades*. The next answer would tie the game. Suva went for Beth since not all the players understood sign language. An elated Suva screamed when Beth signed the answer. Sofia rolled her eyes at the sight of Beth and Suva's victory high five. She wasn't happy to have a deaf outsider at their intimate gathering. She would air her grievance before Thanksgiving supper in case Suva had the bright idea of inviting them to that! Tensions were high; a tiebreaker round was unfamiliar territory for the usually dominant adults. They deployed their best player, Atsila. Standing beside Atsila, Suva's game face was on. As both ladies acted out the same clue, their teammates screamed random, extremely inaccurate answers. Suva focused on Tommy. Tommy's bruised ego from constantly losing, blocked out all distractions, he homed in on Suva. Wait, *he knew the answer.* "Hippopotamus!"

Suva screamed, "Yes, yes, yes!" The teens erupted in hysterical joy, Tommy leaped from the sofa. Suva jumped into his embrace. They kissed. Their energies connected. Wanting more of paradise, Tommy took her tongue into his mouth, thunderous vibrations of sensuality reverberated through their limbs. *Smash!* The room fell silent! Sneakily smiling, Mavis cleaned up the shards of glass at Ayesha's feet. Tommy knew that any effort to move would be futile; his head was spinning. He licked his lips and smiled.

Suva's equilibrium was off. She stood then sat. Suva felt moisture that she didn't recognize. She, too, had a huge smile. Beth signed, asking her what just happened. Suva held up her hands to respond but couldn't remember how to. Beth and Brandon laughed at her.

"That must have been some kiss!" they signed to her in unison. Later that night, Jason sat up, fuming. The night's occurrence tormented him. Suva kissed another man, how audacious and disrespectful! As for Tommy, he had no regard for the bro-code. He needed to be distracted. He woke Mary Beth, her sex did nothing for him. She wasn't Suva. In fact, Mary Beth's time had expired. But he couldn't be bothered to break in another girl for Christmas, so he decided to wait until after the New Year's Eve ball to end it. He would have a fresh girl for Valentine's Day.

By 6 p.m. on Thanksgiving night, supper was already demolished, the men were anxious for the grudge match. At 7 p.m., almost the entire town was crammed into the Southfield stands at Mayberry Academy. Suva and her squad got the crowd excited.
Both teams were huddled around their coaches, getting last-minute encouragements. Coach assigned Tommy as quarterback and Jason receiver. Jason was much displeased, fetching Tommy's balls.

By half time the crowd was enthralled, the game was a nail-biter, the alumni were up by seven points. The teens' only focus in the locker room was to score two touchdowns then run out the clock. Tommy hungered for Suva's kiss, her taste lingered. Coach tapped him with the playbook, "Son, you better get focused before you go back on the gridiron." Tommy sat up straight.

Re-entering the field, Tommy searched for Suva, she was at the top of a pyramid, looking all sweet. On her dismount, he dropped his helmet, lifting her into a long, slow kiss. The squad, the crowd, all went wild. *Damn, this boy can kiss!* Suva again couldn't find her footing. Jason told Tommy that the coach changed the play, Tommy thought it odd but gave the Coach a thumbs-up none the less.

They were now doing the fake left crossover. The stands were quiet with anticipation. The referee blew the whistle, Tommy called out the play. The center pitched him the ball. He faked left and extended the ball to an unaware running back.
*Wham!* Five large alumni guys barreled into him, lifting him then dropping him hard. Shock waves of pain ran through Tommy's nerve endings. Darkness. Tommy's immobility halted the opposition's celebration.

The defense and running back looked quizzical, "Jason, dude! You told us he would run on the play?" Jason walked away, smiling under his helmet. Coach cleared the area, and the paramedics secured Tommy on a gurney. In the ambulance, Melissa examined an unconscious Tommy. A spaced-out Suva held his hand. Wheeling Tommy into the trauma ward, Melissa gave orders to a team of nurses.

"Unconscious eighteen-year-old male, possible concussion. Get Dr. Cyder. Skip the CT and do an MRI." Suva gripped her mother's hand; anxiety narrowing her airways. The increased severity of Suva's fears tightened her chest. In mommy mode Melissa administered the pump, then placed Suva in a private room. Suva cried, wheezed, paced until exhaustion lulled her to sleep. Both football teams and the cheer squad crowded the waiting area. Who changed the play, why wasn't Tommy covered, and where the hell was Jason? These were the questions of the evening. Suva woke as they were wheeling a still unconscious Tommy into the spot beside her. Mavis brought a change of clothes for Suva, but she wouldn't budge. Two hours later Tommy awoke,

"Suva?" Suva hugged him tightly. Melissa pried her away to exam him. Melissa conducted some language and arithmetic exercises.

The extent of the damage was fractured ribs, dislocated shoulder, and sprained wrist. Mentioning some dizziness, Tommy threw up on Suva.

"Yup, he has a concussion."

Suva cleaned him off. Suva's cheerleading uniform was covered in vomit, but she insisted on staying with Tommy. Atsila gave Suva the change of clothes with instructions to shower in Melissa's office. Duncan, Sofia, Ayesha, and Atsila assured her they would hold down the fort till she got back. Mavis accompanied her to the office. Suva took the quickest shower she could take. Again, in the room, she watched Tommy sleep. The medication knocked him out. At midnight, Suva was the last man standing. Melissa was too anxious to go home, so she covered for one of the nurses in the emergency room. Kyle took Atsila home under the guise of getting fresh clothes for Tommy. Atsila was a wreck, Tommy was her entire world. After Atsila's second panic attack, Kyle knew that rest was what she needed.

By 12:30 a.m., Suva's tummy started growling. She was still floating from the kiss, so she didn't have much of a Thanksgiving meal. Thinking of the sizeable succulent turkey she didn't have made her stomach rumble. She checked Tommy's vitals and ensured that he was comfortably tucked in. Running her fingers through his now shoulder-length hair. She replayed that night before the fireplace.

"Wohali, you haven't cut your hair? I don't want you to cut it. It is very sexy this way. Makes you look even hotter." She laughed. "Mi hungry eno!"

"Baby, go eat." Mavis entered the room and sat beside the bed. Suva was about to protest, the loudness of her hunger pains silenced her. She headed for Melissa's office; the good stuff was in the hidden mini-refrigerator stylishly camouflaged as a bookshelf. Melissa's office was closed, Suva went to the ER for the key. She found her mother and three nurses fighting a losing battle with a patient. Suva mentally reflected that this is the reason she would not practice medicine. She had several volunteer hours at the hospital. Suva wanted to be a nurse or a doctor, going on rounds with her mother, until a patient threw up his intestines on her lap.

Since then, much to Deaglan's delight, Suva has strongly considered a law career. Amidst the chaos, Suva noticed four neatly stacked books tied together with a string. It was her all-time favorite trilogy, the *Three Castles*, and the first entry of an encyclopedia series. Suva looked at the chart, Jane Doe, the sole survivor of a major car accident.

"Mom, what's going on?" Suva shouted to her mom over the scuffle.

Melissa stepped away from the examination bed.

"Jane Doe, covered in blood and broken glass, brought here thirty minutes ago but won't allow us to examine her." Suva rubbed her fingers over the Three Castles trilogy, pushed aside images of intestines, took a deep breath, and walked into the line of fire.

Standing beside the kicking, scratching teenager, Suva spoke up, "This reminds me of when Ada the warrior queen was wounded in the battle of Cien and got rescued by ogres." The teen paused. Suva pressed on, "At first, Ada fought them tooth and nail, causing further damage to her wounds, only to realize that the ogres just wanted to help her." The teen settled, her gray eyes entirely focused on Suva. Suva whispered loudly, "Nurse Dickens is an ogre."

The teen didn't respond. Giving up, Suva started walking away. The teen's cold, trembling hand held on to Suva's.

"Borus."

Suva gently squeezed the scrawny hand. "I can't examine you; I'm not a nurse." Confusion rested on the faces of the nurses. "In the story, Ada would only allow one ogre to dress her wounds, Borus." Suva took the chart. "Tell you what, I'll make the notes while Nurse Dickens does the examination." The teen curled into herself, shaking her head profusely.

"Borus or die."

Admitting defeat, the nurses backed away. Suva pulled the curtain around the bed. After putting on latex gloves, she nervously began the examination. The teen took a pen and started filling out the chart. They worked together. "In my nonexpert opinion, all seems to be well. Your vision and breathing seem fine." Suva read the chart. Svetlana Mariska Bucker, fourteen years old, five feet ten inches tall with blonde hair and gray eyes. "Final test of motor skills, are you able to stand?"

Svetlana stood on her own, took two steps to the right, then four steps to the left. Her frame was so frail the band-aids Suva put over the few scratches seemed to weigh her down. "No sah, yuh want some cornmeal porridge, man." Not expecting the teen to understand, Suva rephrased, "You have quite a modelesque physique, Svetlana. Are you a model?" Svetlana self-consciously sat back on the bed.

"Borus, is that all you've got? I know I look malnourished, so you can shove your comments up your as.." Suva interrupted her,

"Wow, Lana, calm down. I meant it as a compliment. With those gray eyes, your built and bone structure, you could be on the runways of Milan tomorrow." Svetlana glared at Suva angrily. Melissa entered the space. Suva handed her the chart. Melissa spoke directly to Svetlana, "I'm sorry about your parents. You have been assigned a caseworker who will meet you at your group home on Monday. The van from the group home will be here at 7:30 a.m. to pick you up."

Back at the nurse's station, Suva was passionately sharing her views with a very busy Melissa. "Mom, that's not fair. Svetlana's going to get lost in the system. Can't you find her a suitable home and bypass the whole group home thing?"

"Suva honey, you have to let the system work. Can we discuss this later, please? Two more nurses won't be able to make it for their shifts."

Melissa kissed Suva on her forehead and gave her the keys to the office. "Baby, get a snack from my secret stash, give Thomas a kiss for me." Suva volunteered to escort Svetlana to her assigned bed in the pediatric ward. A tired overworked Nurse Dickens gladly agreed.

"I'm positive that we are breaking several rules." Suva was sitting on the bed beside Tommy, devouring a large apple. "Lana, do you want to chill with Tommy and me, or would you prefer to be with a bunch of crying babies?" Svetlana gripped her books tighter.

"I'll stay here."

"Good." Suva took a few books out of the book bag Mavis brought. Schoolwork was the perfect distraction. She started with the Additional Mathematics assignments. Svetlana puzzlingly looked on.

"It's a holiday: why homework?" Suva chuckled.

"We are gifted students. I guess they figured we could handle it." Svetlana gazed at the book intensely then got silent. Suva got up and tossed the apple seeds in the trash. "Svetlana, where are you from?" Svetlana began absently writing in the book as she spoke,

"We are from a small rural trailer park town that you've never heard of. We live in a beautifully dilapidated second-hand trailer." She passed the book back to Suva.

"Beautifully dilapidated hhhmmm" Suva was puzzled for at a cursory glance Svetlana's response to the math questions were correct.

"Sorry, a run-down old trailer" Svetlana hugged her books and curled back into herself. With tears flowing, she continued in hoarse whispers. "I have good parents. They liked when I read to them. I read almost all the books in the Town's Library." She touched the Encyclopedia. "I complained about being bored at school; they forced me to go." She smiled here, "Papa says: *Learning is important*"

Suva got goosebumps. She hugged Svetlana.

Svetlana groaned like a caged animal missing the freedom of the wild. "They're gone!" Kicking and screaming, she cried harder.

"The bullies are going to get me now for sure!" Suva held her as tightly as she could.

Suva released her long enough to get a cup of water. The water brought a little calm.  They sat there holding hands in silence. After a long while Suva unraveled her French roll and let her hair free. Recognizing genuine shock of Svetlana's face, she asked,

"Are you okay? Yeah, I know my hair is a hot mess."

Svetlana was mesmerized, "Can I touch it? I've never seen hair like this." Suva moved her head closer to Svetlana's hand.  Svetlana looked around cautiously and started whispering, "I have never met a Spanish person before. You and the doctor are the first."

Suva asked in the same hushed tone, "What other races have you interacted with?"

"Apart from missionaries, our town didn't have many outsiders. This was our first big trip. The outside world came to me through books and old movies."

Suva nodded, not sure of what to say.

"In other words, you are cognitively advanced but socially…" Suva paused, searching for the right word.

"Retarded!" Svetlana chimed in.

Suva laughed. "I wasn't going to say that. I was going to say socially…inexperienced." Suva checked on Tommy; all was well. "First of all, I'm not Latino. Thank you for that compliment. One of my best friends is they are a gorgeous race. I'm biracial. My mother is black, and my father is white." Svetlana inspected Suva, touching her skin and hair again.

"You are beautiful. From an anthropological perspective, you are a perfect creature.  With your wide hips and ample bosom, you are primed for childbearing."

"Prime for what?" Both girls were jolted by Melissa's sudden entrance into the room.

"How did I know that you two were up here? Suva, the nurses, are frantic because a child was missing when the doctors did their 6 a.m. rounds." Both teens were silent. Suva looked at the clock.

"It's 6:30 a.m. already. Mommy, I'm sorry I lost track of time." Svetlana remained quiet. The stern doctor intimidated her.

"Borus, she is your mother?" Melissa hugged Suva and kissed her forehead. "Baby, you can't do this. Please take her to pediatrics. Then go home. I'll be home by 9 a.m. I love you. And as for you, I will see you on Monday at the meeting with your caseworker." Melissa patted Svetlana's head before walking out.

Opening the front door to her house, Suva ensured that the coast was clear. She headed straight for the stairs whispering. When she turned, Svetlana was still at the door. "Lana, what are you doing? Let's get upstairs."

Svetlana spun in a slow circle. "This is your house? My entire trailer park could fit into this living room." Suva dragged her gently up the stairs.

"Whose room is that?" They were passing the room to the immediate left of Suva's.

"That's where I keep my extra clothes." Svetlana peeked in.

"Wow, all my clothes fit in a box." She ran into the room and spun twice, then headed for the bathroom. "You have a tub!"

Suva wanted to tell her to keep it down, but preferred excitement over tears. Sitting on the bed, Suva explained, "The room was initially built for her older brother who died when my mom was seven months pregnant. My dad couldn't bare me being in here, so they gave me their master suite and moved to the third floor.

"I'm sorry, Borus." Suva gave the usual shrug.

"It's okay. You can use this room while you are here. You look like a size two. I'm sure I have brand-new size two clothing in this closet. My mother over shops for me." Suva ran Lana a bath; she had never seen someone so excited to take a bubble bath. Lana stayed under the bubbles for a good minute.

"Suva, this is so good. It smells like lavender." Suva was leaving the bathroom to give her privacy.

"Suva, don't leave. I don't need privacy from you. Suva, your name is so odd." Suva put the toilet top-down and sat.

"Well, it's supposed to be a romantic story, but I think it's gross." Lana made a face and splashed around. Water went all over the floor. She paused cautiously when Suva's smile widened, Lana felt relieved. Suva continued speaking, "After my mom miscarried, she was devastated, no one and nothing would cheer her up. Dad tricked her and took her on a getaway to Fiji. They stayed at a fabulous hotel in Suva, the capital city. According to them, the happiness she felt in Suva gave her the courage to try again. Sweet, right?" Suva saw Lana's confused look.

"Suva, that's a sweet story." Suva walked over to the tub and whispered, Lana, I think I was conceived in Suva hence the name." They both cringed.

"You are going to die in Mayberry!"

Suva and Lana jumped at the sound of Melissa's voice.

"Mom, I can explain. Lana needed to get cleaned up, and—" Realizing defeat Suva gave up. "Mommy, I'm sorry I disobeyed you." She ran into Melissa's arms. "The social worker isn't coming back until the morning." Melissa hugged her child. Releasing her, Melissa took a towel from the shelf.

"Lana, come from under there before you drown." Lana popped out from under the bubbles, looking guilty.

"Ms. Melissa, can I stay a little while longer, please?" Melissa's heart melted.

"Sure thing, honey. Suva, my room now!" Melissa took a quick shower while Suva tried to explain her way out of trouble.

"Mom, can we please talk to Dad about it?" Suva was trying to convince Melissa to become Lana's temporary guardian. On her way out the door, Melissa promised Suva she would think about it. After conducting some preliminary research, Melissa discovered that it wasn't challenging to get temporary custody of Lana. She contacted the caseworker, and within three hours, she was Lana's temporary legal guardian. The girls were elated to hear the news. While Suva and Svetlana were getting ice cream, both pairs of parents, along with Mavis reviewed paperwork around the dinner table.

"Social Services need to be more specific. Temporary until she is placed, that is not a date." Deaglan was combing through the information, commenting more to himself than the others. "They make her sound like a used car and not a person."

Melissa looked at her husband and knew what he thought before he said it. They all felt it, but agreed not to disclose anything to the children until they had reliable information. At the ice cream parlor, Suva decided that swinging by the mall was an excellent idea. Lana was timid at first but eventually warmed up to the idea of owning more than three outfits.

On their way to the boutique, they stopped at the reptile store. Suva loved reptiles; snakes were her all-time favorite. Armed with a white mouse, after convincing the clerk to allow her to feed one of the corn snakes, Suva thought about Tommy. If he were there, he wouldn't have allowed her to go near the black rat snake. Suva secretly liked how protective he got. He was so adorable, with those amazing green eyes and cute lips. Suva had to refocus. She ushered the mouse into his final resting place.

Over dinner that night, Melissa lectured Suva on excessive shopping. "So, Mom, where did the two shopping bags in Lana's closet come from?" The table fell silent. Mavis couldn't help it; she laughed.

"Look at the pot calling the kettle black." Suva explained that she didn't see any harm in getting Lana a few things. She even used her allowance to pay for it.

"Suva, it's not about the money. I don't want Lana to feel smothered by all these things." Melissa winked at Lana. Lana was too busy devouring Mavis's lasagna to add to the conversation. Mavis spoke up,

"All right, ladies, let's agree not to buy anything else until Christmas. We don't want to spoil Lana." Mavis placed another piece of the beef lasagna in Lana's plate. Deaglan entered the dining room with two shopping bags. They had a good laugh. At 2:25 a.m., Suva jumped out of her sleep. Fear flooded her system; Lana's animalistic groans filled the house. A terrified crying Lana was rocking back and forth on the bed. Her eyes were swollen; she was covered in red blotches. Suva's heart dropped, dampening a washcloth with warm water Suva wiped Lana's tears. Suva cradled her. Melissa and Deaglan sat on the floor on either side of the bed, while Mavis went to the kitchen to make some tea.

Lana calmed down a little as she sipped the tea. "They are gone! The vivid scent, their flesh burning, its…its pungent." They allowed her to cycle through her emotions, staying up all night talking because Lana was terrified of going back to sleep. Suva had school that morning, and Lana insisted on coming with her. Deaglan couldn't tell Lana no; after all, she presented a good argument. She postulated that one benefit of paying so much money to send your child to a private school is that they make allowances.

At Mayberry High, Lana sat in Tommy's seat, taking notes for him. By Wednesday, the teachers knew her by name. She even responded to a few questions. Suva convinced her parents to let Lana take the admissions test for Mayberry Middle School. Lana got perfect scores across the board on the grade 7 tests; they gave her grade 8. Same results. Grade 9 & 10, same results. Impressed, the admissions director gave her the grade 12 admissions tests, she was in the 96 percentiles. Lana met with the school's psychologists, who then offered a recommendation that was seconded by the admissions director. The Lanaghans met with the dean, who offered Lana a full scholarship with the recommendation of placement in the tenth grade. She would have to do extra classes over winter break to try and catch up for the spring semester.

"Wouldn't placement opportunities clash with me starting school?"

At the dinner table, Lana reviewed her results. Suva placed the salad on the table. "Yeah, Mommy, would the social worker factor in the proximity to Mayberry Academy in placement?" Deaglan silenced them.

"Look at the mini lawyers with the questions! Can we eat?" Deaglan felt uneasy about the discussion. Dinner was unusually quiet. Although Tommy resumed school, Lana continued being Suva's shadow. Soon, it was winter break. Suva and Tommy didn't go to the winter formal with the other four teens; things were tense since Jason wouldn't admit that he deliberately changed the play. They took Lana to an art exhibit. Suva wasn't a fan of postmodern art, but she appreciated any form of artistic expression. Lana and Tommy were off by themselves, enjoying every sculpture and every painting. Suva watched her from across the room.

Lana was wearing black fitted leather pants with complementary black leather and cotton jacket with pink boots. Lana proudly chose her outfit. Suva noticed that a group of men was also checking Lana out. Suva marched up to them. "Wah a gwan yasso! Why are you stalking a fourteen-year-old?" The men laughed. The flamboyant leader spoke, sassing Suva,

"I'm Spencer T., and I am a talent scout. I have a Christmas catalog that she would be perf for." Suva examined the card, Lana and Tommy joined her. Lana kept shaking her head no once she heard the words photoshoot and modeling. Suva was letting Spencer T. down easily when Carmichael Kissinger walked over.

Carmichael didn't need any introduction; he was Mayberry's celebrity manager. He was well respected in social and professional circles. He was always on the cover of the *Mayberry Ledger*, a picture with him could jumpstart your career. He dismissed his underlings with a wave of his hand.

"Lana, is it? May I speak with your mom?" Oozing charm. He scanned the room.

"Suva is my mom, so you can speak to her." Lana clung to Suva. Carmichael inhaled Suva. He didn't speak; he just examined her.

"You are gorgeous. Your face would sell makeup. Your body would sell lingerie and your—"

Tommy interjected, "Mr. Kissinger, Suva is not interested in anything you have to offer, so can we focus on Lana." Suva erred on the side of caution.

"Mr. Kissinger, we will talk it over with our parents and give you a call." Suva took Tommy's hand and walked away. Carmichael watched her leave. Latin women have the best behind, but this one's smile touched him. Lana talked about the possibility of modeling the drive home. She felt insecure because she was always teased for being too slender.

"Lana, you are a beautiful, intelligent, amazing young lady. Decide based on how you see yourself and not through the lens of your insecurities. We got your back, girl!" Lana loved hearing those words; it reminded her of her parents. They would want her to do what made her happy.

"Plus, I will punch anyone in the face who even thinks of hurting you." Tommy knew he couldn't punch anyone in his current state. Lana laughed and hugged him from the backseat.

"Spoken like a true dad." Over late-night ice cream, the family discussed the opportunity. Deaglan knew Carmichael personally, so he called him up to verify the legitimacy of the offer. With Deaglan's confirmation, Lana decided to do it. Lana was excited; she had a day to prepare for the shoot. She locked herself in the library, reading up on photography, camera angling and lighting, and the art of modeling. Suva and Tommy transformed the treehouse into a studio for a practice session.

"Lana, you are ready!" After the session. Melissa handed Lana a large manila envelope. Lana was exultantly proud as she read her Mayberry Academy invitation letter.

"I got a full scholarship! Well, technically, it's 75 percent because the academic year is...wait, what am I saying? I'm going to be a sophomore?" Melissa explained that it was based on the recommendation of the psychologist and her scores. Mavis commented that it was strange that Suva wasn't allowed to skip even though she got pre-accepted to ManU. She got a "we'll talk about this later" look from Melissa. Lana was too excited to finish dinner. She went straight to her room with the bags containing her school supplies. She felt as if Christmas came early. Lana didn't sleep; she spent the night reviewing the syllabus for each class. She couldn't to start working on all the assignments. Tommy came over, and Suva brought their breakfast to the room. When Lana was in the shower, Suva picked out a simple T-shirt and jeans ensemble. Tommy was standing by the closet with a shoebox in his hand.

"Good, these sneakers I bought will go great with that outfit." Suva gently pushed him against the closet door. She kissed him deeply, ensuring she didn't hurt his right arm that was still in a sling. They pulled apart when the knob on the bathroom door started turning.

"Tommy, why is your face all red?" Lana grabbed her outfit and went back into the bathroom. Exiting through Suva's window, Tommy commented,

"Suva, you are so unfair. Pulling a stunt like that when you know I can't grab you where I want to." Suva took off her robe, holding his gaze, she pulled the first two buttons of her pajama top. *Wham!* Tommy bumped his head on the frame. Suva smiled sexily.

"Look at dat, if you can't handle the visual, how are you going to manage the touch?" She shut the door behind her and went to shower. Tommy was intrigued by this new Suva. Just the thought of her drove him crazy. At this point, he couldn't handle the touch. He took an extra-long cold shower.

## Chapter 20

Hazel, Jay, KG, and Gabe flew in three days before Christmas. A long day of being *Picasso* with an oven introduced various aches and pains to Hazel's body, with such strong encouragement, Hazel enjoyed a soothing evening soak in the hot tub with her grandchildren. "Lana, honey I'm sure the tub feels warmer than your towel." Hazel lovingly coaxed Lana. Lana was attached to her towel like a turtle to its shell, her countenance wrecking of timidity. Suva splashed her with some hot water.

"I don't, don't…" Lana pulled the towel tighter. "Grandma Hazel says I need cornmeal porridge to put some meat on my bones." The ladies laughed hysterically, which was classic Hazel.

"Lana girl, that's what grandmothers do, they always try to fat yuh up." KG playfully pulled on the towel. Hazel got out of the tub, held Lana's hand, walking out of earshot. Hazel hugged Lana. Cradling Lana's face gently between her palms.

"Baby, Grandma's sorry. Didn't mean for you to be self-conscious." Lana averted, doubt selecting her words,

"I know I am not as shapely or busty as Suva and KG, but." Hazel's bear hug cut her off. Hazel's tone matched the comfort of her embrace.

"Child, listen, you are beautiful and amazing. Your body is perfect. God made you just as he had envisioned." Hazel pulled away, tugging the towel from Lana's reluctant grip. "Don't you ever, ever let anyone make you feel uncomfortable about your body."
Hazel pulled her in again. "You may be skin and bones, but you are my skin and bones. I love you!" Lana held on a bit longer. Lana walked over to the girls with extra sass. Mavis brought hot chocolate with marshmallows for the girls and some ginger tea for Hazel.

"Mavis, join us!" Mavis scuffed. The girls exchanged knowing glances. The air was still thick around Mavis and Hazel. "Ahhh, guys, so it is my turn to host the swim team's Secret Santa gathering." KG rolled her eyes and hissed her teeth. "Buck up cause the swim team will be here tomorrow." Suva couldn't decide what to wear to the pool party. KG was of no help. She wanted Suva to wear the same orange two-piece from the birthday party. Tommy wobbled through Suva's window. He uncomfortably adjusted the nuisance supporting his right hand.

"Wohatommy. Please tell her to wear the orange two-piece, instead of this, navy blue one-piece." KG held the item with disgust. Tommy smiled at KG. Disappearing into Suva's closet, he returned with a huge box that was covered in Christmas-themed decorations.

"Wear the red one." Suva grabbed the box excitedly. Underneath a customized annual diary were two red pieces of clothing. KG pulled Tommy in her lap, bear-hugging him from behind. "Yow T a you a di boss!" Tommy stayed in KG's lap, beaming with pride. Suva examined the two-piece. She liked it but didn't want to concede so readily.

"I'm not outvoted just yet. Gabe!"
She called out for Gabe. Tommy chuckled,

"Mi amor, he helped me pick it out." Suva playfully rolled her eyes, accepting defeat. Wearing the team sweats over the swimsuit, Suva checked the food and organized the table where the gifts were to be placed. As the guests started to arrive, she ran to the library to check on Lana.

"Hey, honey, how's it going?" Lana didn't lift her head from the book; she just mumbled, "It's fine." Suva sat around the table.

"What are you having difficulties with?" Lana exhaled harshly, tossing the textbook. "Spanish!" Suva repositioned the book. Placing Lana's hair behind her ear, Suva commented comfortingly,

"Lana, you seem to be an associative learner. You think you have Russian lineage, so you were more receptive to the language. What works for me is finding commonalities between the Russian and Spanish alphabets." Lana's eyes started sparkling. She grabbed another text and flipped a few pages. Suva disappeared, and Spanish filled her brain. Suva hugged her. "I'm so proud of you! Using your Christmas to catch up. We'll tackle global economics after the party." At the door Suva asked convincedly, "Honey, are you sure about the party, a little break is ok." Lana tapped the pen.

"Nope!" Lana tapped harder. "Your charity case won't be tagging along." The words slapped Suva in the face. Guilt pulled Lana out of her seat,

"I'm sorry." Uncertainty held Lana's hands hostage barring them from sealing the apology with a hug. Suva hugged her. "It's ok dear." Suva kissed her forehead. The doorbell rang. Suva answered it to Kiana, a member of the swim team. Two teenagers sandwiched her.

"I hope this is okay. I got stuck with these two. This is Kiyara and Kya."

Suva ran her fingers through their full-bodied afros. "It's no problem. We always have room bundles of adorableness. I love your hair; you guys are so cute!" The girls looked on jadedly. "Kiyara and Kya, follow me. Kiana, pool." Suva took the girls to the library and introduced them the Lana. They corrected Suva,

"Actually. I'm Kiy, and she's Ky." Suva admired their afros one last time.

"Okay, girls, have fun!" She ignored the mortified look on Lana's face.

Suva tottered nervously towards the pool. She felt silly; the team has seen her in a swimsuit. KG was in the hot tub with Gabe and Tommy. KG yanked her,

"Jason brought the tramp!" KG whispered hysterically. Gabe pulled her back into the water.

"This is a team gathering, no outsiders were invited," Suva whispered back, pretending to play with KG's hair. Tommy was observing Suva,

"Atsila, are you going to be okay with this?"

Suva smiled, "At ease Wohali." Confidence straitening her spine, she floated with the grace of a seasoned ballerina. KG whisper shouted, "Take off the damn sweats!" Gabe pushed her under the water this time. Suva's energy electrified the room. She was walking up to the mystery guest. The room froze, anticipatory breaths caught.

"Hi, welcome to my home. Merry Christmas!" Mary Beth blinked away her trepidation and mustered a cordial response. Suva went to the gift table and began distributing the gifts. Kiana was the only person to get a gift card. She was not happy. "Who the hell got me a gift card? Not cool, guys, not cool!" Trenton whistled,

"What I wouldn't give to be Santa Claus. Or even Mrs. Claus for that matter." Coach slapped him on his head. Trenton was referring to the pictures on Suva's swimsuit top. Santa was on the left and Mrs. Clause on the right. Mary Beth was impressed by Suva's body. Yet another thing Jason lied about. He had described Suva as fat and flabby. Suva looked great, her legs were toned, her stomach was flat, and she had a black girl's butt. Jason was so insensitive.

Christmas music was blaring over the laughter from good-natured ribbing and screams from the intense volleyball game. Checking on Lana, Suva was pleased she was engaging in playful conversation with the twins. Re-entering the pool area, Sofia ambushed her, hauling her into the bathroom.

"What is going on?" Sofia, Ayesha, and KG just stared at Suva. Sofia spoke up,

"I am so sick and tired of you and this *Mary Poppins* persona. Why is Mary Beth here? And why the heck are you talking to her?" The other girls spoke up,

"Exactly!" Suva looked at them incredulously.

"Cause I have no beef with her. Jason was the problem." Ayesha was not satisfied with that response.
"Suva, you're such an idiot! She is why your man left you! She's the cause of your public humiliation?" Suva moved her curls out of her face.

"Well, Ayesha, the same way I can be friends with you after you kept Jason's secret and ignored my calls all summer." Ayesha fell silent, reapplying her lipstick.

"Yes, Mayberry Barbie, you betrayed your gender! I still don't agree with Suva for forgiving you!" KG got up in her face. "Plus, you knew what Suva was planning for Jason, you could've spared her. But nooo, you were too busy grinding on some dude, breaking Tommy's heart. What kind of friend are you? Secret Six, my ass!" KG's tone sucked all the repudiations from Ayesha's mind. Sofia was lost.

"Wait, what surprise are you talking about, KG?" Suva eased KG away from Ayesha. Suva ruffled her curls,

"KG, Ayesha, and Sofia didn't know about my plans. I didn't get a chance to tell them." Suva exhaled deeply,

"Tell us what?" Both girls asked in unison. Suva sat beside KG on the counter, leaning against the glass for support to tackle a subject she had long buried,

"Well, for months, Jason kept saying, if I truly loved him, then I would share all of myself with him. So, I was going to give him my virginity on my birthday." Tears welled in Suva's eyes. "I kept calling you girls to discuss it with you, but, Sofia, you were halfway across the world, Ayesha, you…" Vulnerability locked Suva's mouth. Wiping her tears, KG continued,

"She was bedridden from a near-death experience, and guess

which friends weren't there for her?" KG gave Ayesha a nasty look. "She carted that stupid homemade carrot cake to Jason's house. Then *Cruella* sent her to the yacht club." Ayesha felt momentary remorse, she rejected it, popping her gum,

"But, Suva, you have Tommy now. You guys got what you've always wanted." Suva got off the counter.

"Ayesha, narrow-minded as always. Tommy and I are not together. We both need time to heal. You see our hearts were obliterated by two selfish pricks." Sofia was excited.

"Yes! Suva, there is a tigress inside there, after all. Now unleash it on Mary Beth." Suva took KG's hands.

"KG, let's go, these girls don't get it. I am not angry at her. She probably loves him. I wouldn't be surprised if he fed her lies." Ayesha needed to deflect the guilt stirring within her,

"Well, she's probably a racist like Virginia!" The door to stall number 3 opened aggressively. A tearful Mary Beth stumped pass the girls. She cleared the ball of hurt caught in her throat. "You are wrong. I am not a racist...I didn't even know you were biracial." A snot bubble paused her speech. She wiped it; liquified emotions gushed down her face. "I'm sorry, Suva, you are right, I do love him." The pop of Ayesha's gum broke the tension,

"Well, at least we won't have to hear Jason call you Swan anymore." The girls laughed. That ignited a fury in Mary Beth! *Whack!* Mary Beth's palm had a loud conversation with Jason's face. The music player stopped the instant her hand connected with his face.

"That's for all the lies you told!" She kneed him in the groin. "That's for calling me Swan every time we had sex!" The girls had rushed out behind her. Suva was standing front and center for the spectacle. The slap heard around the world was a fitting end to the party.

"Rise and shine, girls, it's Christmas." Mavis gently woke the girls. KG checked, it wasn't snowing, so much for a white Christmas. They hurriedly brushed their teeth and raced downstairs.

"Walk. Ladies don't run; they walk briskly." Hazel's words slowed the girls down for a second; then they sprinted off. Downstairs in the main sitting room, they gathered around the large, overly decorated artificial Christmas tree.

"Merry Christmas, everyone!" Deaglan started the proceedings.

Joyous cheers echoed loudly through the house. "Presents!" Tommy's parents gave Hazel their gift first. Then everyone else followed. When Hazel opened Suva and Tommy's gift, tears came to her eyes. They had painted the family tree with names and faces.

"Babies! There's a picture of my mother…this is beautiful." Suva teared up.

"Well, to be fair, we had a lot of help." Gabe raised his eyebrows at Suva.

"Gabe made the frame." Hazel kissed Gabe on his cheek.

"Thank you, kids. Grandpa would have loved this." Suva handed Tommy his gift.

"Open it gently, please." Tommy cautiously opened his gift. His heart fluttered at the sight of the miniature car, the design redolent of Andre Subryan's car. Joyously dangling the with full-size key. With childlike curiosity he pressed it. The doors opened, and Andre Subryan's voice roared,

"Tommy, let's race!" Appreciation and exuberance ejected him from his seat, Tommy bear-hugged Suva.

"Atsila, thank you!" While Tommy played with his car, without touching it, KG and Gabe opened their gifts from Suva. They hugged her with intense appreciation. Putting on their gold necklace, two diamond-encrusted charms hanging loosely from it. Suva explained that only KG and Gabe had the infinity charm as a sign of their never-ending connectivity. The second charm, the Cherokee symbol for life, they saved her life that dreadful summer day. All four teens tenderly grasped their individual pieces. Melissa and Deaglan gazed in wonderment at their creation.

"Lana, this is yours." Atsila handed Lana a gift that was the size of a book. Lana ripped it open. With sweaty palms, she silently stared at her image on the cover of the Christmas catalog. Sadness entering her fingers as she touched the signature of each family member.

"You look amazing, lady." Kyle ruffled her hair. "Brains and beauty, we go affi fight off di man dem when yuh turn 18." Kyle's attempt fell flat.

"Don't give me false hope!" Lana hissed. She stomped to the kitchen. Returning with two large baking containers. Everyone got a slice of potato pudding and carrot cake. They munched emptily. Hazel needed to save the moment,

"She figured out the recipes and replicated them."

Lana forced a half-smile. Persisting, Hazel handed Lana her gift. Flipping through Hazel's handwritten recipes flushed Lana's face with delight.

"I still have a few more to enter." Hazel massaged her left hand.

Lana cried ferociously.   Hazel's recipes were like the birthright of the family; its apart the legacy.  Lana attempted to speak through her tears,

"The group home – will – have good cooking." A crying Suva wiped Lana's tears.

"Daddy!!!!!" Deaglan wiped his tears, cleared his throat, and said, "Lana, you have one gift left." Melissa handed Lana a thick file jacket.  Lana scanned through the documents, puzzled.

"You – want – to – adopt- me?" The group erupted in laughter and cheers. Deaglan held her hand.

"Yes, Lana, we want you to be a permanent part of our family." Melissa held her other hand.

"I know we get loud at times, and we can get a bit crazy." Lana sobbed harder. She was shaking her head, Yes! They smothered Lana hugs and tearful kisses.

"Family portrait time," Atsila made the announcements.

Deaglan stopped everyone.

"Lana, we haven't officially filed the papers because you need to decide on your name." Lana paced the Persian defense rug. Standing tall, chest high, she declared,

"Svetlana Hazel Lanaghan."

Suva squealed!  The finalized documents were placed in the safe.  At brunch, Suva barely touched the ackee and saltfish, only nibbled on the crushed green plantains. Happiness had the opposite effect on Gabe and Lana. They devoured the callaloo, boiled dumplings, mackerel rundung, kidney, fried dumplings, and yellow yam. Lana had two cups of hot cocoa; it was delicious. Ethnic fatigue swept the table. The adults excused themselves.  Hazel gave instructions.

"I need the kitchen cleaned up, so I can finish dinner and the living room spotless."

"You guys aren't going to help? Why is it..." Suva swiftly covered Lana's mouth. Hazel gave a death stare. With chills running down his spine, Gabe spoke up,

"Nothing grandma wi go clean everything." With Hazel out of sight, the teens attacked Lana.

"Yuh mad or you lick yuh head?" Suva asked, then realized that Lana wasn't versed on Patois yet.

Tommy sympathizing, "Lana, it took me a second to get accustomed to the language and norms too. Let me break it down. It doesn't matter if you used the dishes or contributed to the mess; as a child, you have to clean it up."

Lana still wasn't getting it. She opened her mouth, "But…."

KG cut her off. "Lana, there are no buts in the vocabulary of a Jamaican child. Saying but is the quickest way to get a slap on your behind." Lana looked shocked.

"That's corporal punishment!" The teens laughed at her misguided outrage. Lana continued, "Aren't you half, Jamaican?" Suva stopped clearing the table for a second, hand on hip,

"It doesn't matter if you are 1 percent Jamaican. If there is some Jamaican in the equation, it tends to supersede." KG, Gabe, and Suva did a little dance and stated loudly, "Wi lickle, but we tallawah!" Lana laughed at the craziness and started clearing the table too.

"Is there a book with all the rules and sayings? I have a lot to learn." At Christmas dinner, Lana and Gabe were at it again. It was amazing to see these two scrawny individuals swallow so much food. After the traditional movie, the parents left for their usual Christmas night cruise on Mayor Hunter's yacht. Hazel left for an overnight at Mavis' house. Gabe wanted quality time with KG, Tommy suggested the Tree House. Gabe couldn't grasp the concept of building a house in a tree. "Bwoi, you're unnecessarily spoilt!" In the backyard he was amazed by the two-bedroom spectacle. A large trunk ran through its center, with pieces of wood as steps connecting the two stories. "A TV, really now!"

Suva smiled. "Gabe, just climb!" Gabe climbed protectively behind KG. The room had two lit candles and two champagne glasses with a bottle beside a nicely decorated bunk bed. "Don't get too excited; it's just apple cider! Have fun. We are inside the house."

KG yelled through the window, "Thanks, Suva, take care a yu." Tommy started feeling nervous. Being alone in his room with Suva now had new implications. He fidgeted with the car. "I love you so much for this gift. You can't imagine how much gratitude I want to do to you." Exasperated, Suva freed her mane,

"Wohali, stop talking, and just do it!" Tommy lost interest in the car immediately. Suva was sprawled across the bed on her back. Doubt framed Tommy's words,

"I'm not sure if…with limited knowledge of…" Suva's sharp inhale gave him pause. She shifted to her side, showing off the curves of her silhouette.

"Wohali, your favorite Einstein…" Placing her hand on her thigh, she sultrily lowered tone. "…postulated that '*Imagination is more important than knowledge. For knowledge is limited to all we now know and understand, while…*'" Resting her hand on the buttons securing her chest. "…*while imagination embraces the entire world.*" She unbuttoned her top two buttons, exposing cleavage. "…*and all there ever will be to know and…*" Her fingers lingered on her left breast. "…*and understand.*" Tommy hoped with all hopes that it wasn't another dream.

"My love, if my hand weren't, I would." Hardened by desire, he licked his lips. Suva was pumping with salacious energy.

"Let my hands be yours." Adjusting his snug pants. Intrigue urged him on.

"I would gently caress your cheek." His words remotely guided her hands. "Stroke your hair, remove your shirt." The unveiling gripped Tommy.

She waited. "Unhook your bra." The feathered material hit the floor like a boulder echoing the weight of the moment. It was the first time anyone had seen Suva's bare chest. Tommy luxuriated in their splendor, the cold night breeze altering their form.

Holding Tommy's gaze, she licked a shaky index finger, grazing it over her right mound. Tommy's system abruptly released its overload. His powerful sounds startled Suva, and she ran to him. The look of embarrassment on his face gave her explicit instructions. She retrieved her bra and shirt. Tommy's energy was depleted, but a euphoric buzz replenished him. Suva was happy her flood was hidden. They both needed a shower. An hour later, Suva knocked on his bathroom door. She opened it to find him grinning in the mirror.

"What are you so happy about?" He pulled her close with his left hand, kissing her deeply.

"If we don't stop, I may need another shower." Tommy gazed into her hazel eyes. "You are so beautiful." Suva kissed him again. They fell asleep all cuddled up. At 6 a.m., Gabe woke them both.

"Suva, get up!" Suva yawned and snuggled closer to Tommy. "Suva, your parents are at home." Suva jumped up, almost trampling Tommy to get off the bed. She and KG ran to her room, tossed the cushions off, jumped under the sheets, and tried not to laugh when the door opened.

"Girls, get up! We have an hour to be at the shelter." Suva didn't move; she never wakes on the first call. Atsila went back into the room. "Girls, get up. Grandma made bacon." Both girls emerged from the covers.

"We're up." It was a tradition for the family to spend the day after Christmas at the Mayberry Shelter for the homeless and abused. They worked in teams, distributing clothes, sharing food, reading to the children, and making repairs to the facilities. Suva was relegated to the kitchen because last year, a homeless man slapped her on the butt; Melissa almost gave the man a beat down. They waited until they got home before they told Deaglan, so no one was butchered. Suva didn't mind kitchen duty; washing pots and pans were not that bad. At least, she got to spend time with Tommy, her designated dish drier. Later that night, everyone returned home exhausted. They all soaked in the Whirlpool.

## Chapter 21

Like a thief in the night, the first day of school crept up on them. Lana's anxiety and excitement created a tornado of emotions within her. All outstanding assignments were submitted.  Missed finals would be completed within the first week.
The gym was her only concern, Tommy coached her after she recovered from volunteering at the shelter, but inaptitude lingered. The first week was a success.  Lana passed gym, Jason avoided public humiliation, and the Secret Six were back atop the social hierarchy. Benjamin fished and failed at concretizing the Mary Beth slap story. Suva and Tommy decided to cool it.  They missed KG and Gabe; the foursome made a pact to wait to have sex.

As time progressed, Lana felt unwelcomed by some of her classmates. The publishing of the class standings exacerbated things as she had the second-highest average in the class.  Lana's only source of comfort was the twins. They beseeched Dr. T. to make an exception and allow them to be the only trio lab partners. Suva wanted to make it known that they were sisters, but Lana wouldn't have it. She wanted to gain genuine friends.

Suva started avoiding Tommy once his sling was removed. That Saturday morning, Tommy awoken agitated.  Entering Suva's kitchen, he realized why. "Bonjour Thomas!" Maxwell Thunder and his smug face greeted him.  The conversation became hushed. Flashback of the kiss. They glared at each other, the animosity palpable. Tommy's agitation came out in his voice.

"Maxwell, what the hell are you doing in my kitchen?"

Maxwell took the last sip of the coffee, placing the cup in the sink. Slicked back his hair and chuckled.

"Thomas, bold statement for the governor of the friend zone." Deaglan intervened, while the competition was healthy, they feared blows.

"Cool it, lads." As a distraction, Deaglan and Kyle took Tommy to the country club for some male bonding. Golf didn't do the trick, Tommy was still brooding. In the belly of the sauna, Kyle broached the Maxwell subject. Both men understood his dislike. He and Suva shared a kiss, plus Maxwell was a tad bit obnoxious. Tommy expressed his concern that Suva may be losing interest in him. Maxwell was more sexually experienced and well-traveled, plus that damn French accent.

The men couldn't understand the source of his insecurities. They reassured him that he was the only one for Suva. He was too embarrassed to mention his premature explosions. Their next stop was a swanky restaurant that just opened. Tommy was delighted by the designer outfit placed in his locker. It was Suva's style. Black cotton pants, orange and black button-down shirt with black and orange stitched loafers. The ensemble was comfortable and tailored. He felt good in it. The town car dropped the men off at the largest car dealership in Mayberry. Tommy smiled.

"Did they convert this space into a restaurant?" Kyle was puzzled too.

"Lad, I love cars as much as the other guy, but I'm not eating engine food!"

They both gave Deaglan accusatory looks. Deaglan opened the showroom door. Pitch black. Tommy and Kyle started laughing hysterically. Tommy patted Deaglan on the back. "So much for a swank new resta..." The lights came on to a room filled with people. Deaglan and Kyle left bewildered Tommy standing. A banner dropped, the crowd yelled, "Surprise!" The banner stated, *Thomas, Congrats on Your Double Scholarship!* Shock froze him; then, realization released him. On a long shot he applied for academic and athletic scholarships from Manchester University.

He was flooded with congratulatory hugs. The swim team was happy he was fully recovered, winning State was crucial. The football team regretted that he wasn't playing, but happy for his health. Tommy was over the moon when he saw KG, Gabe, and Hazel sitting with Melissa, Atsila, Deaglan, and Kyle. He kept asking for Suva, and he knew she was the grand orchestrator. The party was raging; the DJ hypnotized the crowd with hits, the food tantalized their palates. Tommy spotted Suva entering the showroom. She looked stunning in a form-fitting cotton orange mini dress with black pumps her hair in a high ponytail. Jason, Ayesha, Sofia, and Duncan were with her. Tommy felt joy...Maxwell! This guy was like a persistent mosquito. The group gathered at their reserved table. Ayesha popped her gum,

"This party is so unnecessary, boo hoo double scholarships! Come on, aren't we all gifted?" Everyone laughed in agreement. Suva agreed with it. Maxwell approached Suva, and they huddled close.

"You just can't seem to close that deal, huh." Jason's comment wouldn't have bothered Tommy on a regular day, but today, they stung. "Tommy, you know what they say, Frenchmen always close the deal. I bet he buttered her croissants good." Duncan interjected,

"Says no one ever! Stop being petty, Jason." Jason persisted,

"All I'm saying is, it's your party, why did she have to invite, him?" Wanting to strengthen Tommy's looks of doubt, Ayesha joined in,

"Exactly, he watches her butt as if his hands know it intimately." Tommy's emotions erupted, spilling out anger and insecurity. Walking over to the still whispering Maxwell and Suva.

"Suva, we need to talk." Ignoring Maxwell, he added, "Private-ly!" Suva looked around the showroom then led him behind a gray curtain. Tommy was still erupting, "Why is Maxwell here? And where have you been since Thursday night? You disappeared after I took my sling off." Suva just stood there silent. "Atsila, answer me." The music was replaced with a voice,

"Perhaps I can be of assistance." The gray curtains fell, and Andre Subryan walked onto the platform. Tommy was speechless! *His race car idol in the flesh!* Andre shook his hand. "Two years ago, a feisty young lady contacted my people wanting to purchase a car similar to my car. It's one of a kind, so not possible. That didn't deter her. She negotiated with us to build a replica instead." Andre pulled off a black tarp, revealing an orange and black Ferrari. The crowd went wild. Tommy walked toward it. High octane exuberance surging through him. The racing theme now evident. The checkered banner, car-shaped napkins, his jacket, Suva's checkered flag earrings.

Following Suva's instructions to suppress the button on his Christmas gift. He jumped when his keys unlocked the car. Tommy giddily inspected the vehicle. His initials were on the mat, seats, and steering wheel. He was smitten by her, 3.4-litre quad-cam, four-valve-per-cylinder V8 engine, her 300hp excited him, he was enthralled by her masterfully crafted curves. Tommy was in heaven. After pictures, Andre announced that he and Tommy were going to take it for its first spin. Tommy apologized but declined. Tommy tossed the key to Suva after opening her door. Suva took her time getting out of the showroom and onto the main, then she hit the gas.

# YESTERDAY

The car took off all 300hp. It was exhilarating. On their way back to the party, Tommy asked Suva to pull in around the back. He got out and opened the door for her. He thanked her endlessly; his heart was so full. Tommy kissed her neck, lifting her against the car. She wrapped her legs around him and held on. Tommy eased off and feverishly unbuckled his pants while Suva licked his neck passionately.  Tommy pulled on Suva's panties, his finger timidly introduced himself to her peach.

"Shit! Fu.." Suva kissed him, stood, and retrieved a bag from the trunk.

"Wohali, let's change."  In the staff bathroom, Suva undid her ruffled ponytail. She replaced her dress with sweats. Tommy cleaned up and changed into sweats also. Tommy kicked the stall door cursing on impact. Suva allowed him his moment, taming her hair with a splash of water. Sitting on the counter, she pulled him close,

"Mi amor, it's fine. We are tyros, so these things will happen." Tommy knew he should let it go, but he couldn't.

"I bet you wish you were with Maxwell, Mr. Sexually Superior." Suva squeezed him close.  She drove, Tommy was still loopy. At the entrance, Suva paused,

"You are my boyfriend, not Maxwell!  I didn't track down his racing idol; I tracked down yours!  I didn't spend my life savings on a custom-made car for Maxwell. I spent it on you. Finally..." Suva gripped his manhood.  "When the time is right, and we are ready for it, it will be you between my legs." Suva walked away. He was enjoying this naughty side.  Inside the party, they joined in on the dance floor.  While Latin dancing with Sofia, Tommy had an epiphany. He pulled Suva close.

"You called me, your boyfriend." Everyone shouted,

"Finally!" Gabe gave him an approving nod. As things were winding down, Andre came over to the group to say good-bye. He handed Tommy a racing jacket.

"You left before I could give you this." It had the word Cherokee inscribed across the back. Tommy looked at Suva in amazement. Andre asked Tommy to walk him out.

"What the hell does Cherokee have to do with racing?" Ayesha popped her gum. Everyone stared at Ayesha in disbelief. KG smirked, asking Suva to explain.  Suva looked at her nails, fully aware that she was baited.

"Well, Tommy is part Native American. He is from the Cherokee tribe." Ayesha was genuinely stunned.

"But how? His father is from Scotland." The group chuckled.  Suva touched her shoulders playfully.

"Ayesha, no, Kyle is Irish, and Atsila is Cherokee." Ayesha started pacing.

"Wait, isn't that the name he calls you when you two are being all Jedi mind tricky?" Suva touched her shoulders again.

"Yes, I was named after his mother." Ayesha hissed and started storming off.

Suva gently grabbed her hand. "A, don't leave, we have to take one more picture."

Ayesha turned, something inside shifted. "Do not touch me! We are not friends! I'm sick of the truth circle; the Secret Six is no more!" There was a collective gasp. Ayesha stormed past Tommy, who was returning to the group to tell Suva Andre wanted to speak with her. Suva left the group and ran outside, just in time to see Ayesha slapping Maxwell in his face. Suva ran to Maxwell.

"What did you do to her?" Still rubbing his jaw, Maxwell looked confused. "Nothing!" Suva ran in front of Ayesha's car before she drove onto the main road. They stared each other down. Ayesha blew her horn, but Suva refused to move.  Ayesha got out and slammed the door.

"Suva, you can't fix this. I'm tired of being your friend. You always do things big just so the rest of us can look bad.  You stealing Tommy is the last straw!"  Suva's jaw dropped. She couldn't believe what she was hearing.

"Ayesha, you cheated on him, then left him publicly. Girl, I love you. That's why I forgave you for leaking all those pictures to the *Tribune*." It was Ayesha's turn to be shocked.

"See, that's what I can't stand about you, Suva. No one is that forgiving! I betrayed you, embarrassed you in the worst way possible, and you remain my friend. Screw the Secret Six." Ayesha handed Suva her ring.  Suva felt as if she was having an out of body experience. She couldn't recall how she got into bed with KG. KG wasn't happy to hear that the friendship was over, but she wasn't sad either. She just wanted Suva to snap out of the trance.  The next day, the family returned to Jamaica.  But they, along with everyone else at the party, would never forget January 12; it was epic.

As the weeks passed, the tension between Ayesha and Suva grew.  Ayesha started hanging out with Avery and Ashley. She only had unavoidable contact with them. Advanced chemistry class was one such occasion. Duncan was trying yet again to be a peacemaker.

"Ayesha, we missed you at study session yesterday." Ayesha popped her gum and ignored Duncan. Her hair was blonder than usual, and her cleavage was more pronounced. "We are meeting up at Tommy's this Saturday, are you coming?"

She popped her gum again but decided to answer, "Sorry, Irish, I have plans with Ashley and Avery. We are going on a double date with Ashley's hot cousin."
Sofia kicked Duncan under the table, and he
turned around.  "Duncan. Just leave her alone; she never belonged in our group anyways." Suva chimed in,

"Sofia, don't say that. She is still our friend." Tommy played with Suva's right ear adding,

"She is just mad at us. It's a huge adjustment." Sofia held her ground,

"Well, maybe if she weren't such a slut, then she would still be your girlfriend, no?"  The four friends gasped. Disappointment rested on Suva,

"Sofia, take that back. That's a very nasty thing to say." Sofia, looking offended, swept her hair to the right.

"Look, I'm just real. Plus, Suva, stop defending her, for this is entirely your fault. I think she could handle you two dating if you guys weren't so 'we are soulmates' about it."  Suva felt pressure building in her chest. *Was Sofia right?* Class started, the teacher made a point about the danger and illegality of mixing two chemicals.  Avery commented,

"Similar to a slave and it's master crossbreeding," Ashley added,

"Tainting the world with illegal halfers."  Per usual, their statements were ignored. The class had grown accustomed to the hate they spewed toward Suva, Tommy, and Sofia.

"Mr. Depti, don't you just miss the good old days?"  The class almost whiplashed at Ayesha's statement.  Suva wanted to say something but couldn't. Ayesha continued. "Repugnant halfers, set of illegal crossbreeds."

Everyone looked at Suva; they were familiar with her mixed

ancestry. Duncan turned to Ayesha, pleading with her with his eyes; she glared back defiantly.

"Duncan, stop defending the halfer, I'm sure 'it' can defend 'itself'!" Tense silence cloaked the room. Ayesha spoke to Suva directly, "Isn't that right, halfer? Tell Duncan you can defend yourself." Ayesha popped her gum again. High fived Avery and Ashley. Suva stared, speechless, liquid pain dripped from her face. Ayesha's face registered no remorse. Suva's heart broke; she walked out of class. Mr. Depti didn't make a fuss; he allowed her four friends to chase after her. Suva asked Tommy to take her home. Sofia couldn't understand what the big deal was. Suva got called that all the time. Jason clarified,

"Idiots versus your best friend, supreme betrayal!" *It probably was worse than his highly publicized cheating scandal.* Suva's parents were not happy about what transpired. They took her to the stables that weekend. She rode her favorite mustang, Shelby, for hours; sampled wine from her father's vintage collection. Her parents informed her that she and Lana would be on their own the following weekend as they would be going to a Valentine's retreat.

That Tuesday in gym class, Suva and Ayesha were on opposing teams in a spirited volleyball game. Ayesha kept deliberately hitting Suva with the ball. Suva got upset and caught the ball. "Listen, Ayesha; you need to stop it!" Ayesha walked under the net and got in Suva's face.

"Or else what!" Pop. Suva stepped back, trying to calm down. Ayesha stepped even closer to her face.

"Gyal, come outta mi face!" Anger colored Suva's cheeks. Avery and Ashley encouraged Ayesha to slap Suva. Ayesha started lifting her right hand toward Suva's face. "Ayesha, I dare you to hit me!" Suva's insides churned. "Which half do you want?" Suva raised her hands. "The right hand is Jamaican, the left Irish!" Suva's chest rose and fell intensely, reflecting her escalating temper. Ayesha backed away. Avery and Ashley were disappointed.

"Next time, halfer."

At home, Suva took a bubble bath. She never loses her temper. While the group was happy, she finally stood up for herself, she felt unsettled. Ayesha eased off her for the next few days. Tommy made a wonderful Valentine's dinner for her and Lana; then they watched *Pretty Woman*. They had fun being in the house by themselves for the weekend.

On Monday, Suva noted Ayesha missed classes. Sofia couldn't understand why Suva even cared.

"Look, Suva, she was a part of our group, we were friends, but that's in the past now." Sofia munched on her Greek salad.

"Sofia, the past? It was last week, jeez." By Wednesday, Tommy and Duncan jumped on the concern train. It was unlike Ayesha to miss classes; as worldly, as she was, she loved school. Calls to her house went unanswered. The parents were probably still in *Dubai* or some other exotic location, not parenting. Wednesday over lunch, Sofia expressed minor concern. Suva's worry overrode her pride; she went straight to the source. Avery pushed his tray away in disgust.

"I've lost my appetite. Halfer, what are you doing on my side of the cafeteria?" Suva whispered a small prayer to God, begging him to control her hands else Avery would get slapped into next Tuesday.

"Look, I need to know where Ayesha is. We heard she was going on a double date with y'all." Suva motioned over Avery and Ashley. Ashley popped her gum.

"Afro kinky, we don't know where she is. Last time we saw her, she was driving away from Lover's Creek." Suva knew Ashley's tone was meant to mock her, but she needed more information.

"Why was she at Lover's Creek?" Avery placed his arm around Ashley.

"While we were getting it on! She was arguing with Joe about wanting to go slowly and getting to know him before they even kissed. What a loser." Suva didn't wait to hear the rest. The group, along with Beth divided into search parties. When no one answered at Ayesha's front door Suva inputted the security code. She signed to Beth that she was going to kill Ayesha when she saw her and then continue being mad at her; both girls laughed.

Entering Ayesha's room, the drapes were drawn, and it smelt musty and stale. Suva blindly searched for and flicked the switch illuminating the room. Beth froze. The room was tossed, Ayesha's clothes were thrown everywhere. Pools of blood were interwoven into the king-sized spread. Ayesha was nestled underneath it, her limp left wrist dangling off the bed. Fear spilled out of Suva, its warmth dripping down her cheek. Suva stopped Beth from touching anything. Suva carefully inched towards Ayesha.

"Ash…why…Ash." Suva gazed at the many cuts and dried blood on Ayesha's wrist. She was confused. If she had cut her wrist, why was there so much blood on the spread and bruises on her face? Suva gently pulled back the sheet. Ayesha was naked; her lower abdomen and legs were covered in blood. Suva looked at Ayesha's pale skin. She had a busted lip, a cracked nose, and a black eye. "What happened, Ash." Shock waves ran through Suva when Ayesha moaned and slowly blinked.

Suva went close to her mouth. "Did Joe do this?" Ayesha could hardly shake her head no. Blood ran out of her mouth when she opened it to speak. Suva heard loud noises coming from next door. "Did Travis do this?" Ayesha trembled, tears ran down her face. With much struggle, she whispered, "I put up a fight the first time…he took a break and came back. He…he left me the razor to finish myself off and make the world…make the world a better place." Ayesha bawled. Beth's knees gave way. She wept on the floor; she had never seen anything so horrific. Suva held Ayesha's hand.

"When did this happen, Ash, when?" Ayesha started trembling again. Suva held on tighter.

"Sunday night and Monday morning." Suva felt dizzy; she wasn't getting enough air. Anger had snuffed out her fears.

"I'm sorry you had to go through this alone. He is going to pay for this." Ayesha squeezed her hand even tighter. Ayesha whispered again,

"No, he won't. He said whores don't get…don't get to say no. When I told him, he was going to pay for this, he said some of us…some of us could afford to." Suva felt her lunch coming up. Suva jumped up, grabbed Beth's hand, and placed Ayesha's hand in it. Suva signed to Beth not to leave Ayesha's side and to not touch anything. Suva ran across the hall into the guest bathroom, and projectile vomited over the floor, counter, and toilet. Then she blacked out. Suva re-entered the room, puffing on her inhaler. She had called her dad, 911, her mom, and then the group.

Her dad's forensics team arrived before the police and ambulance. They took their photos and samples. Melissa came to oversee Ayesha's transport. Deaglan was upset that they sent interns to process the scene because the experts were next door handling an official matter for the Bents.

Ayesha was given sedatives and morphine; she was sleeping

when Suva and the group could see her. Suva read the chart, even Jason broke down.  Ayesha had a mild concussion, fractured ribs, and a broken nose. She had ten stitches in her mouth and 5 in her pubic area.  Melissa wanted to move Ayesha to the private wing, but she had to stay in the trauma ward due to the extent of her injuries. Melissa was still unable to reach Ayesha's parents. Lana and Mavis came with fresh clothes and food. Even though no one had any appetite, they had to eat as they all donated blood for Ayesha.  They took turns showering in Melissa's office so that Ayesha wouldn't be alone.   After her shower, Suva returned to the room to find uniformed officers inside Ayesha's room engaged in heated discourse with Melissa and Deaglan.  Beth focused on their lips through the glass doors and signed what was being discussed. The officers were there to get Ayesha's alibi in connection with the criminal investigation of an attack on the Bents' property earlier that evening.

Melissa was upset and demanded that the men leave the room immediately. The detective cautioned her to tread lightly as this case was being handled by the mayor personally. Melissa walked to the glass door and opened it.

"Officer Kade, you can just tread the hell on out of here." The officer and his entourage slowly exited the room. When the last one left, Melissa called out. "Oh, and Officer Kade, you can tell the mayor if he wants a statement, he should walk the *bleep* down here and get it himself." She walked back to Ayesha's side.  Suva had never heard her mother use those words. She was impressed. Lana mouthed to Suva,

"Who is that lady, and where did that come from?" Duncan chimed in,

"Mi dad would've used more colorful words.  How can they expect to question a victim, the tubes coming out of her are her alibi!" The next day they were summoned to the Mayberry police station to give their statements. Beth and Suva were persons of interest in a criminal assault case filed by Travis Bent and were the main witnesses in the rape case against Travis Bent. Exiting the police station, Suva smiled at her friends, "Let's get back to Ayesha. Guys…what really happened yesterday?" Back at the hospital, Deaglan was as proud as a peacock.  He bragged to Melissa

"Suva is a natural-born lawyer, quite the tactician. You should have seen her." Melissa allowed him the moment. *No way was her baby becoming a lawyer.* Suva announced that signed Lana up for self-defense and taekwondo classes. Melissa confiscated the pocket-sized pepper spray, Suva was going a bit overboard.

Ayesha's parents remained unreachable; she was released into the care of Deaglan and Melissa. They placed her in the upstairs bedroom. The teens camped out in the room and got caught up on outstanding assignments. Ayesha still wasn't talking, not even to the counselor. She just laid there crying. She had night terrors and groaned randomly. She was hooked up to a saline drip because she refused food. Sofia was looking at the cover of the *Mayberry Academy Tribune.*

"Can you guys believe it? Suva, you totally called it. Avery and Ashley are related." Suva had forgotten about that.

"Yes, I guess now he can sue Mayor Hunter." Ayesha released a faint sound that turned into a laugh. Her ribs were still sensitive, so she couldn't laugh as hard as she wanted. "Details…please!" Her voice was raspy. The group was happy to see her smile again. They took turn sharing that students were giving blood on her behalf when the nurse detected something rare in two of the samples. She needed parental consent from the siblings to probe further. Ashley threw up, and Avery smashed a wall. They rolled over with laughter.

"Have they figured out who attacked Travis?" Ayesha whispered his name. Lana held her hand. Duncan spoke,

"No! Suva's dad has his PI on it. Even Tony is using his security contacts."

"I really need to know." Ayesha played with the thin silver ring and sighed. Two weeks later, Ayesha's parents finally made an appearance. Their outrage seemed misplaced. Ayesha was furious when they decided to take her to Aspin for three months. She wanted to stay with her friends; their parents were there for her. The group watched the town car drive away and started missing her immediately.

Deaglan was lead counsel in the case against Travis, he tried getting an expedited hearing but was stonewalled. Mr. Bent had clout in Mayberry, and Deaglan didn't want to play dirty; justice would prevail. The closest hearing date he could get was in three months. Surprisingly, Ayesha was delighted by that news. More time to love herself. Suva was so proud of her. Ayesha kept her word; she phoned every day except for five days when she was unavailable because medical reasons. Sofia commented,

"That's code for getting something else done." Tommy hit Sofia in the face with a pillow. The dynamics of the group had shifted since the incident. Almost losing Ayesha rattled them. Jason mellowed out; he still slept around but in secrecy. Duncan got more protective. Sofia cared but always acted as if nothing mattered. Suva and Tommy were inseparable. The swim team dedicated their championship to Ayesha. The group had to be strategic about AD training because they wanted to be at the forefront of the trial. Suva stayed up with Deaglan the night before going over case law and detailing Ayesha's social history. Deaglan still didn't ask Suva what she knew about Travis's attack…plausible deniability.

The courthouse was a circus; all of Mayberry's media outlets were present. Half the Mayberry Academy populace was cutting school to either be in support of Ayesha or Travis. Each side was equally full. The group sat right behind Deaglan and waited anxiously. Judge Barnes instructed Deaglan to begin his opening.

"Your Honor, before we begin, I would like to present the court with an emergency injunction delaying these proceedings until the assailant responsible for Mr. Bent's brutal attack is behind bars!" The defense attorney spoke before Deaglan even opened his mouth. Deaglan objected,

"Your Honor, this is a delay tactic. No conclusive correlation has been made between the two events. Thus, both trials can run concurrently." The defense lawyer put his game face on.

"Your Honor, these are signed letters from the mayor and the attorney general urging you to delay this trial." Judge Barnes knew his back was against the wall. He banged his gavel.

"We will begin at 3 p.m.. We are adjourned."
The attorney handed Deaglan a subpoena; it was for Suva to appear at the pre-trial hearing. Suva assuaged Deaglan's concerns about her readiness by reminding him about her interrogation. During the break, they called Ayesha to fill her in. She was still terrified to come back; she had not seen Travis since the incident. She knew she would need to testify; according to Suva, the jury needed to put a face to the accusations. Suva encouraged her just to be herself, and the jury would love her. Ayesha still refused to testify.

The defense, now the prosecution, wasted no time. He called Beth to the stand. The court-appointed translator relayed her testimony. Beth's statements remained unchanged. Ayesha missed three days from school; on the third day, the group separated and searched for her. She and Suva entered the room; Ayesha was covered in blood and severely beaten. Suva ran to the bathroom. She didn't keep track of the time that Suva was gone because Ayesha was crying and squeezing her hands. Beth didn't see anyone next door because all the blinds were drawn. She didn't hear anything because she is deaf. His final question baffled Beth.

"How many boyfriends did Ayesha have three months before the incident?"

"I don't know, maybe two or three." Deaglan and Suva exchanged looks; they now had confirmation of what the lawyer's game plan was. Suva took the stand, her anger bubbling beneath the surface. She relayed a similar story to Beth's, the only difference being she threw up in the bathroom, had an asthma attack, and woke up on the floor. Which is not uncommon based on her medical history. The lawyer switched gears.

"Suva, isn't it true that you walked in on Ayesha having sex with a random stranger while she was in a relationship with Tommy?" Suva noted the biased wording, and she searched for her most polite response,

"I fail to see the relevance of that incident to this case." The lawyer stared at her,

"Your Honor, please compel the witness to answer!" Judge Barnes reminded him that this was a pre-trial hearing, so he should minimize the theatrics, then he instructed Suva to answer. Suva smiled.

"Ken wasn't a random boy, and yes, I walked in on them." The lawyer flipped through his documents.

"And isn't it true that Ayesha referred to you by several derogatory, racist names." Suva looked at the judge and back at the lawyer. Leaning forward,

"So that's your plan. To use this pre-trial to establish Ayesha as a promiscuous racist so that you won't look like a complete jerk by badgering her directly, grow some ba"

"Objection!" The crowd mumbled loudly. Judge Barnes pointed out that he was objecting himself. The lawyer calmed himself, riffled through some more paper, then asked,

"Suva, isn't it true that Ayesha threatened you verbally and would have assaulted you physically if the gym teacher hadn't pulled her away?" Suva smiled; he said what she wanted him to say precisely.

"Yes, she did." The lawyer smiled; he had cemented his defense for his client. Suva continued speaking, "Sir, Ayesha forgot my birthday, called me names, embarrassed me publicly, and almost assaulted me." The lawyer was pleased Suva's words were frosting on the cake. "If she and I aren't friends, why then would I attack Travis? Wouldn't I be grateful to him for getting rid of my bully?"

The lawyer said nothing. Suva turned to the judge, "Your Honor, may I step down now; this was nothing but a fishing expedition." Before Judge Barnes responded, Deaglan indicated that he had some questions for Suva. Suva was taken off guard.

"Suva, which hand is your dominant hand."

"My left."

"Do you have any experience with knives."

"No, other than cutting ropes as a *Girl Scout*." Deaglan thanked Suva.

"Judge Barnes, since Travis' attacker is a right-handed and seemed to be a knife yielding expert, the defense asks that you render an expedited ruling as there is insufficient evidence against my client to take the case to trial.

"So granted." Judge Barnes was thoroughly entertained.

## Chapter 22

The teens completed all their assignments and negotiated with Dr. T. to schedule training around the trial. As expected, Travis's lawyer painted Ayesha as a confused promiscuous girl who had consenting sex with Travis and damaged herself because Travis refused to be her boyfriend. Deaglan quickly adjusted his opening statements to focus on the crime, not the individuals. The lawyer's first move was to call Ayesha to the stand, being fully aware that Ayesha was not present. He then went into a passionate diatribe that Ayesha's absence was disrespectful to the court, the judge, and, most importantly the jurors. Hence, a dismissal of the case would be fitting. Deaglan strongly objected,

"Grandstanding, Your Honor! Ayesha isn't here because she was raped, beaten, and left for dead. She's too fearful of facing her attacker!" Judge Barnes banged his gavel.

"Sustained. Call your next witness." The lawyer called several witnesses that identified a scantily clad, heavily made-up, gum popping Ayesha from enlarged photographs. Ayesha was not looking favorable. The mostly conservative jury started judging Ayesha and buying into Travis' story. On day three the lawyer called Ayesha to the witness stand again to reinforce his point. Judge Barnes threatened to hold him in contempt. He called Aaron Yardley to the stand. Aaron was the boy who took Ayesha's virginity. Deaglan had no grounds to make his testimony inadmissible. Aaron testified that after offering him sex to be her boyfriend, Ayesha graciously offered herself to his friends to close the deal. Deaglan stood.

"Objection, Your Honor. Hearsay!" Judge Barnes agreed and asked that the last statement be stricken from the record. The lawyer moved on.

"Aaron, what happened when you refused to comply with Ayesha's wishes?" Aaron turned to the jury, still furious that Ayesha's father got him and his family kicked out of Mayberry.

"She told me she would tell everyone that I raped her." The jurors' mouths hung in shock and the uproar of the gallery drowned out Deaglan's objections. He attempted damage control during cross; but the impact was too explosive. At home later that night, Deaglan pulled Melissa close,

"Honey, Aaron's testimony imploded my case." Melissa rubbed his temple.

"Convince Ayesha to testify? It would be very impactful." Deaglan sat up.

"Babe, she's deathly afraid of him. She breaks at the mention of his name." He sighed. Melissa sat in Deaglan's lap and kissed him deeply.

"I'll talk to her tomorrow." Deaglan kissed her again, pulling the hair clip, he lifted her on the bed. Day four. The lawyer was in high spirits. He eagerly called Suva to the stand, the testimony she gave in the pre-trial hearing would just put the nail in the coffin of Ayesha's ruined reputation. After being sworn in, Suva relaxed her cheeks; she didn't want the jury to see her disdain.

"Savu, would you consider Ayesha to be a good person?" The lawyer got straight to the point. Suva smiled unrattled,

"Suva…being, a good person, is a relative term." The lawyer was prepared.

"Suva…did you not testify that you walked in on Ayesha having sex with someone she wasn't dating? Did you also testify that she threatened to assault you after calling you racist names, and that brought your friendship to an end?" Deaglan objected, he was overruled. Suva paused, thought carefully,

"Your Honor, I move to make any testimonies from case 120179ARL are inadmissible."

"On what grounds, Your Honor?" The lawyer responded without realizing that Suva made the statement and not Deaglan. Suva spoke up before the judge, searching for the reason with every word,

"On-the-grounds, that…" She was excited when she found the cause. "Because all witnesses in that pre-trial were under the age of 18 and consent must be given by their parents." She paused for a moment; the judge was about to speak, she interrupted him. "Also, there is a motion to seal those records because the witnesses were under 18." Judge Barnes waited for her to finish,

"Mr. Lanaghan, I have not seen such a motion," Suva spoke up again. "It has been prepared, Your Honor, on account of the full docket for today, maybe-that's-why you haven't seen it." Suva knew she was grasping at straws. But it worked; the judge ruled that all testimonies relating to the Travis Bent assault case inadmissible. Deaglan turned to one of his associates, who scurried off to prepare and file the motion. Deaglan winked at Suva for her quick thinking.

The lawyer rifled through his papers, buying time. He asked Suva the same questions he asked in the assault case. Suva was very strategic with her responses, pointing out that yes, she and Ayesha had a spat and weren't on speaking terms. However, they were teenage girls; it was encoded in their DNA to have disputes and periodically malice each other. The lawyer kept pressing. He asked if she viewed Ayesha's sexual activities as being promiscuous. Suva sat back in her chair and exhaled, she responded from her heart,

"I believe Ayesha has made some mistakes and some horrible choices." The lawyer got a tad bit hostile.

"Yes, but is she promiscuous!"

"Sir, I cannot provide a definitive response as I only witnessed one interaction." The jurors smiled. The lawyer took a step back, sized up Suva, she smirked, daring him to bring it.

"Suva, how would you classify a girl who wears heavy makeup, cleavage-baring clothes, and excessively high heels?" Suva studied the pictures,

"A rebellious teenager who is going through what *Erick Erickson* would term as an identity crisis." He smiled,

"So, Suva, are you saying she should be treated the same as every other teenage girl. Look at how you are dressed." Suva bit back her impatience,

"We are all individuals who are entitled to equal treatment regardless of our past and how we choose to dress." She leaned forward in the stand, "Let's talk about you. You failed the bar thrice, should your colleagues and the jury tune you and your *Armoni* knock-off? Embarrassment shoved the lawyer into his seat. "You see, sir, regardless of how Ayesha dresses and how many people she has allegedly slept with, it doesn't negate the fact that Travis Bent brutally raped and beat her, leaving her with a razor with instructions to kill herself!" Tears silenced Suva. The jury was touched. The lawyer had no further questions; Judge Barnes ordered a recess until the following morning.

Deaglan scolded Suva for her disrespectful behavior on the stand. Suva overtly objected.

"Are you kidding me? It was a Hail Mary that saved our asses!" Melissa walked into Deaglan's home office, cautiously. Suva and Deaglan rarely had disagreements.

"Suva, I have raised you to be a lady, not to berate people and exploit their weaknesses." Suva rolled her eyes and pouted her lips.

"Dad, he spent the entire week doing just that. You taught me to analyze my opponent. That's exactly what I did." Suva huffed. Deaglan was very calm despite Suva's attitude.

"Suva honey, that was a low blow. I don't operate like that." Suva hissed her teeth. "Low blow, my ass, he got exactly what he deserved." Deaglan looked up, his hazel eyes turning a dark shade. Melissa grabbed Suva in her chest, pulling her closer by a fistful of her clothing.

"Yuh nuh have no manners pickney?" The power of Melissa's grip exorcised the attitude from Suva's body. Swallowing a lump in her throat, Suva did her best to sound as calm and respectful as possible.

"No, ma'am, I mean, yes, ma'am." Still holding Suva in place, Melissa glanced over at Deaglan, he raised his brow, she released Suva.

"Now, apologize to your father." Even though Melissa released her grip, Suva didn't move; she was even afraid to break eye contact with her mother.

"Daddy, I'm sorry for my behavior just now as well as for how I behaved today."

Deaglan exhaled. "Apology accepted, Suva." Melissa walked around the large desk and leaned against Deaglan's arm. Suva remained in place.

"May-I-be excused…please?" Deaglan looked at Melissa and tilted his head; she got the message.

"Yes, you may be excused. Some grapes are being chilled for you." Suva sheepishly walked away.

"Thank you, ma'am." Deaglan sat back in his chair.

"Your daughter has such a feisty attitude," he commented. Melissa laughed.

"So she's my daughter when she acts all fiery, huh?" Deaglan smiled and positioned her directly in front of him.

"I forgot how sexy you are when you get all disciplinarian." He playfully bit her tummy. Melissa giggled loudly.

"Don't do that, Dea, you know what it does to me."

"Mel, you know I can't remember the last time we had fun on this desk. Let me refresh our memories." He stood and kissed her.

The following morning, Deaglan woke up revived. Travis' lawyer did not rest his case, as expected since Suva was his last witness. Instead, he called Ayesha to the stand. Judge Barnes held him in contempt of court. He refuted, stating he was giving her the treatment she justly deserved. Deaglan objected at his underhanded ploy.

"I'm here, Your Honor." The room fell silent, Ayesha, the elusive ghost made her way to the stand. The jury couldn't reconcile this young lady with the pictures and the descriptions given. Tommy's libido perked up. It was an aesthetically pleasing transformation. Her natural honey-blonde shoulder-length hair replaced the usual back-length bleached extensions. She allowed her natural eyebrows to flourish instead of the gaudy drawn on ones. Her light gray eyes were no longer hidden behind blue contacts. Her makeup was still immaculately done, but the shades were more subdued. Her silhouette was softer, and her chest was now a natural full B cup instead of the double Ds. In true Ayesha form, her figure-hugging fuchsia dress was complemented by red bottom stilettoes.

The anticipation in the room was palpable. The lawyer shuffled papers.

"Your Honor, may we have a brief…" Deaglan smirked,

"A brief what Your Honor?" Judge Barnes grimaced,

"Counselor, don't waste the court's time!" The lawyer straightened his jacket and displayed all the pictures of her scantily clad.

"Ayesha, can you explain why you choose to wear these outfits?" Ayesha was very calm, both in tone and demeanor.

"I don't need to justify my attire. It was and is my personal choice. Do you have to justify why you chose to wear that knock-off designer suit today?" The jurors chuckled. Suva felt vindicated but held her peace; her mom was in the courtroom.

"Would you say you are promiscuous?" She was honest about her exploits.

"I did go through a period of rebellion, where I thought the only way to feel loved was through sex. I didn't and…still don't fully understand myself." The lawyer was surprised at how honest she was; the jury was eating it up. He switched gears.

"Ayesha, did you have sex with my client on several occasions before the alleged incident?" She detailed all the dates. Tommy was a little hurt, for the majority they were a couple.

The lawyer had her right where he wanted, and he stood in front of the jury to ask his remaining questions.

"Ayesha, did you want to be in a relationship with my client?"

"I did, but then I reconsidered." The lawyer pressed on.

"Even though you changed your mind, did you not threaten Travis Bent that if he didn't comply, you would tell everyone that he raped you?" Ayesha looked at Travis in complete shock.

"No, that is absurd. I didn't want to be in a relationship with Travis because…he never…he never wanted to kiss me." She and Tommy locked eyes.

The lawyer felt uneasy. But Mr. Bent was paying him a lot of money.

"Didn't you enjoy it when he got rough with you?" She laughed in disbelief.

"Yes, yes, I did." The jurors' mouth dropped. People were on the edge of their seat. Phones vibrated unanswered. Ayesha twirled her circle around her finger. "There is a difference between talking dirty or him ripping off my shirt and him breaking four of my ribs…fracturing my nose and…splitting my lips."

He kept pressing, not giving the jury time to express sympathy.

"Ayesha, wasn't the incident in fact yet another time when you engaged in consenting sex with Travis Bent?"

"No! Travis came over unannounced looking for sex, I told him no and asked him to leave. He then assaulted and raped me, because whores don't get to say no! He left me there…bleeding and in pain!" Judge Barnes gave her a tissue. She paused, twirled her circle, and continued. "He returned the following morning and did the same thing all over again. When I said I wanted to die, he left a razor blade and told me to do the world a favor!" The courtroom irrupted, *Liar! He should rot in jail! Bastard!*

"Order! Order! I will clear the room order!" Ayesha continued speaking after the noise died down.

"It doesn't matter if I dressed like a prostitute, and if I were promiscuous, it does not give anybody-the-right-to-do-what-he-did-to me." The lawyer went back to his desk.

"No further questions." Deaglan remained seated.

"Ayesha, do you hate Travis Bent?" Ayesha looked over at Travis.

"I did hate him at first and was happy he got what he deserved. But now, I don't." Deaglan urged her to explain. "If it weren't for this incident, I wouldn't have found myself. All that hurt and pain has brought enlightenment. I, however, think that he should be punished to the fullest extent of the law to show people that no matter how rich and powerful you are, actions do have consequences." Travis's lawyer saw an opportunity to humanize Travis,

"Redirect, Your Honor." He remained seated so as not to seem intimidating. "Ayesha, what do you mean by Travis getting what he deserved?" Deaglan objected because the judge already ruled that case inadmissible.

"Your Honor, the witness opened the gates, and since she didn't testify then, her testimony now is relevant." Judge Barnes allowed it.

"Honestly, I feel no sympathy towards him being attacked." The lawyer placed the picture of Travis's groin area at the front of the display.

"You have no sympathy for an innocent young man who was attacked on his tennis court by a muscular red-headed French woman, who incapacitated his two friends, broke his nose and mutilated him?" Ayesha stared at the picture intently.

"Ayesha, did you hire someone to attack Travis?"

"No, on account that I was bleeding half to death." The lawyer paused,

"My client was mutilated with a sharp object that left him with permanent scars. Ayesha, can you explain what the scars mean?" Deaglan spoke up passionately,

"Objection Your Honor, Ayesha, is neither a hyalographic expert nor is she on trial here!" Judge Barnes accepted the objection,

"Counselor, tread carefully."

"Ayesha, do you recognize any of these scars?" Ayesha massaged her forehead, "The abrasions on his upper left thigh could be my initials AJ. The carving of the razor blade on his right thigh could be a reminder to him of the desolation I felt when he left a razor blade for me to kill myself." Discomfort from flashbacks shifted her in the seat. "The NO in the center may signify the repeated no's I screamed."

"Based on the graphic nature of the remaining scars, that

picture cannot be displayed. Ayesha, do triple dollar signs bare any significance?"

"Where were those carved?"

"Into the skin of my client's penis." Ayesha and Suva made tearful eye contact. Ayesha twirled her ring and responded in a low tone,

"I know what it means. When he was through with me, I told him he would pay for it, he punched me in the mouth and said that some of us could afford to!" That was the breaking point in the case. The lawyer rested. The jury took what felt like the longest day ever to deliberate; they came back with a guilty verdict. Travis would serve two consecutive sentences, four years for rape and two years for assault and battery. He was also ordered to take 400 hours of anger management courses.

After the verdict had been rendered, the bailiff handed Deaglan a note: Judge Barnes requested to see him and Suva in his chambers. Judge Barnes spoke to her as a father to his child.

"While we were not able to prove it, I know you know more than you let on about the Travis' assault. I won't dig any deeper this time, but, if your name should ever come across my desk again, I will bring the full weight of the justice system down on you!" Silence. When he was finished speaking, Suva ran behind his desk and hugged him.

"Thanks, Barnzy!" Deaglan froze; only lawyers called Judge Barnes that. He was going to be held in contempt.

"I won't hold you in contempt as long as you ensure that she pursues law. She has a lot of promise." Deaglan quickly left his office, pinching Suva for her slip.

## Chapter 23

Weeks after the trial, the Academic Decathlon was a welcome sign of normalcy. Jason got his revenge on Mollyby keeping her up the entire first night. Maxwell kept his flirting to a minimum after Suva warned him. Ayesha was pleasantly surprised by the quality guys who had overlooked her before that were perusing her now. Not that she needed validation, but it was certainly an ego boost.

The final round was an exciting rematch between Hartford and Mayberry. No tiebreaker was needed this time, Mayberry dominated! The absence of Avery and Ashley made the air less tense. As they celebrated their win, Dr. Theopolis lamented that this championship team would be graduating soon. At the awards ceremony, one of the presenters stood out in Suva's mind; he was a member of the Manchester University admissions committee. Glenford Archibald was a short stumpy man that wore extremely thick lens glasses. He uses his superior intellect to compensate for his height. She approached with caution and introduced herself. They had a delightful conversation.

Glendford congratulated her on leading her team to two consecutive victories. He proudly admitted that he was the head of the ManU admissions committee, and it was just this week he was looking at her file. He loudly whispered that she was on the Student Ambassador shortlist and that she would be contacted soon to come in for her interview.

On the plane ride home, Suva was on cloud nine. Jason commented that Tommy had finally popped that cherry. Suva didn't hear his comment because she was too busy planning her interview outfit. Two days later, her official invitation arrived. After reviewing the packet, she realized she had to go shopping. The position of Student Ambassador was a huge deal, and all candidates went through rigorous interviews. The interview process was a weekend-long event where candidates were observed at various functions, culminating in a panel interview the Sunday evening.

The gang went with her for the big weekend. ManU was five hours away by car and forty-five minutes by plane. Suva was too nervous to talk; she kept replaying her earlier conversation with KG and Hazel. They both believed in her and supported her wholeheartedly.

Hazel prayed with her on the phone and would be submitting a prayer request to her prayer group. Suva felt reassured, knowing that she was covered. During the flight, Tommy squeezed her hand,

"Atsila, whatever the outcome, I'm just happy that we'll be on the same campus." Suva snuggled up against him. The Manchester University campus spanned several acres. Its prominence engulfs you upon entering the large thick walls that fortified the school, much like European Scottish castles. The founding fathers were of Irish, Scottish, and British descent. The men wore kilts at all significant ceremonies, and bagpipes play over the PA in recognition of specific historical dates. The Boeghans and the Lanaghans were extremely excited about the campus tour. The ManU campus made Mayberry Academy look like a parking lot.

As the tour progressed, they transitioned through time. The freshman and second-year dorms were apartment buildings equipped with laundry rooms, cafeteria, pools, and gyms. The third- and fourth-year students lived in mini-communities based on their area of specialization. Their apartments were more old-school. They lived in brick-style houses that were converted into flats. The Ferguson House was where Melissa and Atsila lived right across the street from The United Residence where Kyle and Deaglan lived. Tommy and Suva wanted to live there too.

To their surprise, there was an addition of a coed apartment building; it was for the ManU athletes. Gary the tour guide explained with exuberance,

"Thomas, this two-bedroom apartment is yours on account of your dual scholarships."

"How far is it from the freshman dorms?"

"Thirty minutes."

"I'll stay at the freshman dorms then." Tommy held Suva's hand tighter. The final stop on tour was the Ambassadors' complex. It was five conjoined flats, with one flight of stairs leading up to the door. To the left of the stairs were double parking spaces. When they opened the thick glass door, they were sold.

Standing at the door, you could view the entire apartment. A spacious living room furnished with a large couch and fireplace was to the left. To the immediate right, there was an intimate dining table for four; beyond the dining room was the modern kitchen. Suva loved the eight-burner stove and oven. There was a straight line from the main door to the exquisitely furnished master bedroom.

A bathroom with a hot tub was just inches away from the queen-sized bed. Suva couldn't believe how well the Ambassadors were treated when they visited. After all, they were academic Ambassadors, not the Head of State. Peeking into the second room, then into the office, Suva asked,

"Gary, why do the Ambassadors need a second room and office? Do they usually bring their families with them?" Gary chuckled at her question,

"Ms. Lanaghan, this apartment is not for the Ambassadors. It is for our Student Ambassador." The group halted. Gary explained further,

"Our representatives must maintain a 3.8 GPA, participate in at least three co-curricular activities, and carry out their duties effectively. We want them to have no distractions. However, we do encourage positive social interactions. Hence, the second room is there to accommodate family weekend visits." Lana squealed,

"Suva, you get to live here? That is totally wicked! I call dibs on the bedroom!"

Gary broke character for two seconds and smiled; then, he was back to being the stuffy aristocrat. Suva felt the pressure of the weekend all over again. She didn't like interviews and wasn't comfortable with the idea of selling herself. After the tour, they went back to the freshman dorms to get dressed for the official welcome dinner. At dinner, Suva was seated beside a feisty Russian woman who was quite the chatterbox. Since Suva was too nervous to eat, she enjoyed the chatter; they even spoke in Russian for a bit but switched back to English when no one else understood.

Saturday went by very quickly. In the morning, Suva had breakfast with the other applicants. In the afternoon, they went to an orphanage ran by ManU. It had orphans from all over the globe who were seeking asylum. That is why it was important for the Student Ambassador to be multilingual.

The parents had a special dinner planned for the kids at their old hangout. It was Paddy's Diner. The diner looked more like an Irish pub than a traditional diner. There was a wall in the back of the diner that the parents wanted to show them. It had a picture of the foursome their senior year in college. It was signed by all four, and the message read, "To our children, we are so proud of you and happy that you are best friends now and will be married one day."

Suva inspected the picture carefully. There was no way they would have known. Tommy and Lana urged by disbelief attempted to remove the image, but Paddy himself appeared and told them that no photo has ever been removed from that wall. Once it is placed there, it stays there. The children were still very skeptical as to the authenticity of the message.

Suva breathed deeply. It was her turn to be interviewed. Her legs got weak with each step she took. She had perfect 20-20 vision, yet she couldn't see the people on the panel. She sat in the chair provided.  The panel had fifteen members cheered by the president of the university. They were sitting behind a long horizontal table facing Suva. She couldn't breathe even though she was overly prepared having stayed up all night practicing. The president took his glasses off. Everything after that was a blur of nervousness.

She would have to wait a few weeks for their decision. She was grateful for the distraction of KG's graduation. Attending KG's graduation and seeing Hazel took Suva's mind off things. They had loads of fun, but before they knew it, they had to fly home to prepare for Suva's graduation.  The graduates had to wear the dreaded Mayberry Academy gown. No matter how they protested, they were reminded that it was a matter of tradition. The unsupervised after-party at the cabin got them through the ordeal. The entire senior class was at the party. KG volunteered to be the bartender or drinks disburser since no alcohol was being served. Everyone took pictures and reminisced about all the scandals and good times. The most significant uproar was about the location of Avery and Ashley and the greatest prank ever. They edited Ashley's certificate and name card to read Ashley Hunter. The school erupted when the announcer kept repeating Ashley Hunter.

Suva and Ayesha danced in circles, hair flashing. Sofia joined them after feeling left out. Duncan, Jason, and Tommy watched them from the couch. Jason was secretly lusting after Suva; she was doing a Latin dance, looking all spicy. He was going to get her back; he loved envisioning them as a married couple. He somehow made himself the center of their circle and made his best Latin moves. The girls cheered him on. He twirled Suva, pulling her close for the *Salsa*.
The music changed to Dancehall, Duncan and Tommy joined them, and they paired off.  Dancehall music electrified Suva.  She turned her back to Tommy and rubbed her bottom against his crotch. After a minute, Tommy stilled her hips.

She turned and jumped into his arms. They both laughed, remembering the last time she did that. Suva whispered,

"Baby, I want to feel your body next to mine." Tommy cradled her behind.

"Suva, I want that too, but speedway won't allow it." Suva kissed him softly.

"Tommy, it's all cognitive. Train your mind and body so that you can enjoy these moments without speedway erupting." He bit her bottom lip and focused. Easing her down, he turned her around and danced on her from behind. The beat was excellent; the song was about a *sexy body girl*. Suva kept going lower and lower while still maintaining the grind. Tommy thanked God for yoga, or else he wouldn't be flexible enough to keep up. The rhythm hypnotized Tommy, he stood behind her firmly, bending her until she touched her toes. From the floor, Suva looked back at him and started jiggling her butt. The crowd went wild. Tommy gave her bottom a little tap. Cheers all around!

Some of the guys from the football team teased him that virgins only got pants touching. Jason concurred.

"Yup, Tommy is getting absolutely no action!" Teens pointed and laughed. Suva held her hands up, silencing the crowd, circling Tommy as she spoke.

"Hold up, guys. Hold up. First, Talbot, you aren't one to talk. Your first kiss was with your cousin, so zip it." The fullback tried playing off his obvious embarrassment,

"She was my one, two three…my third cousin!" His teammate covered his mouth.

"Jason, we were together forever, and you never even got to second base!" Suva held up two fingers to be dramatic. The crowd laughed and pointed at Jason, whose face was stained with anger. Suva stopped in front of Tommy and placed his hands on her hips. Her legs were looking magnificent in her red Daisy Dukes.

"I'm grateful to Tommy for being so kind and understanding. If all I was doing tonight was dancing, can you imagine what I'm going to be like when I decide to demonstrate all…this…gratitude." She ran Tommy's hands from the middle of her chest down to her midriff. Pity was replaced by envy. The males hooted when Suva jumped on him, wrapping her legs around him.

 "Come on, baby, let's go somewhere private, I'm suddenly feeling thankful." Tommy followed her lead and headed for the back room.

He got approving cheers and whistles. Tommy's and his ego were delighted by her little display. He was the one that was grateful to have some distance from her. He almost didn't make it; she was all sorts of sexy and alluring in her Daisy Dukes. It was at that moment he decided to add an extra hour to his workout; Suva was quite the tigress.

One week later, Gabe came up. The foursome rehearsed their speeches; Lana played the role of the parents. Lana took her part seriously.

"Guys, come on. I'm not convinced."

They sat on Suva's bed, taking in all of Lana's tips on persuasion. After a third try, they got the seal of approval. Mavis asked them to set an extra plate for a special guest. The guest was late, Atsila kept whispering to Kyle. Melissa would smile then hide it. Lana and Gabe couldn't wait to chow down. Mavis was an awesome cook. When the doorbell rang, Suva was instructed to get it. She started rolling through all the languages she knew; guests always feel super special when they were greeted in their native tongue. When she opened the door, it was the ManU Vice-Chancellor.

Mrs. Pennicut commended Suva on representing herself well and standing her ground under fire during the extensive interview process. Suva was elated by the news that she was now the official Student Ambassador. Suva did her victory dance then got down to business. The family left the two ladies to talk. The ladies reviewed Suva's welcome packet, the rules, and regulations, the long laundry list of countries and languages that Suva would have to become familiar. The only sad news was that it was the end of June, and Suva would assume duties on August third.

Amidst the jubilation, Suva saw her opportunity. She gingerly interjected their road trip plans in between cheers. The parents weren't buying it; a cross-country road trip was unsafe. After a very lengthy debate, the teens won. However, Tony, their military-trained personal driver would chaperone as the navigator. Lana and the remainder of the secret six would accompany them, and they had to check in twice daily.

**Chapter 24**

After a wonderful Fourth of July weekend filled with fireworks and delicious burgers, the gang loaded up the bus. It had ten bunk beds, two bathrooms, a kitchenette, and a spacious common area. Waving good-bye, Suva threw up. Everybody stared down Tommy accusatorily. After a three-hour delay, they were off. Suva's period had started; her parents wanted her to stay home because they knew how sick she could get. Tommy's assurances of care persuaded them.

The first week on the road was awesome; they stopped at water parks and a major zoo. Jason was annoyed at Tommy for not leaving Suva's side. Tommy was missing out on all the fun so that she could have a personal butler. Sure she was weak and kept vomiting, but she wasn't terminally ill. A very misguided Jason shared his thoughts over dinner one night.

"Come on, how painful can a period be? Girls always get so dramatic about it. It happens every twenty-eight days, get over it!" He was brutally shut down by everyone, including Tony. KG shook her head,

"Jason did it hurt when I punched you in the nose, shoulder, and groin." Jason covered his groin instinctively. "Now imagine me doing that to you for five straight days every single month." Jason made a face, and the matter rested. By week 2, Suva was up and running. Lana was glad because their next stop was a *Lazer Tag* championship. They got slaughtered in the first round. They did better at the national Paintball tournament where they placed third. Duncan bruised an opponent and became instant friends when he nursed her wounds. Olivia Hylton was a hardcore paintballer, so she was surprised that Duncan was able to clip her. She was even more surprised at how caring and kind he was.

At the end of week 2, the gang got a suite at a hotel because they got food poisoning, and the two bathrooms on the bus weren't adequate. When they weren't on the toilet or throwing up, they had a good laugh about it. For their third and final week, they decided to take it easy and visit hot springs and lakes. They underestimated how hot the second spring was, and Duncan and Jason got scorched on their feet for showing off and plunging in first. Burns aside, they had fun that day.

On the last night of the trip, Tony took them to a massive

camping ground. They watched the sunset, built a campfire, ate s'mores, and reminisce about the good times they had. They appropriately thanked Tony for a fun ride by dumping him in the lake. Over dinner, Ayesha asked yet again,

"Guys, what happened the night you found me, who attacked Travis?"

"Ayesha, for the millionth time, we don't know. Let-it-go!" Sofia responded aggressively.

"Shut up, Sofia! I don't believe you!" Ayesha started crying. "I will never be more than just Travis' victim. All my yesterdays have been wiped out by that one god damn day!" Duncan spoke softly,

"Ayesha, like we told the police we were nowhere near that property when he was attacked." The fire blazed higher, matching the intensity of Ayesha crying. Suva sat beside her on the log and soothed her.

"Ayesha, focus on the fact that we loved you yesterday, today, and forever!"

"You guys tolerate me; you never loved me." Ayesha removed a block of wood from the fire and dropped it. It lit the ground and blazed a circle around the group. Tony stood outside the flames with an extinguisher. Jason shouted at Tony,

"Really Tony!" Tony shrugged. Ayesha stood defiantly.

"I'm evoking the sanctity of the Truth Circle." Silence. "Suva, you always preach about standing in your truth. Well cut the bullshit guys. I want to know who defended me, Tony's Private Investigators and the police couldn't find anything. Who…guys you only showed up to court because…" Ayesha sat on the log. "…because I'm a loser, and no one loves me!" She wept! Jason was perturbed,

"Am I the only one concerned about this big ass circle of fire?" Sofia slapped him. Silence filled the circle as the orange creature danced majestically around them. Drums of anxiety were beating in Lana's tummy. She gripped Suva's hand. Ayesha sobbed intermittently. Duncan spoke up,

"Damn, we must honor the truth circle!" They all sat beside Ayesha. Emotions surged through Suva as the words flowed from her heart,

"Ayesha, you have never truly known your worth." Sofia's walls collapsed,

"Mi hermana, mi corazón sangró cuando te lastimaste."

Ayesha sniffled and asked again,

"What-really-happened?" Suva sighed deeply recalling it like it was yesterday,

"Beth and I found you half dead. Hearing that creep having fun with his friends after what you told me, broke something in me. On my way to the bathroom, I called Tommy.  I had texted him on the T phone '911 Ayesha's house' the moment I saw the bloody spread. All six of us spoke outside your bathroom. Then we moved quietly and with much precision. In the bathroom I ensured that my vomit was evenly disbursed. After washing my hands, mouth, and face. I used water to smooth my hair down and wrapped it in a neat bun." Tommy's voice crackled a bit when he spoke,

"I speedily undressed Suva, leaving her bra and panty only. I used the towel to open the cabinet under the face basin and retrieved a pack of white gloves and some Band-Aids. After using the Band-Aids to cover her knuckles, I put the gloves on her hands. The temperature fell, the wind tossing Sofia's hair went unnoticed, she was deep in her memories as she recounted,

"I then retrieved two costumes and wig from the closet that Mrs. Jacobs keeps her Christmas Decorations and Halloween Costumes.  We dressed Suva, and three minutes later, she emerged from the bathroom unrecognizable in a bodysuit, red wig, and sweats. The base in Duncan's voice echoed into the night,

"Suva hurried downstairs to me in the kitchen. I had poured three specific cleaning liquids from the maid's supply closet into a casserole dish. When the concoction started bubbling, I added a powdered detergent from under the kitchen sink.  Suva then fetched a small carving knife from the large wooden box at the bottom of the china display in the master dining room that no one ever uses. The knife was very sharp with a sturdy handle.

While Suva carefully put the box back in its place. Jason sprinted back to the kitchen with the knife, and I dipped the blade into the bubbling mixture. Cautiously, holding the blade in place so that the mixture didn't splash, as lacerations would be flesh deep and permanent." Jason twirled his ring around his finger, and he held Ayesha's hand while he spoke,

"I used foil wrap to create a case for the blade. Then hoisted Suva through the bathroom window in the maid's room, I used the pool stick to change the angle of the camera so she could enter the Bent's property around the back of the pool house and under the shrubs. She ended up on the far side of the Bents' tennis court. Travis Bent was drinking and playing tennis with two of his buddies.

"Travis, you are such a lady's man. You have girls coming out of your bushes," His friends joked, stroking his ego. Suva sauntered, flashing the red hair. Ignoring the others, she homed in on Travis. He had a racket in his right hand and a beer in the other. Suva allowed him to get an eyeful of her enhanced bosom. Suva spoke in her most impressive French accent; in her mind, the redhead was French.

"I'm looking for a partee. I want to...how you say have a gud time." She swayed her hips to imaginary party music. Travis liked what he was seeing. He put his beer down and pulled her closer.

"Stick with me, baby, and you'll have the time of your life." Suva had to dig deep, not to poke his eyes out. She got serious but maintained the French accent.

"Really? Did you show Ayesha the time of her  life?" He shoved Suva away.

"Frenchie, you made a huge mistake coming over here. I still have some more in me, and this time, I have reinforcements." He signaled, his boys started their approach. He tossed the racket from side to side. "Can't you see you are outnumbered?" He swung the racket at Suva. She shifted, dodging the blow. "There are three of us and only one of you." Suva smiled.

"That's what makes it fair." Suva punched him in his gut and snatched the racket.  She forcefully connected her knee with his nose bridge when he was bent over. She quickly got two balls from the ground, and power slammed them into his friends' groins one after the other. Suva stood over him.

"That's all the fight you have you piece of sh...? Suva rolled him on his back.  She pulled his shorts down, exposing his groin.  He started protesting, and Ayesha's bruised faced flashed before Suva, she punched him in his mouth. Suva edged AJ on the left side of his groin. She drew a razor blade on the right side of his thigh; in the center, she carved NO. Suva started feeling guilty because she knew the skin would never heal then,

"My dad is going to have your head for this. Whores don't get to say no to a Bent." He spat blood. Suva knelt back down and took his penis in her hand and carved three dollar signs. Suva left him screaming. She told his friend to call the ambulance quickly, or else he's going to bleed out. Suva exited the court on the other side. Jason inhaled deeply, exhaling slowly he picked up from Suva,

"Then I pulled her back through the window. Sofia and I undressed her. Tommy removed the gloves, and Band-Aids then clipped her nails. Duncan collected the knife, costumes, and shoes in a garbage bag then placed it in a duffle. Sofia redressed her and pulled her hair out." Suva wiped back tears,

"They left, and I sprinted back upstairs, causing me to genuinely puff on my inhaler, your stairs are no joke. Returning from the bathroom I called my dad, the police and my mom. Later that night at the hospital, when it was my turn to shower, I disposed of the duffle bag in the hospital's hazardous waste incinerator." Lana, KG, and Gabe stared at the five strangers before them. Ayesha stood timidly smiling,

"Beth?" Suva shook her head,

"She was none the wiser. Ayesha, no one should ever experience the injustice you went through.  Stand in your truth as a survivor!  Yesterday will not break you. Instead, it will lay the foundation for the extraordinary warrior you will become. Like the phoenix rise from the ashes of your yesterday!" Ayesha held out her hand, placed her ring in her palm. The other five followed suit.

"Thank you!" They engulfed in the blanket of their embrace. Tommy lifted Suva and kissed her deeply. Jason asked,

"Did you guys mess around while we were together?" Suva hissed,

"Jason, we don't need a truth circle to answer that. No, we didn't" Jason rolled his eyes,

"Have you guys at least had sex yet?" Tommy grabbed Suva's butt,

"What's the rush…she's mine yesterday, today, and forever!" Suva cupped his face,

"Wohali, I love you with all of me. You are my best friend, my soul mate, and I can't wait to be your wife and spend the rest of my life with you. We belong together…yesterday, today, and forever!"

## Epilogue

Suva gently woke her husband. "Baby turn on the lights, someone has been calling incessantly." He switched on the lights.

"It's 3 am, maybe Lana has an emergency." Not finding the cordless phone in the room, he retrieved the one from the bathroom. Seeing the caller ID, anger flushed his face. He handed her the phone, she held her necklace. The machine beeped, and the message played out.

"Atsila, pick up, please…Atsila pick up!" Suva held the necklace tighter. "Atsila I." Her husband ripped the phone from her hand and smashed it against the wall.

"Swan, why is he calling our home?" Still holding the necklace, Suva pulled the sheet over her head and left him there fuming. Her husband can be so dramatic. Suva couldn't believe the turn *Today* had taken.

Sofia was mercilessly dumping Duncan for some random dude. But Duncan found his bliss by marrying Olivia Hylton; it's the happiest anyone had ever seen him. Ayesha, a successful human rights activist stationed in Milan, with Lana as her Intern. Lana was a brilliant Law student by day and a high-fashion model by night. Suva looked at the massive rock on her finger. *How did she become Mrs. Jason Henri?*

In the bathroom, Jason splashed water on his face and smiled at his reflection; he knew precisely why Tommy was calling. His smile got sinister; Suva was his. *Surprised? I told you I would get her back! It makes you wonder what happened after yesterday…*